FOREIGN HOME

This Foreign Universe – Book 3

A Novel by

J.S. SHERWOOD

FOREIGN HOME
This Foreign Universe – Book 3
Copyright © 2022 J.S. Sherwood

FIRST EDITION SOFTCOVER
ISBN: 1622537475
ISBN-13: 978-1-62253-747-1

Editor: Becky Stephens
Cover Artist: Sam Keiser
Interior Designer: Lane Diamond

EVOLVED PUBLISHING™

www.EvolvedPub.com
Evolved Publishing LLC
Butler, Wisconsin, USA

Printed in Book Antiqua font.

BOOKS BY J.S. SHERWOOD

ARC ONE: THE BATTLES THEY FOUGHT
Book 1: *Foreign Land*
Book 2: *Foreign Planet*
Book 3: *Foreign Home*

ARC TWO: THE EARTH THEY LEFT BEHIND
Book 4: *Almost Pathless*
Book 5: *Almost Homeless*
Book 6: *Almost Earthless*

ARC THREE: THE SEEDS THEY PLANTED
Book 7: *The Engineer*
Book 8: *The Explorer*
Book 9: *The Sage*

DEDICATION

For Meaghan,
Through All the Dimensions

PART ONE

Chapter 1

Abe and Winona stood side by side, hands clasped tightly together, eyes wide as they watched the five Singers descend the stairs to the stasis chambers. They had agreed to have five humans present at the awakening of their people: Abe, Winona, Tashon, Rosa and Johann. The rest waited outside the caves with a few dozen Crawlers. The rest of the four-legged species remained in their own land, repairing the city and looking after the injured, orphaned and widowed.

Abe smiled at Winona and the rest of his companions, amazed and triumphant that he had been a part of making the awakening possible but pained that Ballas was not there. When they had returned victorious, one of the first things Abe did was check on Ballas. But when he arrived in the small cavern, Ballas was dead, with no clear cause.

He turned back to the Singers as they approached the far corner of the room. As he did, he had to remind himself of their new names. Atom, the eldest Singer. Wave, previously known as Scar, and Comet, with her cropped hair. The hardest for him to remember were the new names of Mohawk and Braids. He had spent so much time with them that to suddenly change how he referred to them was proving to be a large adjustment. Yet the names made sense, and it felt better to refer to them by names that resembled their true selves and not just their physical appearance. Braids was now known as Lioness: strong-minded, willing to do anything to protect her family. The note for Mohawk's new name was more difficult to pin down. It created a feeling of whimsical kind-heartedness that Abe and the others decided to take more literally. They named him 'Whims.'

Atom pushed her hand against a stasis chamber. The drawer holding the sleeping Singer slid out and its occupant, a thin woman, sat up. Wave pulled the tube out of the new Singer's chest. She gasped and her eyes shot open. She turned around, at first singing notes of familiarity as she saw her fellow Singers. Then she glimpsed the humans and gracefully climbed out and stood.

Staring at Abe and his companions, she let out notes of gratitude. None had told her the humans had played a role in allowing her to awaken, yet she knew. Abe smiled, filled with his own thankfulness that, despite all the tragedy, he was able to be a part of something so historical. He squeezed Winona's hand and turned to see her eyes wet, her face alight with joy. His heart leaped at the sight.

When the Singer's notes were complete, she joined the humans on the stairs. Wave moved to the next chamber and opened it, while Comet removed the hose. Just as the first awakened Singer had done, this one sang gratitude for the help of the humans. The pattern continued, each of the five Singers taking turns opening drawers and disconnecting tubes. Soon, the staircase was packed full of fifty-three Singers and five humans.

Comet walked to the foot of the stairs and sang the Singer note for 'Crawler.' Instantly, the Singers around Abe tensed, and he felt their fear. Hushed notes rippled and grew louder until Atom let one loud note ring out. The room went silent. Again, Comet made the note for 'Crawler,' but this time connected with a distinctly different emotion: trust. Notes of confusion and fear rippled through the awakened Singers. The fear turned to distrust of the five Singers.

"They're questioning them?" Winona asked, surprise evident in her voice.

Johann nodded and scratched his beard. "They've spent far more time distrusting and fearing the Crawlers than not. That won't go away easily."

Rosa turned to Tashon. "Have you seen any more visions?"

"No, ma'am. But I think it'll be okay."

"Me too," Rosa said.

Abe wasn't sure he agreed, but he kept his doubt to himself.

"Okay," Johann said loudly. "We're going to take you to our ship, our home. There are many humans there, and a few Crawlers." Johann paused, letting Whims translate, then continued. "I know that you're probably fearful of meeting them, but these Crawlers saved our lives. I trust them."

Whims called for the Singers to follow, and they made their way to the Ship of Nations, the five humans taking up the rear.

"Abe," Johann called. "How many more are there?"

"Hundreds, at least."

Johann whistled and shook his head.

Theresa sighed and swore under her breath. *At least she's opening up to the idea*, Abe thought. Not that she has much of a choice.

The Singers mumbled notes of trepidation as they walked, which turned to trembling fear as three Crawlers came into view. They all stopped short, watching silently as Whims approached the Crawler in front.

Abe looked at the Crawler's legs, confirming that it was the same one that had held the Singer book two days before. *Only two days?* Two days, and nearly half a species had been wiped out. Abe exhaled, dispelling the thought. What mattered next was building up the relationships between the three species.

Whims sang two notes to the Crawler. The first, 'welcome to our home.' The second, 'thank you.'

The Crawler responded with a spattering of clicks and clacks, then produced the Singer book from the hidden pouch between its legs and head. Almost simultaneously, a unanimous note of shock echoed from each of the fifty-three Singers.

"This," the Crawler said, "showed us. Changed us. Sorry for bad of past."

Whims translated the words, weaving intricate emotions of sorrow and regret to signify the Crawler's full meaning. Silence followed.

Abe looked around, fearing the Singers would doubt the Crawler. He pulled Winona closer, their shoulders touching.

A Singer with waist-length black hair stepped out of the group and approached the Crawler. They stood close enough to reach out and shake hands if they wanted. Instead, the Singer pulled out its own copy of the book, flipped to a specific page, and sang.

Minutes passed. The very air around the Singer seemed to swirl and explode outward, filling the entire forest with a sense of deep, familial connection. The Singer stopped and closed the book, the rest of its present species echoing the same sentiment: *you are our family now.*

Whims called and led the Singer to the ship, the five humans remaining where they were.

Abe exhaled and smiled. "That went purely," he said.

"Better than I had imagined," Rosa said.

Johann and Winona agreed.

Tashon remained silent.

Winona stretched and sat on a rock. "I hope the rest of the groups react as good."

Smith and Theresa walked to the group, one smiling and the other biting her lip.

"You think, what, another twenty groups?" Smith asked.

"If they're the same size as this one, yeah," Abe said.

Theresa shook her head. "Shit, a thousand Singers." She looked at those around her. "I know, I know. They probably don't pose a threat. But shit. The cultural integration of three species is going to create problems we don't even realize yet."

Abe nodded. "Yeah. I wish Ballas were here to help."

Smith nodded. "Any sign of him in the Fourth, Tash?"

"No," Tashon said. "Like most of the others, nothing."

Abe closed his eyes. Winona pulled him into her, and he rested his head on her shoulder. He knew things were looking up, but they'd already lost so much. And the fear of losing more weighed heavier and heavier on his mind.

Chapter 2

Smith stood by the farm just outside the ship, the peach trees and vegetable bushes covered in a thin layer of snow. They would grow fine, though, given the warmth the biotech plants produced internally. A breakthrough made by Smith's teacher ages ago.

The area was teeming with humans, Crawlers and Singers. Five groups of Singers were awake and out of the caves. Each accepted the Crawlers, though some with more trepidation than others.

To his left, Minow and Yeance stood with two Singers and a Crawler. Smith smiled as he watched them go through the introductions of those who speak different languages. It was made easier, though, because it seemed Singers understood the Crawler language even better than that of the humans. And all evidence suggested that the Crawlers could read the Singer language.

Smith joined them as the Crawler apologized to the Singers for all his species had done.

Both Singers released a string of forgiving notes that caused the Crawler to tremble, its head vibrating. Smith got the feeling it was an emotional response, like tears pooling in a human's eyes.

"Gratitude," the Crawler said. "Your acceptance is," the Crawler paused, and looked to Minow. "Right word?"

Minow smiled. "Your acceptance of the Crawlers is appreciated," she said. "It's life changing for them. World changing for all of us."

The Crawler trembled again. "Yes. Changes us, like Singer book changes us."

The Singers expressed their forgiveness again, said goodbye, and left.

Yeance and Minow looked at each other, and Smith realized they were holding hands. "When did this happen?" he asked with a smile.

Yeance shrugged. "It just... did," he said.

"No," Minow said. "You were a mess after the fighting ended, and you broke down sobbing, telling me you were in love with me."

Yeance grinned. "Yeah, that's right. But you cried too, and then you kissed me."

"Allegedly," she said with a smile.

The couple laughed softly together. Smith congratulated them and they walked off, hand in hand.

Smith stood alone with the Crawler, who silently stared at him. The species, Smith noticed, seemed not to understand awkwardness the way humans did.

Smith cleared his throat. "Abe says he can tell you all apart by the patterns on your legs. I have to say, though, I'm having a hard time."

The Crawler made a fast hammering sound, their version of a laugh. "You all look same. Your name is?"

He laughed. "Smith," he said.

"Smit," the Crawler said.

Smith looked at the Crawler and considered correcting the mispronunciation. But what was the point? It wouldn't do anything to improve the relationship. Plus, what if the Crawler simply couldn't pronounce it the correct way?

"Right," Smith said to the Crawler. "What's your name?"

The Crawler responded with a litany of clicking clacks that Smith knew he would never remember, especially when placed against other names that would undoubtedly sound similar.

He decided to give the honest answer. "I won't be able to say that."

Again, the Crawler laughed, its mouth pounding open and shut. "Is no problem," it said. "Crawlers all talk of making new name human can say."

Smith raised his eyebrows. "That's kind of you," he said.

The Crawler breathed out. "Is small thing. A name is just word."

"Unless you're a Singer," Smith said.

"Yes," the Crawler said with a tick. "Singers beautiful. Better than Crawler and human."

Smith smiled and nodded, aware that the comment could have bothered him or hurt him. Yet the Crawler spoke truth. With a sigh, Smith thought of how inferior human language was when held up to that of the Singers. Or was it simply different, no better, no worse? Perhaps that was the better way to look at it, he realized.

"Just different," he said to the Crawler.

The Crawler spoke a phrase in its native tongue but did not translate.

"Don't agree?" Smith asked.

"Don't know," the Crawler answered. "Crawler don't usual think on such — *click* — right word?"

"Philosophy," Smith said.

"Losophy," the Crawler said.

Smith laughed, unable to stop himself. The Crawler joined in, two different species brought together by fate or chance or choice, sharing a small moment of pure amusement.

The Crawler stopped suddenly. "Our leaders?"

"Imprisoned," Smith said. "Locked up."

"Yes. Do what with them?"

"We—" Smith said, but he was cut short by a screeching melody.

A lone Singer ran into the clearing, his mouth open wide in a screaming tune of pure fear and rage. He jumped on a Crawler's back, wrapped both arms around its head, and squeezed. The Crawler's voice crackled. It bit the Singer's arm and shook violently until the Singer fell off. The Singer jumped to his feet, preparing to attack again.

The Crawler clicked loudly. "No," it said. "Don't want hurt you."

The Singer remained poised to pounce. Slowly, while melodizing an apology, he stood straight and stared at the Crawler.

"Know," the Crawler said, "we hurt Singers. Sorry leaders hurt Singers. You not fear us again. Stopped leaders."

The Singer made the note that translated, approximately, to 'okay.' He took a few steps closer to the Crawler and shared his doubts, openly and honestly, with the Crawler. A melody that filled Smith with doubt, making him question the Crawlers' intentions. What if they only drew the Singers out to ensure they killed every last one? What if those who had helped changed their minds, and turned again to killing the Singers? Smith understood the Singer's fear, though he did not feel it himself. Abe had told of how these Crawlers had killed others of their own species to protect human and Singer life. And Smith trusted his son far more than he trusted the fear of a Singer, no matter how reasonable that fear might be.

"Understand," the Crawler said and pulled out a copy of the Singer book. "Please. Like Mother said, 'hurt not any, not those who first hurt, not any.'"

The Singer collapsed to his knees, erupting in a frantic cry of notes laden with regret. He attacked a living creature, broke his covenant of pacifism. And Smith felt the Singer's overpowering self-hatred seep into his heart.

Braids—Lioness—joined the grieving Singer and helped him to his feet, quietly whispering notes as they walked toward the caves.

Smith closed his eyes and sighed.

Mercy, it seemed, was something every species on Aethera could understand better.

***

Night had fallen. All the Singers were awake, and no others had attempted to harm a Crawler. Not physically, at least.

The three species were gathered in a large inner hallway of the ship, eyes focused on four restrained Crawlers. The leaders imprisoned for their crimes against intelligent species. Smith, Johann and Theresa stood near the prisoners. Next to them, one Crawler, plus Singers Wave and Atom.

Johann cleared his throat. "We need to agree on a punishment for the former Crawler leaders." He paused and waited for Wave to translate. "But first, do we all agree punishment is deserved?"

Wave translated the question, and the overwhelming answer was 'yes.'

Smith stepped forward. "Okay. We need to decide how the punishment is dealt." Smith inhaled. How they dealt with the Crawler leaders would lay the foundation for all future interactions between the three species. "Many humans want to create a society that encourages and instills mercy. We want to utilize that system now. But we are not the only ones affected by these Crawlers' actions."

Wave translated, and the room went silent. Slowly, the Singers and the Crawlers started muttering among themselves. Wave joined Smith and Johann and made a simple note of questioning. What would such a system look like?

Smith nodded, then looked at Johann. "I never read the comic book," he said.

Johann laughed. "All right, I'll explain it to everyone."

Wave nodded and called out to the crowd. Everyone went quiet.

"The idea is that the hurt party in a crime is given the opportunity to pass judgment on the offender," Johann said. "We hope to do this in a way that encourages mercy."

Johann turned to Theresa.

"Yes," she said. "In our case, the Singers are truly the offended party. And." She paused, inhaled. "Everything the Singers have shown gives me confidence that they will choose a punishment that will begin a legacy of peace and mercy that will define the future of each of our species."

Smith locked eyes with her, then smiled and nodded. Something had shifted in her opinion of the Singers during the last few days. Smith thought it was from living in close quarters with the Singers, but perhaps it was just her way of politicking.

Wave approached the former Crawler leaders and sang a melody that raised a question in Smith's mind: Am I willing to change? Smith looked to the four Crawlers, then back to Lioness. She went quiet.

One of the restrained Crawlers lifted its feet up and down, looked at the floor, then erupted into fierce, violent clacks. Its head shook violently back and forth. The verbal tirade lasted over a minute, and ended with the Crawler spitting a thick glob of saliva into Wave's face. He lifted his hand as if to strike the Crawler, then let it drop. Silently and calmly, he wiped it off his face and turned away.

Johann sucked air in through his teeth. "Damn, it's gonna be hard to find mercy for them."

Chapter 3

The first rays of sunlight broke over the horizon. Alone, Tashon sat atop the ship and shivered against the cold breeze. Most everyone was asleep, in the ship or in the caves. Three species living in relative peace. A time of excitement and planning for the future.

Yet Tashon found himself confused, and longing for that higher plane. Part of his mind, as always, hovered above in the Fourth. It gave him a view of the rising sun, the ship casting a long shadow among the yellow trees. But he ached to lift fully into the Fourth, or even to lose himself in the nothing between dimensions. After his last sojourns from the Third, though, he didn't have the energy to do so.

Plus, there had been no sign of the Singer who had shown him the visions of the Crawlers. The visions that proved to be only partially correct. That frustrated Tashon more than he would have expected. They had saved the Singers, after all, in large part due to the visions he'd been given. So why should it matter that the visions were not entirely accurate?

It mattered, he realized, because of what it meant. He didn't like being referred to as a prophet, but he had accepted that his ability and his visions could be of great benefit to those on Aethera. With the inaccuracies in his visions, though, how could he trust future visions to provide valid knowledge of the future?

He sighed and shook his head.

Laos appeared in the Fourth.

Tashon smiled and closed his eyes. *"Any sign of her, Laos?"*

"No," Laos replied. *"Nor of the being that aided you."*

Tashon nodded, his frustrations rising. It seemed that the higher being would have the answers Tashon sought. And, even though it did not like Tashon being in the Fourth, Tashon felt and understood the being's concern for him. For every living being. Damn, he wished he could find that grand being. His mind twisted inside his skull and nausea swept over him. He needed to calm down and, without being able to rise to the Fourth, he had to settle on meditation.

"I'll talk to you later, Laos."

Tashon closed his eyes. Adjusted the focal point of his fourth-dimensional camera, placing himself almost out of sight. Focused on his breathing, focused his camera on a specific strand of sunlight illuminating a dead yellow leaf resting on the white snow. All else disappeared. The only thing that mattered in that moment was a dead leaf resting in the snow, the sunlight reflecting off the white illuminating the dead leaf as if its spirit were rising into the Fourth.

The beauty of Aethera was grand, he reminded himself. Its raw, natural beauty surpassed anything man could ever make, and brought peace in ways the thought of man never would. Even if the Fourth's other-worldliness took precedence in his mind, he could not let himself forget that. If he did, he feared he would lose all desire to help those in his own dimension.

He inhaled, exhaled. Fell into a slow, steady breathing pattern, and let everything but the glowing leaf disappear. Disappear into almost nothing. Not the full nothing he found between dimensions, but enough to quiet his mind and calm his body.

When he opened his eyes, the sun was directly above him and a group stood on the other side of the ship, staring at him. Rosa, Yeance and Minow stood at the front. Yeance quietly waved at Tashon and asked if they could join him. He nodded and the group formed a semicircle in front of him.

Rosa smiled. "How are you, Tashon?"

Tashon half-smiled back. "I'm okay, Rosa. You all right?"

She nodded in reply, opened her mouth to speak, then closed it. He knew what the group was expecting, though, and after everything they'd been through, he felt they deserved it.

"Questions?" he asked.

A teen girl spoke, her voice squeaking with excitement. "What is it like actually being in the Fourth?"

Tashon smiled, shrugging. "Impossible to explain," he said. "Colors I never imagined. Shapes beyond reckoning. Imagine you're a child's drawing. Like a stick figure. Then something...unknowable pulls you off the page and into the Third. You would see the cubes, the spheres, and understand them as best you could. But when you go back to the page, how would you explain to the others?"

Some nodded as though they understood. Tashon knew that they did as best as they could. It was impossible to truly understand without going to the Fourth.

Yeance spoke next. "We've all heard you talk about seeing the dead there. Do you think it's their souls?"

"I do," Tashon said.

"Is the Fourth heaven?" Yeance smiled.

Tashon shook his head. "The souls of the good and bad are all there. Of every species, I think." He paused. "Aleron's monster is there too, I'm sure. I haven't seen it though."

"Have you seen everyone who's died?" a boy asked.

"Only a few. Laos is always there. Evalee comes and goes. Grace — my sister — and my parents, once. And others from a distance."

"And that Singer," Rosa said.

"Right."

"What's it like for the souls?" Minow asked.

Tashon inhaled. "*Laos?*"

"*It's better but still confusing. We can still grow. Better ourselves. Pain is...different. More intense, but not as lasting.*"

Tashon relayed the information.

"So this life isn't all there is to improve ourselves," Rosa said with a smile.

Tashon nodded. "Right. And it seems that there are places even higher than the Fourth."

"Really?" Yeance said.

Tashon shrugged. "I get that idea, but I don't know for sure."

Everyone nodded, seemingly lost in thought. Tashon wondered if sharing what he knew of the Fourth would be beneficial or harmful. He needed to make sure it didn't spiral into a belief system that created bigotry and violence. No crusades, terrorists or forced conversions. But how could he do that? He had no idea, but he would do all he could to teach only peace and goodwill.

Rosa started that conversation for him. "You've seemed more peaceful since learning your connection to the Fourth."

"I have." Tashon stopped, closed his eyes. He knew what he was about to say would change his role, the future of his life. Yet doing so felt inevitable. "I think I can help you all find that same peace. If you want."

Yeance nodded and smiled. "Doesn't everyone want more peace?"

Everyone agreed, their eyes bright with anticipation.

Tashon nodded, breathing to calm himself before he stepped fully onto the road that would put him in a more culturally significant place than he ever expected himself to be. "Close your eyes," he said.

They did, and Tashon realized he had no idea what to say. Meditation was almost as new to him as it was to them, and he was only able to do it effectively because of his connection to the Fourth.

"How should we sit?" the boy asked.

Tashon kept his eyes closed and looked at the group from above. Each copied his posture exactly: legs crossed, arms pulled tight across his chest to keep warm. He'd never thought of a meditative position before, had always simply positioned himself in whatever way felt most comfortable. From his experience, it didn't matter.

"Comfortably," he said.

Each adjusted to whatever position they wanted and remained silent. Tashon knew they were expecting him to say something. But what? He had no amazing insights that would change their lives forever, not even words of wisdom that would comfort them for the week ahead of them. All that came to mind was his memory of nothing.

He inhaled, exhaled. "Nothing and everything," he said quietly, monotoned. "Everything and nothing. Everything is nothing, nothing is everything. Think only this."

He tried to remember what else he had felt floating in that emptiness.

"Everything matters and nothing matters. You are significant. You are insignificant."

He smiled and breathed. Breathing right was important.

"Slow, steady breaths," he whispered. He let his mind wander the Fourth and spoke whatever words came to him. "Universes, dimensions, all more vast than any comprehend. We are nothing in the vastness." He smiled at the thought. In the distance of the Fourth, his mind saw a concord of souls leaving a multi-pyramidal shape en masse, a cloud of blacks, grays and whites. "Our nothing makes up everything. Insignificant, significant." He stopped. No more words came. The pyramids and flying souls disappeared. Had they been there at all?

He turned his attention back to the overhead view of the meditative group. They all appeared serene, but he couldn't help but wonder if his words were helping. He'd never studied much religion, had rarely taken the role of a teacher. And now, Rosa, a woman he'd admired since she stood up for him on the ship, was looking to him as a prophet. She'd even convinced others of his supposed prophetic status. It was humbling, and he would do what he could to help those who believed in him. Would it have any lasting effect? Or would it crumble and fall apart soon after his death?

These thoughts threatened his own peace, and he knew he couldn't provide peace to the others in that state of mind. He opened his eyes. "That's all I have," he said.

Eyes opened, arms and legs stretched. Faces appeared relaxed and tranquil. One by one, the group left, each offering sincere thanks to Tashon. Then only Rosa remained with him.

She smiled. "Beautiful, Tashon."

Tashon shrugged and nodded. "Thanks."

"Thank you too," she said. "I have a feeling more people'll come next time."

"Next time?"

"You didn't think it was one time only?"

Tashon shrugged again. "No. This is new. What do we do from here? Start a church? Write my meditations down? My visions? I'm no prophet, Rosa."

"We'll figure that out as it comes. Let's start with this: when do you want to help people mediate again?"

Tashon considered. All he wanted to do was sleep and see what new insights he could gain from the Fourth. He didn't exactly want to lead a meditation again, but he didn't not want to either. He knew it was only right to share what understanding and peace he had with everyone that wanted to listen.

"Give me three days," he said.

She smiled. "I'll spread the word, Sage."

She stood and walked away.

Sage, Tashon thought. *Better than prophet.*

Chapter 4

Abe lifted a small box of packaged food into a Crawler vessel. The vehicle was rectangular, the bottom curved and full of divots. His dad walked to his side, then tossed in a pile of blankets.

Abe nodded to him. "You really good if I go?" he asked.

Smith smiled. "I am."

"Pure O_2," Abe said.

He smiled as his dad gave him a hug. Life was working out. For the moment, at least. Yet he still couldn't shake the feeling that something else was coming. They'd suffered a shipwreck. Two, to be precise. Fought off Aleron and his shadow beast. Taken out half a species that wanted them all dead. For all of the fighting and darkness and chaos to be suddenly over felt wrong. As if a piece of his life were missing. Abe knew it didn't make sense, and it only made him think that more darkness would come.

One night, when he was half asleep, he wondered if his fear of more darkness would cause him to see darkness where there was none. To make more problems than there actually were.

So, with the fear of darkness in his mind, he needed to do something. Anything more than sitting around waiting for the trial and judgment of the Crawler leaders. To meet that need, Abe invited himself to return to the Crawler land to aid in the repairs of their city.

His dad patted his back. "I'll see you when you get back," he said.

Abe nodded, smiled and turned back to the vehicle. Its flat deck was packed with supplies, Singers, Crawlers and humans. Smokies encircled it, reminding Abe of when he had first encountered the nanotech creatures in the desert. He climbed onto the vessel and found Winona at the far end.

"Hi," he said as he sat next to her.

She smiled. "Hey, you ready?"

"Of course," he said, returning the smile.

A Crawler walked toward them and rested its midsection on a crate.

Abe quickly looked at its legs. This was the Crawler who had been their guide when they tunneled into the Crawler capital.

"Leave soon," it said. "Thank you to help."

"You're welcome," Abe said. "Thank you for saving all of us."

The Crawler chattered. "Is good for all of us."

"It is," Winona said.

Abe looked at her then back at the Crawler. "What's your name?" he asked.

"We all choose name human can say," it said. "My human name Lollawk."

"Lollawk?" Abe repeated.

"Lollawk."

"Why Lollawk?" Winona asked.

The Crawler pounded a laugh. "I like Lollawk sounds."

"Me too," Winona said. "Do you know our names?"

"Yes, yes," Lollawk said. "Abe. Winona. All Crawler know you."

Abe raised his eyebrows. "They do?"

"Yes, yes."

"Why?"

"You not know?"

"Know what?" Winona asked, her voice rising with curiosity.

"Singer book," Lollawk said. "Singer Mother. Knew you two come here."

Abe and Winona glanced at each other, then back to Lollawk.

"What?" Abe said.

Lollawk pulled the book out, flipped through the pages and handed it to Winona. Abe leaned over. It was a drawing. A detailed sketch of two humans, one male and one female. Both were bald. The male had only one arm, the other gone just below the elbow. It looked exactly like Abe and Winona.

"Damn," Abe said.

"The hell?" Winona asked.

Lollawk reached out and turned the page, revealing the same picture, with one difference: the male was holding a baby in his one good arm. Abe turned his head away, a wave of excited embarrassment rushing over him. Was his relationship with Winona fated? Foretold by some Singer prophet?

Winona giggled, then coughed. "We're going to have a child?"

"First child of new era," Lollawk said.

"But first we'd have to, uh...." Winona coughed and shook her head.

"Yeah," Abe said.

Another Crawler jumped aboard the carrier. "Time go now."

The vessel vibrated and shot straight up, stopping a dozen feet above the trees.

"Grab tight," Lollawk said.

Abe grabbed a rod on the side of his seat. Winona did the same, and leaned her shoulder into his chest. They accelerated suddenly and Abe almost fell to the floor, but was held steady by Winona wrapping an arm around his waist. They smiled at each other and laughed. After a few minutes, Abe grew used to their speed and was able to stand on steady legs. He walked to the edge and looked down.

They sped over the hills that had taken them days to cover by foot. In the cold and the snow there was no sign of the bush creatures or of any more supersonic birds, of which Abe was grateful. He hoped to catch glimpses of one in the bushes, but they soon crossed over the rocks, passed the waterfall cliff, and were above open water without seeing another living creature. He decided they must hibernate during the winter, or perhaps migrate to warmer climates.

Winona stood silently next to him the entire ride, hand gripping his. He liked how he felt around her, liked being with her, liked *her*. Yet he could sense the awkwardness between them since Lollawk said it had been prophesied they would bring a baby into the world. They'd gone through their own hells, apart and together. The only person he trusted more, cared for more, was his dad. Did he love her? Did he want to raise a kid with her?

He had no idea.

"We're only sixteen," Winona said.

"Huh?"

"We're not having a kid anytime soon," she said.

Abe laughed nervously. "That means we're not, uh...." he said.

"Having sex anytime soon?" she asked.

Abe shrugged.

Winona rolled her eyes. "Are you saying you want to?"

Abe looked at the ocean below, then around at the Crawlers, Singers and humans that surrounded them. He looked back at Winona, considering the question.

"Sex doesn't feel all that important," he said. "With everything else."

Winona smiled. "Yeah," she said. "But at some point new humans will need to start being born on Aethera."

"Yeah," he said. *Seems less romantic that way*, he thought.

The stone pillars of the Crawler land appeared on the horizon. Some stood tall while others were broken to pieces. Abe focused on Winona.

Her eyes, her smile, her strength. He wasn't ready to make a lifelong commitment with anyone, but he knew that when he was he would be ecstatic if that person were Winona. As soon as he came to this realization, an entirely new image burst into his mind: Aleron's shadows breaking back into the Third, black tentacles piercing Winona, converting her body into another limp puppet.

He swallowed hard and closed his eyes, wondering if his mind would always be drawn to the dark and pessimistic.

***

Without the adrenaline of battle pumping through his veins, Abe plainly saw what the cost of the battle had been: destruction and death. There, at the scene of the fight, all feelings of victory and revelry vanished. One section of the city was dedicated to cremating the corpses of the dead. Others for treating the injured, or keeping the enemy Crawlers locked away. All of these stood off in the distance.

Abe, Winona and all who were still living and free worked to clear the rubble from the structures that still stood. The entrance to the pillar Abe worked on was blocked by the remains of another stone tower. According to Lollawk, it was an entrance to the storage tunnels that held emergency food supplies. Other entrances remained open, but this one was closer to the hub of activity.

With a grunt, Abe reached his only arm around a boulder and pulled it off the pile, sending it tumbling to the ground. From there a row of Crawlers, Singers and humans passed it down and out of the way. Abe wiped the sweat from his forehead and sent another boulder rolling. As soon as the rock was out of the way, a gush of air rushed out of the opening that appeared. It was warmer than the winter air surrounding him and smelled of smoke.

"Got an opening, Lollawk!" he called.

The Crawler clicked and climbed to the hole. "Yes, yes. Good." He pulled a cone out of his hidden pouch. "Drink."

Abe took it in his hand and examined it. Thinking of the Crawlers' weapons he'd already seen, he squeezed his hand tight around it. A small hole opened on the flat edge. He lifted it to his lips and gulped the cool water.

He sighed and smiled. "Thank you."

Something crunched inside the tunnel. A metal ball flew out of the hole, bounced on the ground and rolled to a stop. A resounding click burst from Lollawk's mouth. Another Crawler clicked back, ran to the ball and kicked it into the air. It exploded ten feet above the ground.

Lollawk forced Abe down the pile, rushing behind him. The pile trembled. Then exploded outward, boulders, rocks and pebbles raining down on them. Abe turned and found Winona a few yards away. He ran to cover her but a soaring rock struck his shoulder, sending him face-first into the dirt. Winona ran to him, throwing her body on top of his. Abe felt a rush of embarrassment, then of gratitude as he realized she cared enough for him to cover his body with hers. *Perhaps we are fated to be together*, he thought. And that thought terrified him, almost more than the thought of Aleron and his shadows returning to Aethera.

The rocks and pebbles succumbed to gravity and the air filled with dust. Winona pushed herself off Abe. Both jumped to their feet and turned to the newly uncovered tunnel. Three Crawlers charged out, surrounded by half a dozen biotech birds with fangs and razors for wings. The birds shot forward, their wings cutting the throats of one Crawler, two humans and two Singers. Harsh clicks and screeching melodies filled the air.

Lollawk leaped on top of an attacking Crawler, jabbing skinny fingers into its eyes and pulling it to the ground. The birds turned around and came back for another slicing pass. Abe grabbed two rocks and threw them in quick succession. Each struck a bird, the two crashing to the dirt and sparking. To his left, a Singer snatched a bird from the air and slammed it into the ground.

Abe turned to face the next enemy, but the fight was already over. Two Crawlers lay on the ground, dead and bleeding from the eyes. Lollawk had the last enemy Crawler pinned to the ground, a cable coming from his forehead piercing the head of his foe. Looking for information, Abe guessed.

The survivors gathered in a circle. A man gasped and ran to a body on the ground. A woman about his age. He fell next to her, dropped his forehead to hers and silently sobbed. A Singer walked to his side and quietly sang comfort.

Abe looked away, blinking away tears. He thought of his first day on Aethera, his dad slowly covering his mom's body in dirt, scoop by scoop. He took a deep breath and wiped his cheeks. The three remaining birds perched peacefully on a boulder, no sign of aggression in them.

A Crawler looked at Abe. "Birds under control. Controller died. It go still."

Abe nodded, his mind still on the day his mom died.

Lollawk made a loud, rasping sound as the cable retracted into his head.

"What learn?" another Crawler asked.

"Some more not accept surrender," Lollawk said. "Not know where."

The other Crawler clicked and stomped its feet. Lollawk repeated the speech and action.

"We'll keep an eye out," Abe said.

"Why didn't they accept the surrender?" Winona asked.

"Hate strong," Lollawk said, looking at the Crawler pinned beneath him. "Do what with her?"

Abe looked at the blood-soaked bodies and was ready to tell Lollawk to kill her. Then he remembered the legacy of mercy Johann and his dad wanted to leave on Aethera.

The man crying over the woman stood and wiped his nose. "Prison," he said. "Like your leaders."

Lollawk yanked the Crawler up and dragged her toward the dome that housed the Crawler prisoners.

Abe looked back at the weeping man, and asked himself, *Would I have that kind of mercy if I were him?* He liked to think he would, but he was pretty certain he'd succumb to grief and rage if he were in the man's shoes.

Chapter 5

"So, what do we do with them?" Theresa asked. "They're not admitting to any wrongdoing. They're convinced they were right in trying to kill off all human and Singer life."

Smith rubbed his eyes. He understood how she was feeling. There seemed to be no right answer, and Smith was more and more convinced that any answer could be right *or* wrong. He looked to the Singers and Crawlers who sat in the caves with them.

"You see the world differently than we do," he said. "What do you all think?"

A Crawler by the name of Hutsep answered first. "Singers against all violence. Even in punishment. Even in retaliation."

Lioness stood, responding to the statement with notes of disagreement. Peace had been the way of all Singers, but their species was changing. She did not like being grouped in as one with all Singers.

"You think we should kill them?" Johann asked.

Lioness replied with one note: 'no.'

"Keep former leaders locked," Hutsep said.

Smith considered the option. "Is imprisonment more merciful than death?"

The crowd talked among themselves but soon grew quiet.

"How do we define mercy?" Minow asked.

"That's a good question," Johann said.

Theresa coughed. "It's kindness, despite not receiving any."

A memory sprang into Smith's mind. "Evalee and I talked about this once," he said. "Mercy is getting—how did she say it?—not as harsh a judgment as you deserve."

Minow sighed. "But what do they deserve?"

"Execution? Life in prison?" Theresa asked. "Hutsep? Or another Crawler?"

Hutsep pointed at another Crawler. "Ulot answer."

"Crawlers talk much on this," the Crawler Ulot said. "Crawler law would kill leaders. Singer teach not kill. Cannot let leaders free. Keep in prison, yes. But that mercy?"

"Any thoughts?" Johann asked, looking at everyone around him.

An elderly man stood up. "I studied Earth history for years. Taught it. War criminals, or those who committed crimes against humanity were usually executed. Sometimes sentenced to life in prison. Historically, either of those could be considered deserved. But we're talking less than they deserve," he said, and remained standing.

"And what would be less?" Smith asked.

"Maybe, just an idea, they could be prisoners but not locked up. They could be tethered to a guard always, somehow. But still be able to go outside, eat real meals, but not be confined to one small area."

"Like a pet," Minow said. "Not a prisoner."

Some laughed softly at that, but Smith thought it was a decent idea.

"That could work," he said. "Ulot? Hutsep?"

"Guard must be Crawler," Ulot said.

Hutsep clicked. "Yes, tether from Crawler guard to prisoner. Might work."

"Might?" Theresa asked.

"Would limit guard much," Hutsep replied. "Guard would need partner not tethered to keep guard and prisoner safe."

Theresa sighed. "Does this seem like a smart idea? Safe?"

Someone else stood and leaned against the rock wall. "Hutsep, Ulot, if we do it like this, are the leaders gonna escape and murder us?"

Hutsep and Ulot clicked quietly with the other Crawlers.

Theresa turned to Johann and Smith. "Are we really sure about showing this much mercy?"

Johann shrugged and smiled. "We're trying something different, right? Trying to create a society different and better than any on Earth. The real question is, do we think placing more importance on mercy will help us do that? I think it will."

Smith nodded. Johann was right. It was different and terrifying and potentially dangerous, but if showing mercy created a more peaceful society, it would be worth the risk. Wouldn't it? Smith sighed quietly. When Johann first told him of the system of mercy, Smith had expected the first trial of it be the result of a drunken brawl or petty theft. Not to decide the fate of tyrannical leaders who fought for the genocide of two species.

Ulot turned back to the group. "Yes, can work. What do Singers think?"

Atom immediately let out a resounding 'yes.' Lioness followed with a string of notes saying she would see how it went, but if the Crawlers made any indication of hurting again, she would be willing to execute them herself.

"Okay," Smith said. "Tomorrow, we'll give them their merciful imprisonment and let them live with us."

"But on constant guard," Theresa added.

The group split off into smaller circles, each discussing the potential positive and negative consequences that could spring from their decision. Smith was happy to hear that, despite the bad it might bring, most everyone was open to trying out the new system. In Smith's mind, that was because all the humans knew that it was a lack of understanding and mercy that eventually led to most of the war and bloodshed on Earth. Since each of them had left Earth in an attempt to create a better society on a new planet, it only made sense that they would be willing to try to create a society with the goal of preventing those issues.

As Smith meandered through the cavern, listening to people's hopes, fears and theories, he saw Lioness sitting alone against a wall. He walked to her and sat down, sensing something was wrong.

With as much emotion as he could, he asked her if she was okay. The notes that came from her were almost a whisper, but he felt her hurt. Her pain. Her confusion. Yes, she made the decision to commit violent acts. It was against the Singer ways, but she was doing it to protect her species. To her, it was justified.

Most of the other Singers didn't see it that way. Lioness went silent for a few moments. Smith thought she was done, but her melody returned louder than the first time. She sang of how most of the Singers had been treating her since they learned of her violent acts. They spoke poorly of her, some even choosing to shun her completely. The Singers refrained from physical violence, but that did not mean they were always kind.

"I'm sorry," Smith said.

She thanked him and asked how he was doing. Since she had been so open with her answer, he saw no reason to respond any differently.

"I'm excited about the future," he said. "But also terrified. I have no idea if this plan of mercy will work out how we want it to. In a hundred years, will it be a society I want my grandchildren living in?" He shook his head and shrugged. "Sometimes I wish Tashon's Fourth sight showed him the future."

Lioness let out a note of confusion, indicating she didn't understand what Smith was saying about Tashon. As quickly and simply as he could, Smith explained Tashon's connection to the Fourth. Told of the visions he'd seen, the idea that the Fourth was a type of afterlife. When he told of the Singer soul Tashon communicated with, Lioness made a note like a gasp and jumped to her feet.

"Lioness? What's wrong?"

Staring off into the distance, she made two notes that meant one word: Mother.

Chapter 6

Tashon awoke feeling energized, physically and mentally, ready to return completely to the Fourth. He made his way quickly out of the ship and into the woods. After an hour of walking silently, he decided he was far enough away from anyone else to find the peace he wanted.

There were no questions in his mind of whether rising again to the Fourth was a good idea. To him, it was a need. He needed to feel the air of that higher plane. Needed to find answers, find the being that had aided him. And to find the Singer who showed him the visions.

He found a spot of ground, free of snow due to the warmth of the rising sun. With a smile and tremor of excitement, he sat down and crossed his legs.

"Are you sure about this?" Laos's words swam into his mind.

"Yes," Tashon answered aloud.

He had an idea of how to better prepare his mind and body for his time in the Fourth. A way to heighten his strength and increase his ability to occupy the Fourth for extended periods of time. First, he had to return to nothing.

He closed his eyes, stretched his mind higher to the piece of his essence in the Fourth. Pulling his body from the Third, he watched from his higher view as his form disappeared from Aetheran soil. Everything flashed white and he stopped his form from rising higher. He floated in nothing.

Sound disappeared, as did color, touch and smell. He let everything in him wash away. Pain. Worry. Fear. Aware only that he existed, accepting that being allowed to exist was enough. Seconds — or hours, or weeks — later, a voice called to his mind. Bit by bit, he let himself be pulled back into awareness of physical dimensions. First, he felt the wind of the Fourth, then saw the colors, and then recognized the voice that had been calling to him.

The godlike being towered in its mountainous form before Tashon.

"You're back," it said.

Tashon nodded. *"I've been looking for you."*

"*Yes. I've been gone searching.*"

"*For what?*"

"*For others. Others like you.*"

"*Like me?*"

"*Of the third dimension, able to willingly access and enter the Fourth.*" The being spun, twisted and shrank to Tashon's size. "*I found none. How did you obtain this ability?*"

Tashon raised his eyebrows, surprised that the being did not already know. "*A black being came to the Third from the Fourth. Made human puppets, pierced its appendages into their brains. It got me, but didn't fully connect before our tesseract engine sent it back to the Fourth.*"

The being's body shimmered and twisted. "*I see. That is where that monster came from.*"

"*You've seen it?*" Tashon's heart raced as he looked around. "*Here?*"

"*Seen and taken care of.*"

"*How?*"

"*With the help of many.*"

Tashon shook his head in wonder, wanting to ask more but somehow knowing that's all the being would say about Aleron. "*Why aren't you sending me back this time?*"

The being laughed. "*You are stronger this time. Being here does not seem to be wasting you away as before. Why is that?*"

"*I found nothing.*"

"*Ah. The in between. Nirvana. Paradise. The Resting Place.*"

"*That's Nirvana?*"

"*The closest anyone will ever get to such a place. Nothing, the only place where there is no good and no evil. No want nor desire. The place sought by mystics and sages and prophets. Dangerous. Impermanent.*"

"*Dangerous?*"

"*Yes, dangerous.*" The wind twirled around the being, and it flew away.

Tashon sat down, exhausted. The dizziness and nausea from previous trips to the Fourth were gone, but being there still drained his body. His mind, though, had never felt more invigorated. He was filled with questions, with imaginings both wonderful and terrifying. Felt as if he were on the brink of understanding everything, yet knowing he would never fully comprehend anything in the vast dimensions of the universe.

He smiled. Laughed until he couldn't breathe. He coughed, then wiped tears off his face. When he opened his eyes, he found Laos and Evalee in front of him.

He sensed Laos's confusion and felt Evalee's amusement.

"Tash, it's good to see you smile," Evalee said to Tashon's mind.

"It's true," Laos said. *"But what's so funny?"*

Tashon paused, thinking, then answered, *"I feel the happiest I've felt in a long time."*

The essences of Laos and Evalee smiled, a soft shimmer surrounding their forms.

Tashon smiled back. *"Evalee, where do you go when you're not over Aethera?"*

"To see what's out there. This dimension is vast and beautiful."

"What've you found?"

"More places like the Higher Spheres."

"Really? What are they like?"

"Each one a different shape, each with its own sense of wonder. As if each has come from its own, unique place. I don't think I can explain any better."

Tashon nodded. It was like him trying to explain being in the Fourth to those who only knew the Third.

Soon, his exhaustion got the best of him. He said goodbye, closed his eyes and pulled himself back to the Third.

He opened his eyes and looked up. The rising moon was low in the sky. A full day come and gone while he floated in nothing and communicated with beings in the Fourth. He walked back to the ship, a calm in his heart he hadn't felt since before he killed Laos. And, for once, he didn't question whether he deserved to feel that calm in his heart.

The air was warmer than many nights before it and Tashon arrived at the ship to a large group made up of all three species. They ate, talked and laughed. He looked for Rosa, but before he found her, Lioness ran up to him. The Singer sang notes quickly, filling Tashon with a vast range of emotions that left him confused and exhausted.

He held his hands up. "Stop. Wait."

She went silent.

"I can't follow," he said calmly. "Too fast."

She sang one note.

Tashon thought he understood. "Mother?"

Lioness sang, "yes," followed by a note Tashon didn't recognize.

It made Tashon calm, centered and sure of himself. He thought 'confident' might be the word, but it didn't feel right. Lioness repeated the note, but still he couldn't make sense of what she was saying, and he could sense the frustration in her voice. He looked around and called the nearest Crawler over.

"Yes, Tashon?" it asked.

Tashon felt he should know the Crawler before engaging in a discussion of translation. "What's your name?"

"Hutsep," the Crawler said.

"Hutsep, you understand the Singer language, right?"

"Yes, yes," it replied.

Tashon looked at Lioness and back to Hutsep. "I don't understand what she's trying to tell me."

"Lioness," Hutsep said. "What say you?"

Lioness sang a long string of notes, the meaning making only the simplest of emotional sense to Tashon.

Hutsep made a scratching click and looked at Tashon. "Truth?"

"Is what true?"

Hutsep looked up. "You go above?"

"I can," Tashon said.

Hutsep clicked quietly. "Wonder, wonder."

Lioness sang again, louder and with more urgency, her notes tumbling into one another. A melodic rap of severe curiosity, a yearning for answers. Answers about 'mother.'

Tashon shook his head. "I don't understand."

"I understand." Hutsep pulled out another copy of the Singer book. "You know this?"

"The book?" Tashon shook his head. "It has to do with the Singers' pacifism. That's all I know."

"Much more." Hutsep reverently turned the pages. "Peaceful goal of Singers, yes. Also Singer history. Singer future. All told by Singers' first mother."

"Future?" Tashon asked. "Like prophecies?"

"Not know word," Hutsep said. "Future. Mother wrote your people to come. To save Singers."

Tashon inhaled quickly. This 'Mother' foretold the coming of the humans? Prophesied their coming to rescue the Singers from the Crawlers? It seemed impossible, yet for some reason it registered to him as truth.

Then he understood what Lioness was asking. "She wants to know if I've seen their first mother," he said.

Hutsep clicked happily. "She believes you already seen first mother."

"I... what?" He looked to Lioness.

The Singer went into another ranting melody, but now knowing the context of her notes, Tashon understood more clearly. He felt her amazement at hearing Tashon had seen a Singer in the Fourth. Knew of her rising doubts since she had seen reason for violence, since she had seen the goodness of many of the Crawlers. Understood her burning desire to know if the Singer Tashon saw in the Fourth was her first mother.

Tashon didn't know for sure, but he did know what he was beginning to believe. "I think it was your first mother," he said.

Chapter 7

Abe and Winona took shelter from an icy rain inside a Crawler dome, surrounded by dozens more, all trying to stay warm. Wind blew the frozen drops into the building through crumbled walls on one side. A handful of Crawlers leaned over a biotech creature. A massive feline, prone and unmoving, its back split open, revealing a complex maze of wires and veins, batteries and organs.

"I saw one like that rip the head off a Crawler," Abe said.

Winona stared at the falling ice. "It's odd seeing it like that. Realizing it's not just a wild animal."

"Yeah," Abe said.

"Do you think they're self-aware?"

Abe looked at her. "Huh?"

"The biotech. I know they're part engineered material, part computer. But what about the organic part? Is that part aware that they're not a natural creature? Do they care? Do they want? Get scared? Feel love?"

Abe sighed and shrugged. "No idea."

An older woman sitting nearby scooted her way to the couple. "I was wondering the same thing, hons," she said. "They have to have some type of natural mental capacity to do what they do, don't ya think?"

"I'd think so," Winona said.

"Probably," Abe said. "But for them to always follow the commands from the Crawlers, there has to be something engineered in them to ensure they obey."

"I agree," the woman said. "But how self-aware are they? Do they know they're being controlled?"

"Slaves or machines?" Winona asked.

"That's where I was going," the woman said. "I'm Londey, by the way."

"Abe."

"Winona."

"You're wondering," Abe said. "About whether it's right to create and use the biotech creatures?"

Londey nodded. "Right. Is it ethical?"

Abe considered the question, wondering how Ballas might answer. "But maybe the Crawlers have a completely different idea on ethics. Or even what 'alive' means."

Winona shook her head. "But they do have some sort of ethics. At least these do. They fought and died for us and the Singers."

Abe and Londey agreed, but the mention of the Singers turned Abe's thoughts to what their book said of him and Winona. How was it possible that a book written long before he was born, by a different species, had a drawing of him and Winona? It shouldn't be, but something told Abe the images in the book were what Lollawk said they were. But that thought made Abe question his own free will, and the idea that his life choices were dictated by destiny made him feel no different than the biotech that murdered on command.

He watched the Crawlers digging around inside the computer animal's body. Did the hybrid creature have any say in its destiny? *Do I?* Abe thought. He had no answer to the question.

"Abe!" Winona shouted, startling at Abe.

"Huh?" he said, confused.

"You disappeared," Londey said. "Where'd you go?"

Abe looked at Winona, then at Londey, and back at Winona.

"Oh," Winona said, then laughed awkwardly.

"What?" Londey asked.

Abe cleared his throat and shook his head. "That Singer book *talks about us.*"

Londey nodded. "You mean the prophesy that humans would come save them from the Crawlers?"

"What?" Abe said.

Surprised, Londey asked, "You didn't know? What were *you* talking about?"

Abe looked at Winona.

Winona sighed. "The book specifically talks about me and Abe. Has drawings that look like us."

"I don't understand this place," Londey said. "What's the book say about you?"

Abe and Winona exchanged another awkward glance.

"It says," Abe said. "That, uh, we'll be the parents of Aethera's first child."

"Of the new era," Winona added.

Londey looked at both of them and broke into loud laughter. "I'm sorry," she said, trying to catch her breath. "I can see how uncomfortable that makes both of you."

"Yeah," Abe and Winona whispered at once.

A moment of silence followed, and Abe couldn't help but feel his future had already planned itself out, without ever asking his opinion. And no matter what he did, there was no escaping that plan. The Singers had seen that the humans would arrive and save them from the Crawlers, and that vision happened as they saw it would. Did they see it because it was fated to happen, or was it fated to happen because they had seen it? Was there a difference?

Londey shook her head. "No, sure as hell don't understand it," she said.

Lollawk walked through the room, checking on everyone, making sure they were warm and fed. Abe waited nervously as the Crawler approached.

He stopped and clicked. "Abe. Winona. Londey. You feel good?"

Abe shrugged and shook his head, and then realized Lollawk wouldn't know what that meant. "No," he said.

"What do to help?"

Abe took a deep breath. "Tell me more about the Singer book. How'd the Singers know we would come?"

"Not know. Guesses. Theories. Nothing more."

"Have you asked the Singers?" Winona asked.

"Yes. Singer say Mother saw Singer future. To Singers, that fact."

Londey cleared her throat. "They don't look for any explanation?"

"No," Lollawk said. "Some do, now. Yet most Singers don't like such questions."

"Lollawk," Abe said. "Do you have a theory?"

Lollawk patted his feet up and down, quickly breaths escalating his mouth. "No. Yes. Not good one. Maybe Singer Mother move in time. Maybe Singer Mother dream of future. Maybe, maybe, maybe. Think maybe never know."

"Maybe she was like Tashon," Winona said.

"Tashon can't see the future," Abe retorted.

Winona smiled. "Not yet. But what if he could? What if he figures how to move in the Fourth in a way that moved him through physical space but also time?"

"That's a lot of ifs," Londey said.

"As good a theory as any," Abe said. "But you're starting to sound like Rosa," he added with a smile.

Across the room, a Crawler clicked loudly and Lollawk walked away. Londey soon left as well, leaving Abe and Winona to ponder their destiny and whether the outcome of their lives was already determined by some all-seeing power.

They moved to the edge of the dome, lay down and fell asleep.

***

Abe was a child again, back on the Ship of Nations. He stood with his mom on the top level, holding her hand as they looked out through the glass at a large star. It seemed too close to be safe, yet no harm came to them or the ship. He looked up at his mom, she looked down at him and they both smiled. Then he turned forward again, soaking up the warmth of the light that illuminated them. Light. Warmth. Comfort. All he ever needed was right there.

Then the light was obscured by hundreds of black shadows tethered together. They broke through the glass, sending shards everywhere. They stared at Abe and his mom. She pushed him behind her. The forms surrounded her and pulled her out into the cold and the dark. Abe screamed as the light of the star died out.

***

An explosion, then screeching clicks and bleating clacks shook Abe awake. For a moment, he thought it was Aleron, come again to finish what he started. He jumped to his feet and, through eyes still blurry with sleep, saw a small squad of Crawlers charging through a new hole in the dome wall. Not Aleron, but still a problem.

Small, bulbous biotech ran beneath their feet, glowing a soft yellow. An older lanky man jumped to his feet and kicked at one of the creatures, but just before his foot made contact it leapt into the air and landed on his scalp. A yellow liquid drained from beneath the biotech, soaking the man's face and sizzling his skin. He screamed as Abe ran to help. But before he could get to him, a Crawler kicked him to the ground.

Abe quickly rolled over and jumped back to his feet. Lollawk ran to his side and screeched so loud it vibrated Abe's chest. He gave Abe the weapon he'd used when they first attacked the city, what Abe now thought of as the 'thorn exploder.'

"We are more than them," Lollawk said, looking around at the dome filled with friendly Crawlers, Singers and humans.

Abe gripped the metal disc in his one hand and fired a stream of darts at the biotech. Three of them blew apart, spraying the urine yellow liquid on the legs of two enemy Crawlers. It slowed them down, but they kept charging. Abe fired again, taking out more biotech, fearing one would find its way onto his head. Or Winona's. He looked for her only to find that she had a weapon similar to Abe's. She fired at Crawler legs, and brought two to their knees.

Lollawk ran at an oncoming Crawler as if to plow right into it, but at the last second leaped into the air and landed a quick kick square in its face. Its head snapped back, and the Crawler went limp. More friendly Crawlers charged in, kicking and gnashing. Abe finished off the biotech quickly and turned his aim to the Crawler legs, but soon realized he wasn't needed.

The biotech feline leaped into the fight and let out a screech that belonged to the mouth of a bird. The remaining enemies stopped their advance, turned and ran to the freshly made hole. Their retreat failed as the feline landed on the back of one, bit into its head, jumping off before the body collapsed. Its feet found purchase on the next nearest Crawler, and soon the head of each attacking Crawler was crushed, the attached bodies limp and motionless.

The Crawlers dead, the biotech bulb detached from the prone man's head and sat on the ground, its yellow glow blinking brighter and dimmer, brighter and dimmer. The man rolled to his side and moaned. Abe ran to him and knelt down. A layer of skin had melted off his face, leaving blisters and spots of bright red.

Abe placed a hand on his shoulder. "Are you okay?"

The man nodded.

"I know you, a bit. What's your name?"

The man inhaled shallowly and then coughed. "An... Anton."

Lollawk joined Abe, then crouched and examined Anton's face. "We have plant to help heal."

Anton nodded.

Lollawk clicked at a nearby Crawler, who ran off. "Jute get it."

"The hell," Anton whispered. "The hell they keep comin' from?"

Lollawk stood straight. "Not know. Need to discover."

"We should send out patrols," Abe said. "Find any more that are left."

"Yes, yes. Send some out at dark."

"I'll come."

Lollawk clicked loudly. "No."

"What?"

"Need Abe, Winona safe. Need first parents safe." Lollawk turned and left, ending the discussion.

Abe remained by Anton, left not only to worry about unknown attacks on his freewill but also on the blatant command from Lollawk. *Would it be better if a Singer told me to stay put, making me believe the decision was my own?* Abe asked himself. He didn't think so.

Chapter 8

Smith's heart raced as Ulot walked out of the ship and into the clearing, a cable connecting his forehead to one of the Crawler prisoners. Another Crawler—Smith wasn't sure which one—walked a few feet behind the two. They stopped face to face with Atom, Wave and Comet. Humans, Singers and Crawlers lined the edges of clearing. Smith stepped forward, for the moment acting as mediator. Now that the leaders were connected to Crawlers who understood human language, no Crawler would need to translate Smith's words.

"Former first leader," he said, repeating the term he'd heard Ulot say. "You sought the death of two species. The Singers and my own. Killed many of them. Murdered them, murdered your own kind. Justice would ask for execution, or life in a cell. But"—he took a breath, hoping they were making the right choice—"mercy has won out over justice. You will be a prisoner, but not imprisoned. You will be under constant guard, but still able to enjoy being around others and fresh air. Perhaps you will even change your thinking, your ways." Smith stepped directly in front of the first leader and lowered his voice, speaking the words Theresa said he should. "But if you attempt to harm anyone, this gift of mercy will be rescinded."

The first leader clicked quietly, but made no other movement. Smith turned to the three Singers. In unison, they sang a long, lulling melody with one meaning: forgiveness. Every few notes, a few Singers stepped into the clearing and joined in the song.

Smith looked at the circle of spectators. Many human eyes were wet with tears. Some Crawlers silently swayed back and forth, as if dancing. And in the shadows of the trees, Lioness and Whims stood with two dozen other Singers, Crawlers and humans. All completely still and silent. Smith understood their unwillingness to forgive, had even considered tossing the idea of a merciful society to the wind. But he was determined to do all he could to create a society and culture that would be less likely to collapse due to hate and violence. He still had doubts whether it would succeed, but his hopes outweighed them.

The remaining Crawler leaders were brought out one by one, each given the same speech, the same notes of forgiveness. None seemed, to Smith, to completely comprehend what was happening. But perhaps they did, and were only shocked by the kindness offered by their enemies. Or they were already planning their escape.

Once the singing for the last Crawler ended, Johann moved to the center of the circle. "This is a defining moment in the future of all our races," he said. "Tonight, we'll all share a meal."

The crowd slowly spilled into the clearing, species mingling with species. Smith and Johann remained close to the prisoners, as much to protect them as the civilians. It wouldn't surprise Smith if Lioness or one of her peers decided to attack one of the former Crawler leaders.

He turned to Johann. "You planned a feast?"

Johann smiled. "Yeah. Seemed like a good idea."

Hutsep suddenly appeared beside them, legs bouncing up and down. "You eat food? With everyone?"

"Yeah. A sign of welcome from us to you and the Singers," Johann said.

Hutsep clicked quietly. "Crawlers never eat together. Always alone."

"What?" Smith asked.

"Not Crawler way to eat together. Other Crawlers"—he clicked to himself—"not happy for tonight."

Johann shook his head. "Damn it," he said.

"Hutsep," Smith said. "What should we do?"

"All like gift of food. Don't see insult when eat alone."

"Okay," Smith said.

Johann nodded. "We'll let everyone know."

Hutsep thanked them and walked away.

Johann turned to Smith. "Merging cultures will not be the easiest."

"Easier now that they don't want to kill us, though," Smith said, then laughed.

Johann humored him with a small chuckle. "I just hope we get it all figured out."

Smith pointed to the group in the shadows of the trees. "Should we be worried about them?"

Johann sighed. "I don't think so." He shrugged. "Maybe. You think they'd attack the Crawler leaders?"

"I'd be tempted to."

"I *have* been tempted to," Johann said. "In the military, we killed dozens of humans just like those Crawlers. No trial. No jury. No mercy."

Smith looked at the ground. "I forget you were military on Earth."

"I sometimes forget I was ever on Earth."

Smith smiled. "Why decide now to not execute when you did on Earth?"

"Earth was different," Johann said. "Worse, in most ways. And there was no precedent for mercy. I just remember reading that comic book and wishing the world could figure out mercy. I want to set the precedent now, at the beginning."

"Let's hope the precedent sticks around for another few hundred years," Smith said. "Or more."

They stood in contented silence, watching the roots of mercy take root within their new culture.

***

Smith, Theresa, Whims and Atom sat on their own stumps, each holding a small plate of roasted vegetables and imitation meat. Each Crawler had taken a plate and carried it into the trees to eat by themselves. It was a simple difference between the species, but it seemed large to Smith. For humans, meals were a time to gather and bond, and he knew the humans were hoping to have such an experience with the Crawlers. But at least the Singers joined them.

He looked to Theresa. "You doing all right with all this?" he asked through bites of green carrots.

She swallowed her food. "It makes me nervous. I like what we're trying to do, but I'm still afraid it's just an impossible dream. I'm still not comfortable around them—Singers and Crawlers." She paused and took a drink. "Yesterday I came around a corner and ran into a Crawler. I screamed, and my first thought was that it was going to kill me." She shook her head, embarrassed at herself.

"But you're more used to them than you were," Smith said.

Whims put his plate on the ground and sang a few notes. They were the sounds of confusion and fear, but also of hope.

Theresa smiled. "Thanks, Whims. I'm hoping too. Hoping through the fear."

A Crawler emerged from the trees, carrying a plate full of food. As it settled down next to them, Smith saw that it was Hutsep.

"Hutsep?" he asked, surprised the Crawler was joining them.

Hutsep held the plate in front of his face. "Try human way."

With a hiss, his mouth snapped open, twelve inches from bottom lip to top.

Theresa yelped and fell off her log.

Smith instinctively jumped to his feet. Five thin, white tongues burst from Hutsep's throat. Each wrapped around a piece of food and sucked it back down. He closed his mouth and inhaled deeply.

Hutsep looked at Smith and Theresa. "Good taste."

"Shit," Theresa said, getting back on her stump.

Smith sat down. "You think Hutsep was going to eat you?"

"For a second it seemed like a possibility."

Smith laughed quietly, but knew she wasn't the only one fighting fears of the new and uncertain. *As long as the fear doesn't turn to violence*, he thought.

"Crawler eat no meat," Hutsep said. "Not good for us."

"Really?" Smith asked.

Theresa scoffed. "No shit?"

"True, true," Hutsep said.

They continued to eat, Theresa flinching each time Hutsep opened his mouth. But she refused to leave, Smith realized. She was determined not to ruin what Hutsep was trying to accomplish.

As Smith looked around at the humans and Singers eating together, he caught a glimpse of Minow and Yeance quietly sneaking into a side airlock of the ship. He smiled and shook his head, reminded of his first weeks with Evalee. *Damn, she would've loved all of this*, he thought.

With his five tongues, Hutsep finished much quicker than the others. He set his plate on the ground and watched the others eat.

Smith swallowed and cleared his throat. "Tell us more about your culture, Hutsep."

"Culture?"

"The way you live. Eating alone, not eating meat. What other things are a part of Crawler life?"

Hutsep clicked and went silent, as if thinking of something to say.

"Genders," Smith said. "Male and female. How do you tell a difference?"

"I know human language has words. She, he. Her, him. Crawler language have no such words. I am female. I lay eggs. Call me he or she or anything else. All okay."

"Do all Crawlers feel this way?" Smith asked.

"Yes, yes. All just words."

Smith nodded. "Okay."

Theresa coughed quietly and looked up from her plate. "You lay eggs?"

"Yes, yes. Human not?"

Theresa looked at Smith and raised her eyebrows.

"You brought it up," he said.

Theresa sighed and went into an explanation of the pregnancy and birthing experience for a human female.

Hutsep clicked loudly. "Is terrifying."

Smith and Theresa laughed, both agreeing with shrugs and nods.

Once he caught his breath, another question arose in Smith's mind. "How old are you, Hutsep?"

"Age? Maybe two hundred rotations."

"Of Aethera around the sun?"

"Yes," Hutsep said.

Theresa raised her eyebrows in surprise. "How long do Crawlers live?"

"Maybe three hundred. How long humans live?"

Smith ran the numbers in his head. Aethera moved around its sun faster than Earth, about 250 days. "One hundred thirty rotations. Approximately."

"True?" Crawler asked. "Change how species live together. Singers live six hundred or more."

Smith and Theresa locked eyes. For the first time, Smith felt humans might end up being the weakest of the intelligent species on Aethera. Individual humans would have far less time to make an impact on their world in comparison to the other species. But would that negatively affect their success as a species? He hoped not, and decided to enjoy the present and worry about those implications later. The sun sunk lower in the sky and, for the evening, the three species were at peace with each other.

Chapter 9

Tashon sat atop a large boulder, legs crossed, staring out at an audience dozens strong. Each of the three species was represented almost equally. And each of them was there to hear Tashon tell of his time in the Fourth. Of how he had found peace, how *they* could find peace. Nerves shivered through his stomach. He focused on his breathing and reminded himself that he was the only one to do what he could. To keep that to himself wouldn't be right.

"I went back to the Fourth," he said. "But before that, I went to the space in between dimensions."

A young teen raised his hand. "What place?"

"A place of nothing. A being I saw in the Fourth told me it's Nirvana. Paradise."

"What being?"

"Like a god, but it refuses that title," he said. "I get the idea while I speak with the being that it was once like we are now."

Someone in the crowd asked why he thought that. Tashon shared, with every detail he remembered, everything he knew of the being. Everything it did and said.

"So we'll be like it, more evolved, more godlike, one day?" Yeance asked.

Tashon bit his lip, then inhaled deeply. "Maybe, I think. Laos has said that progression and growth don't stop. But, I don't know if that means we can progress to some type of godhood."

A Crawler clicked. "That your theory?"

Tashon nodded. "Yes. Almost everything I tell you are my theories. The only things I feel are true are that the Fourth is some type of afterlife. And that understanding the, uh, duality of the universe can help us find peace. Everything else is my belief. Based on what I've observed."

"Duality?" the same Crawler asked.

Tashon ran his hand through his hair, thinking of how best to explain it. "Two sides to every coin," he said, cringing at the use of an old cliché.

"Coin?" another Crawler asked.

"Never mind," Tashon said. "Duality is two differences within the same thing or idea. Like, the Crawlers. Your species. At first, we thought all Crawlers were out to murder our entire species. But once we discovered and understood that nearly half your species were fighting to protect and preserve us, we found a type of peace."

"Understand," the Crawler said. "Think understand."

Tashon spotted Lioness in the back of the crowd, and another comparison formed in his mind. The Singers were not all pacifists. Some struggled with the concept and had turned against it. But Tashon felt bringing that up would raise tensions. Most Singers were against the actions of Lioness, even if they never directly said so. And they had gathered in front of him to meditate, not discuss the varying intricacies of the duality of intelligent life.

"Close your eyes," he said, closing his own to set the example. "Nothing. Nothing is the only place, the only thing between the duality of the universe." He stopped, letting them ponder on that thought. "No good, no evil. No pain, no pleasure. No ecstasy, no sadness. It simply *is*. But also *is not*. Push all the thoughts out of your mind. Imagine what nothing might look like." Tashon tried to call up his own memory of nothing, but could grasp nothing concrete. Just vague absences and abstractions. It was definable not by what it *was*, but by what it *was not*. "Do you understand? Can you feel nothing?"

Soft murmurs spread through the crowd. Tashon caught some words, and all he could tell was that no one meditator felt the same as any other. How to explain nothing to those who had not experienced it? How to explain the absence of all fear and hope, joy and sadness, when merely existing in the Third brought all those emotions and more? He decided the best he could do to help them find a peaceful meditation was to return to the duality of the universe.

"Okay, breathe," he said. "Focus only on your breaths. Only your lungs expanding when you inhale and contracting when you exhale." He paused, and thought of the other two species present. "Or whatever part of you controls your breathing." He laughed quietly, as did some in the crowd. "I found peace when I understood opposites are the same while also being different. Life and death. Violence and peace." In the Fourth, the pyramids he'd seen before returned, closer this time. "Light and darkness. All of it exists. We cannot change that." He smiled, accepting the words he said as true though he'd never before spoken them. A simple truth he'd never considered. He opened his eyes without speaking, splitting his attention between the meditators in the Third and the pyramids in the Fourth.

It struck him as somewhat insane that so many chose to sit and meditate with him. That so many believed his words when he himself had questioned his own sanity. Why did they so readily believe him?

Then the pyramids. In some ways, they resembled the Higher Spheres. But Tashon only saw two souls enter the Spheres. Souls poured in and out of the pyramids, from deepest black to brightest white. The most souls he'd ever seen at one time.

He closed his eyes again. *"Laos? What is that?"*

"I don't have a name for it. But it's a place I'll have to go, I think."

"Have to?"

"It's calling to me."

"Evalee?"

"She's with Smith. When I see her again I'll ask her."

"Let her know I'm looking for her too."

"I thought I was your only fourth-dimensional friend?"

"Just my best. Not my only."

Laos laughed. *"I'm going to go closer to the pyramids. See what I can figure out."*

"Okay."

Laos left. Tashon opened his eyes. "Welcome back, everyone," he said.

Slowly, eyes opened and looked around. On the humans, he saw looks of peace, confusion and frustration. Some had found what they were looking for. Others had not. But had he really expected everyone to find peace in one sitting with him? No, but he hoped they would return. He looked at the other two species, unable to discern any emotions from their faces, though he guessed they were feeling joy or frustration as well.

He stood and jumped off the boulder. Lioness, Klen and a few others of each species were in front of him almost immediately. Thanking him, asking questions, offering their own opinions and theories.

Rosa pushed past the group and put a hand on his shoulder. "He'll talk with everyone later," she said, pulling him away. "Right now, he needs a break."

Some shouted questions as they walked off, but all Tashon caught was a melody of restrained hope from Lioness.

***

Tashon lay on the cool floor of a small, secluded cave deep in the red mountains. He had wandered through the tunnels for over an hour until he found somewhere that seemed quiet, far enough away from everyone else. Being in the cave helped rest his mind because his Fourth vision couldn't see through mountains. Sometimes he needed to not look down on himself. But as he lay there, slowly reenergizing his mind and body, he wondered if he could pull himself to the Fourth through the stone of the mountain. What were the limits of his ability? The question filled him with a burning desire to find and push those limits. If he could do and learn more, he could pass that knowledge on to those who looked to him for understanding. He could, he hoped, come back to them with more than mere theories.

If Laos were here, he thought, *he'd probably say this is a bad idea.*

But Laos still hadn't returned from the pyramids, so Tashon could try his skills without judgment. Also, without anyone to stop him from pushing too far.

Remaining on his back, he stretched his arms toward the walls and closed his eyes. From above, he stared at the mountain range that housed the cave system the Singers called home. The range stretched for more than a hundred miles, but Tashon saw them for how small they truly were. He was less than a speck in the immensity of dimensions, the mountains no more than a strand of hair. And if everything was so small, was there a way for him to expand his vision past what was directly around his physical form?

For a moment, he lost himself in the possibilities that would bring, but soon forced himself to face the problem at hand. Could he pull himself to the Fourth even while within a structure? He mentally replayed each time he'd gone to the Fourth. Did his body rise higher in the Third, then move into the Fourth? Or did it move out of the Third first, and then up? If it were the former, he wouldn't rise higher than the stone ceiling above him. But as he focused on his memories of transferring between dimensions, he became certain that moving into the Fourth from within a structure was possible.

He slowed his breaths, cleared his thoughts. Used the piece of him in the Fourth to pull on his physical form, slower than he had in the past. His body lifted mere inches off the ground, vibrated and lifted to the Fourth. The mountains didn't hold him, nor could they have. He popped out of the Third, floated amidst the nothing he had grown to love. But the words of that higher being swam into his mind and he resisted the urge.

He dropped onto the ground surface of the Fourth, dizzy and

breathing heavily. Spending time in nothing did better prepare him for the Fourth, then. He would have to rest in its emptiness before returning to the Third. He looked around. The pyramids were a short distance off, the same mass of souls surrounding it.

A form appeared in front of him, the deep sense of sincere apology emanating from it. Tashon looked at it, confused for a moment, and then realized it was the Singer who had given him the visions.

"*Where did you go?*" he asked.

Another melody of apologetic sorrow burst from her essence.

"*It's okay,*" Tashon told her. And he meant it. "*I wouldn't have known there was a threat at all if you hadn't shown me. I don't care if it wasn't wholly accurate.*"

Her form rose, descended, rose, descended. She thanked him, and Tashon could see the weight she'd been carrying lift off her in dark colors, impossible in the Third. She turned to leave, but Tashon called after her.

"*The Singer book. The book of your people that the Crawlers have. Did you write it?*"

Her form shifted, but she didn't respond.

"*Are you the one they call Mother?*"

She sent out one note: yes. And she turned, flying off to the pyramids far too fast for Tashon to catch. She left a tune in her wake. A tune that told Tashon he would never see her again.

All he could do, then, was what he came to the Fourth to do. Test his skills and push his limits. Discover all he could learn and do in the higher plane that was feeling more and more like home.

Chapter 10

Abe walked alongside the biotech feline that had been open on the floor the day before. The creature hefted a large slab of a dome wall over its head while Abe carried a bucket full of biotech pieces, both organic and mechanical. They plodded toward the nearest dome, now fifty feet ahead of them. Abe glanced at his fierce companion, again wondering how aware it was of its surroundings. How capable of slitting his throat or tearing his heart out. If a rogue Crawler came on them, would it be able to command the creature to kill Abe? Would the creature be able to resist if it wanted?

Winona waved as they reached the dome. Abe handed the bucket to a Crawler, who quickly went to work digging through its contents. The feline carried the slab to a hole in the dome, lifted it, and pushed into the structure's jagged edge. As soon as the edges touched, they glowed a soft red and melted together, becoming a single piece, leaving the hole no larger than a human head.

Winona laughed. "Amazing."

Abe agreed and smiled at her, unable to deny her beauty. But were those his thoughts, or the desire of destiny? Was there a difference? Did it even matter whether being with Winona was predestined if being with her brought him joy?

The Crawler with the bucket clicked loudly. "Found it!"

Abe turned. "Found what?"

The Crawler stretched out its skinny arm, showing off a small, roughly cylindrical jagged piece of metal. It was etched with symbols that were meaningless to Abe.

"What is it?" Winona asked.

"Key," the Crawler said.

"To what?" Abe asked.

"Come, come," the Crawler said as it ran into the dome.

Abe and Winona followed. The biotech feline walked the other way, no doubt in search of more rubble to repair the hole. Abe shook off the feeling that the creature was a slave and turned his attention back to the

Crawler and its key. With a resounding click, the Crawler stopped in the center of the dome and every Crawler in earshot went still. The humans and Singers inside the dome looked around, confused whispers and notes spreading among them.

"Key," the Crawler said again. "Key. First leader palace. Key."

Abe shook his head. "A key to the palace of the Crawler leaders?"

"It sounds like it," Winona said.

Lollawk joined the Crawler holding the key. "Best discovery. Go now to palace."

The Crawlers walked out of the dome, followed by the humans and Singers. They moved quickly through the rubble and destruction, the Crawlers calling out their destination as they passed other groups working to repair the damage from the battle. By the time they reached the massive dome atop the pyramid of stairs, the crowd was hundreds strong.

Lollawk led the march up the stairs and stopped in front of the door, a black circle etched with symbols matching the key. The Crawler pushed the stone-like key into a hole at the bottom of the door. The door spun silently, accelerating every second. It became nothing but a blur, and then disappeared. The opening it left behind led to a large room, empty save for something in the center that Abe couldn't make out through the dim light. All of the Crawlers stomped their feet, clicking or laughing loudly. Abe realized that, for them, this was a momentous event. And that realization filled Abe with excited curiosity.

He turned to Winona and smiled, trying to think of something clever or poignant to say. Nothing came, so he said what was on his mind. "Wonder if the Singer book saw this happening?"

Winona laughed awkwardly and looked like she was about to speak, but no words came out.

"You okay?" Abe asked.

She shrugged. "Yeah, I... I'll tell you later."

Lollawk clicked. "Go in!"

Calmly, almost reverently, the Crawlers followed Lollawk in. Abe and Winona fell in line with them. As his eyes adjusted to the darkness, Abe saw what filled the center of the room. A raised platform with four chairs on top of it. At least, what Abe thought were chairs. He wouldn't have made the connection if he hadn't already seen the seat on top of the Crawler wheels.

He turned to the Crawler nearest him. "Chairs?"

The Crawler made a quiet, vibrating sound. "Leader chairs."

Abe nodded in understanding. "Thrones."

"Are you choosing new leaders?" Winona asked.

"Not yet."

"Why are we here?" Abe asked.

"Watch."

Lollawk walked forward, stopping a few yards before the platform. He placed his feet on four distinct markings, then lifted one foot at a time and pushed them back down. The markings glowed and the platform slid to the side, revealing a staircase that descended into darkness. "Follow," he said, walking into the dark hole.

The staircase was short and ended in a short, square room. The walls were lined with crates of soil, with hallways spaced evenly between the gardens. Plants unlike any Abe had ever seen grew from the soil. As the son of a biotech farmer, he never thought that would happen. Hair-thin vines slithered out of one crate and up the wall, glowing bright orange. In another crate, white porous spheres grew in a haphazard tower that almost touched the ceiling. A plant that was nothing but long, red thorns.

"Food," Lollawk said, followed by a click. "Eat!"

The Crawlers ran to the various garden boxes, ripped plants from the soil and disappeared down the hallways.

Lollawk was the only Crawler that remained. "Used to be for leaders only. Or ones leaders chose. Too much when others went hungry. Change that." He paused, pulled one of the thorn plants out with a *snap* and handed it to an older human woman. "These most rare for us. Hard grow."

The woman looked around. "Can I eat it without dying?"

Winona pulled Ballas's food tester out of her pocket. "Put it in this."

"Where'd you get that?" Abe asked.

Winona closed the thorn into the device. "Grabbed it from Ballas's bag before we left. Thought we'd be eating here and it'd be good to have."

"You stole from a dead man?" Abe asked.

"Yeah," Winona said. "So that *we* don't end up dead too."

"Okay. Thanks, then, I guess."

"And that'll tell me if this food'll kill me?" the woman asked.

"Exactly," Winona said. "Lollawk, where'd all the Crawlers go?"

"Crawlers eat alone."

"They do?" Abe asked. "Why?"

Lollawk made a hissing noise. "Is Crawler way."

The device in Winona's hand dinged. "It's safe," she said, reading the small screen. "But it might cause heartburn."

The woman gasped. "It can tell that much from a scan?"

Winona nodded, pulled the thorn out and handed it back to the woman. She took it, put the thick end between her teeth and bit down. It crunched as she chewed silently, then her eyes went wide. She coughed and Abe thought she was going to spit it out, but she held her composure.

"Spicy," she said. "Burns your throat. Thank you, Lollawk."

Abe held his hand out. "I'll try it," he said.

She handed it over. Abe turned it between his fingers and, without considering the consequences, put the entire thorn in his mouth. The outside of it crunched between his teeth, releasing a thick liquid. At first, it was salty, with a hint of sweetness. Then the heat hit. He coughed, considered spitting, but wasn't sure if that would offend Lollawk, so he swallowed. The heat traveled down his esophagus and into his gut.

He coughed again. "Heartburn. That's putting it lightly."

Winona, the other woman and Lollawk laughed.

"Here," Lollawk said, walking to the crate that held the white spheres. He pulled on one. It popped off with a sucking sound. "This help."

Abe took the food and lifted it to his nose, inhaling the scent. It was sweet and earthy, reminding him of the white meat they got from the bush creatures. He bit into it and tore a piece off, chewing the stringy flesh. It immediately soothed his burning throat and he let out a sigh of relief. Then he realized Winona hadn't tested it.

"Ah, shit," he said. "It better not kill me."

Winona broke off a piece and put it in the tester.

"Too late for that," Abe said.

Winona shrugged. "No. If it tells us it's unsafe, we'll make you puke." She smiled.

Abe rolled his eyes and decided to ignore the comment. "What's your favorite food here, Lollawk?"

"Come," Lollawk said, walking to the other side of the room. He stopped in front of a small, glowing bush. Purple fruit hanging from blue leaves gave off a citrus scent. Lollawk plucked off a berry and held it in front of his face, inhaling deeply.

The testing device beeped and Winona looked down. "Oh, shit," she said.

Abe's stomach dropped. "Shit, what?"

Winona smiled. "I won't get to make you puke."

Abe stared at her while she laughed. "Yeah, I don't think I'm ever having a kid with you." He smiled and shook his head.

Winona playfully pushed him and smiled. Her smile flushed his veins, filling him with excitement. But then the thought: *I'm only fated to feel this way for her.* His smile disappeared.

"What's wrong?" Winona asked.

Ten Crawlers walked into the room, each holding a cable wrapped around another Crawler.

One of the five communicated back and forth with Lollawk.

"Prisoners," Lollawk said. "Enemy. See where they go?"

"Yes," Abe said, grateful he didn't have to answer Winona's question.

They followed the prisoners down one of the hallways that, to Abe, looked no different than the others. Just wide enough for one Crawler, they walked single-file until they reached a square door. The Crawler in front slid fingers across its surface in seemingly random patterns, and it slid open.

Across the threshold was a long, rectangular room. Cables hung from the low ceiling, spaced evenly down the center of the room. A few dozen of the cables were already attached to the foreheads of Crawlers, some of the prisoners clicking quietly.

"The ones who surrendered?" Abe whispered.

"Yeah." Winona nodded.

They watched silently as Lollawk walked to a circle engraved on the left wall. He traced his fingers in meandering swirls and zigzags until the circle spun and swung outward, revealing a glass cube. Within it were ten-legged discs covered in blinking moss. Lollawk pulled one out and carried it to the closest prisoner. The enemy Crawler screeched as Lollawk placed a disc on its forehead. The disc spun around, not unlike the beetle had done to Abe's now severed arm. The screeching intensified as wings popped out of the disc and flew off, connecting the Crawler's forehead cable to a ceiling cable. A thin line of blood trickled from the Crawler's forehead. Abe watched silently as the process repeated for the remaining prisoners and, seeing the brutal nature of it, wondered whether imprisonment was a merciful option.

Chapter 11

"Are we all going to live as separate nations based on species?" Theresa asked.

Smith shook his head and looked to the others in the conference of room of the ship. Klen and Hutsep were joined by Atom and Comet.

"No," Smith said. "I think that defeats the purpose of us all living together. We need to exist together in peace. Separating species will cause us to see each other based on differences."

"Yes, yes," Klen said.

Atom and Comet both melodized their agreements.

"Okay," Theresa said. "Okay. But that just leaves us two continents."

"Three," Smith said. "Remember Aethera from above? Three continents." Smith looked to Aethera's native species. "What's on the other continent?"

"No," Klen said.

"Unlivable," Hutsep agreed.

"Why?" Theresa asked.

Atom sang in a way that made Smith feel scared, unsafe.

"Dangerous?" he asked.

"Yes, yes," Klen said.

Theresa scratched her elbow and leaned forward. "What's dangerous about it?"

"It moves," Klen said. "Floats. No dirt. No ground."

"What?" Smith asked. "How?"

"All sticks. Vines. Twisted together, floating."

"Huh," Smith said. "Maybe at some point we can send others out to explore it, map it."

"Not the focus now, Smith," Theresa said.

"I know, I know. It just sounds like something I'd like to see."

"No," Klen said. "Monsters there."

"Monsters?"

"Not let you go," Hutsep said, followed by a loud click of his teeth.

Comet agreed with a single, firm note.

"Okay, okay," Smith said. He wanted to know more of the floating continent, but it wasn't worth endangering the budding relationship between the three species. "We won't go."

"Good," Hutsep said. "Now, how humans get leaders?"

"Popular vote," Theresa said.

"Vote? Not know word."

Smith looked to the Singers. "Vote?"

Both indicated they did not understand.

"We let citizens decide who they want to lead them," Smith said.

"Odd," Hutsep said. "New idea."

Smith shook his head in shock. "New? How do you choose a leader?"

"Firstborns."

"Huh?" Theresa said.

"Four Crawler families. Each generation firstborn is leader."

"Do you want to keep doing it that way? The Crawlers?"

Klen and Hutsep looked at each other, then back to smith and Theresa.

"No," Klen said. "But vote? New."

"You don't have to do it the same as humans." Smith could see the comment bother Theresa, but she stayed silent.

"True," Klen said.

"How do Singers do it?" Theresa asked.

Atom sang slow and calm.

Smith caught some of the words. Wise. Old. "The eldest Singer?" he asked.

Comet sang yes. Smith smiled and nodded. With how long the Singers lived, it made some sort of sense to him.

"Do you want to keep doing it that way?" Theresa asked.

Again, Comet answered affirmatively.

"Do the rest of the Singers agree?" Smith asked, thinking mostly of Lioness and the other Singers who were questioning the life of pacifism.

Comet sang wavering notes that filled Smith with uncertainty. The Singer didn't know.

Theresa stretched her arms above her head. "If the Singers want to do it a different way, will you?"

Comet began the same uncertain melody but was interrupted by a louder tune coming from Atom. Her answer: absolutely.

"You're the eldest Singer, right, Atom?" Smith asked.

She was.

"And if the Singers wanted a new leader, you would step down?" Theresa asked.

Atom would.

Smith nodded and took a deep breath, preparing himself to bring up his next concern. "Okay," he said. "Once each species has a leader, what then?"

"Meaning?" Klen asked.

"Meaning," Smith said. "Meaning, I'm worried about us humans. We live much shorter lives than both Crawlers and Singers. I'm afraid of the weak place that puts us within Aetheran society."

Atom responded immediately with notes that calmed Smith's worries, made him understand that she did not intend to use human lifespan against them. And Smith never thought she did. But as the society and culture grew, as power-hungry individuals vied for leadership, he saw the humans ending up in a position of weakness.

Klen twitched her head back and forth. "Understand. Part of why leaders sought Singer death. Long Singer life brought fear."

Smith nodded. "Atom, Klen. I trust the Singers and Crawlers *now*. But what about the future? I just want to make sure humanity's future is secure."

Theresa looked at Smith and smiled. "Thanks, Smith. So, what can we do to spread power equally among the species?"

"Without forcing the species to change aspects of their culture they don't want to," Smith said.

"Crawler land has four seats of power," Hutsep said. "Three species."

"What about the fourth?" Smith asked.

"One leader for each species," Theresa said. "Then a fourth chosen by *all* of Aethera?"

"That could work," Smith said.

It went silent. Smith considered how effective such a system would be. And, more importantly to him, how it would affect human life. Not only did humans have the shortest lifespan, they were also the minority on Aethera. At least with the way suggested by Theresa, the humans would always have a representative regardless of their population count. But something about it still felt *off* to Smith. Too familiar. Too many opportunities to revert back to how things were on Earth.

Or was that just fear talking? Was it even possible to avoid the pitfalls brought on by human imperfection? Or, in their case, the imperfection of intelligent species as a whole?

"How do we keep those leaders safe?" Smith asked. "And keep them from gaining too much power, like the Crawler leaders did?"

"Most Earth nations set up different branches of government," Theresa said. "Tried to keep the balance that way."

Smith nodded. "But we're trying for something better than what was on Earth with our mercy-based criminal system," he said. "How can we improve on Earth's leadership structure?"

"Civilian choosing leader improvement for Crawlers," Klen said.

Smith couldn't argue the point. Atom and Comet indicated they felt the same way.

Theresa sighed. "I think...." She paused. "I don't think it's possible to prevent all tragedies. To stop every possible future governmental threat. We can try, and I want to. I think it's better to put faith in civilians. I mean, look at what the Crawlers did for us when they realized what their leaders were planning."

"Thank you," Hutsep said. "No decision yet. Talk with civilians. Let all give ideas."

Smith stood. "Let's go."

***

Within a few hours, they had a list of all ideas for government they heard while talking with a large group of civilians gathered in the Singers' main cavern. The former Crawler leaders stood against the wall farthest from Smith, mercifully imprisoned with their guards. Lioness and her groups stood on the opposite wall, speaking and singing quietly.

Johann stood up and walked to the center of the room. "We all want what's best for the future of each of our species," he said. "And we're trying to figure out what that is. Humanity's current leaders have spoken with Atom, Comet, Klen and Hutsep. We believe it's best we all live together, create a society that accepts all three species. After talking with all of you, it seems you feel the same."

Quiet muttering ran through Lioness's group. Feelings of frustration and uncertainty. A hint of rage. Smith shook his head, hoping they kept calm. Hoping they realized how detrimental an act of violence would be for *all* the species on Aethera.

Johann went on as if he heard nothing, scratching his beard as he spoke. "We've heard many good ideas. Some great ones. Some insane ones too," he said with a smile. "The first thing we've agreed on is how our main leaders will be chosen. Singers will continue to give their eldest member the honor to lead. Is that right, Singers?"

All the Singers, including Lioness and her peers, gave a calm and resounding affirmative. *At least they're not going against the other Singers,* Smith thought. *Yet.*

Johann nodded. "And the Crawlers have decided to vote, to choose for themselves, who will be their leader."

All four former Crawler leaders hissed and gnashed at the comment. The hissing turned to screeching and one of the leaders lunged off the wall, yanking his attached guard to the ground. The leader charged at the nearest free Crawler, but was stopped as a blue shock of light ran down the cable into his skull. He dropped, body twitching, a gurgling click escaping his throat.

The guard stood up, breathing heavily. "Sorry. No concern, not dead."

Two other Crawlers helped drag the limp body back to the wall. The remaining three leaders hissed angrily but didn't move. Across the cavern, Lioness was a dozen feet away from the wall she's been standing by, fists clenched tight. If the leader hadn't been stopped, Smith was certain she would've taken it into her own hands to take his life.

Johann coughed. "Well, *most* Crawlers have decided to vote." He laughed nervously, scratching his beard and eyeing the crowd. "Let's, uh, let's continue this talk tomorrow."

The crowd remained still and silent as the guards escorted the Crawler prisoners out of the caves. As soon as they were out of sight, whispers spread throughout the crowd. Whispering turned to talking then turned to shouting.

Calls for full imprisonment echoed off the walls. Smith waited patiently, listening. And realized the only voices shouting for something less merciful belonged to humans. His own people so quickly turned from their idealistic mission. He joined Johann in the center of the crowd and both shouted out, trying to get everyone's attention. None paid them any heed.

"Didn't happen like this in those comic books," Johann said.

Smith shook his head but said nothing. If he did, his frustration at the humans now refusing their mercy would boil over. He understood where they were coming from, of course. But where they were coming from was a place of fear, and that rarely led down a positive path. If ever it did.

Atom emerged from the crowd, bellowing out one crisp, vibrato note. The ground and walls seemed to shake with the power of it. The room went silent, eyes focused on the eldest Singer. She waited, motionless. And then, almost silently, a note slid from her throat. Gradually grew louder, shifting tones up and down. A wave of safety spread out from her, soaking into Smith. And, he hoped, into everyone in the room. He hoped they felt they were in no real danger. Yes, the prisoner tried to attack a civilian. But the guard performed his duty. Stopped the prisoner. They were in no real danger. *Or are we?* Smith wondered.

Eventually, those in the cavern broke into smaller groups, talking among themselves. Smith wandered around, saying casual greetings as people waved or called his name. He tried to hear what was being said. How many truly wanted to end their plan for a merciful culture before it even began?

He spoke and listened. Some were willing to continue laying the foundation of a merciful society. Others wanted such a society, but only to an extent. For them, crimes such as the ones committed by the Crawler leaders should be given no mercy. A few, but enough to worry Smith, were consumed with fear that they hid with rage, pleading for executions. Calling for harsh and swift justice.

He eventually ended up in a circle with Rosa, Theresa, Yeance, Lioness, Minow, a few other humans and three Crawlers.

"We weren't in any real danger," Minow said. "The guard took care of it. He did what he was supposed to do. It *worked*."

"Yes," a Crawler said.

A man scoffed. "This time, yeah. But what about next time? Once they have time to plan, to figure out a way to escape? *We can't risk that*."

Yeance shook his head. "But can we risk reverting to extreme justice that in a few hundred years could put Aethera right where Earth was?"

"Really?" The man threw his hands in the air. "Punishing them for seeking *genocide* will not have that effect."

"What if it does?" Minow asked.

A Crawler clicked quietly, and Smith thought it was agreeing with Minow.

Rosa laughed and shook her head. "We can't play in what-ifs. This is our safety. Our safety right now. Not in a generation or two."

"Rosa," Yeance said. "I thought you wanted to create a merciful society? One of understanding and forgiveness."

"I did, I do. Shit, we all want that. But we can't let them keep tormenting us."

"No torment," a Crawler said. "Safe."

Yeance held up a hand. "So you're saying we, essentially, break their wrist like you did that girl on the ship?"

Smith sucked in a breath of air. He knew Rosa hated that she did that to Cosima. He also knew Yeance made a mistake bringing it up.

Rosa stepped forward. "Shut the hell up. That was a mistake. But she did end up sacrificing herself to save us."

"But was that because you snapped her wrist, or because Tashon and Abe showed her kindness?"

Rosa took a deep breath and stepped back. "I... don't know."

"It was probably from the kindness she found," Minow said.

Smith cleared his throat. "We can't know that for sure. I mean, look, we're trying to decide what's best for our future. And I get it. I'm scared too. About the future. About the former Crawler leaders. All of it. I've asked myself whether it's worth it or not too. I think it is."

Rosa shook her head, confusion spread blatantly across her face.

"It's not," the man said.

Minow looked around the room. "But what if it is? Worth the risk? What if this act of mercy sets up the future of Aethera as a planet of peace and kindness that surpasses Earth?"

No one answered. Smith liked what Minow said, but it was all still what-ifs. "We can go back and forth guessing what result our actions will have tomorrow and hundreds of years from now," he said. "But we'll never know that. We can't know that. But we can do our best to create such a future for Aethera."

The man looked down and took a deep breath. "Smith. We all like the idea of such a merciful society. The *idea*. But keeping them out, around us," he said, raising his voice. "Isn't mercy for them, it's danger for *us*. The idea is just an ideal that won't work in reality."

Smith nodded and looked at the others in the room.

Rosa sighed. "I still don't think it'll work. A lot of us don't."

"Why?" Minow asked, her voice trembling.

"Give too much mercy, and they'll turn it against us."

"Don't give enough," Minow said. "And we become vengeful."

Theresa spoke for the first time. "Both are true. But Crawlers? Are you all really okay giving your former leaders this much kindness?"

"We," a Crawler said, then paused. "Most, yes. Some angry, some scared."

"Lioness?" Smith said. "What do you think we should do?"

As if she'd been waiting to communicate, a tumbling melody burst from her throat. She was stuck and confused. Both sides made sense to her, and she didn't see one clear answer. Smith understood. He knew what they were doing could backfire, realized that it almost had already. And he also knew they all wanted the same outcome: the best possible future for Aethera.

"We need to figure out—together, all species—what we want to do. With the Crawler leaders, and with everything else moving forward."

The night went on, people came and left, each giving their thoughts on how to move forward. The conversations continued through the night and long past the rising of the sun.

Chapter 12

Tashon stood on the surface of the Fourth, eyes closed, his mind conjuring up an image of what the part of him that was always in the Fourth might look like. The part of him that acted as his own third-person camera floated in his mind's eye, behind him. A somewhat round, green-blue mass with a surface that constantly rippled. If he could truly see it, he was certain it would look as he imagined it. And why wouldn't it? He saw reality within his mind in ways no one else could.

He forced it to rotate one way, then the other. Pulled at the edges, attempting to stretch it out, widen the lens through which he saw himself. It gave, slightly, becoming more elliptical than circular. His heart and head pounded with the effort, but he pulled again, this time at opposite ends. It stretched more, returning somewhat to its circular size. He rotated it, pulled in those directions that existed only in the Fourth dimension. *Or any higher dimensions, if any exist*, Tashon thought. He pulled and his head spun with the effort. He slowed his breaths, pushed all unneeded thoughts away. It stretched out, barely. He paused and examined it. He adjusted his mental grip on it and pulled again. It fought him, as if it had no desire to be pulled. But after an unknowable length of time, it gave ever so slightly. Tashon stopped and looked at it. *Bigger, at least*, he thought.

With a smile, he opened his eyes and sat down. The pyramids, surrounded with the constant concourses of beings, stood closer than they had, casting multiple pointed shadows across the ground.

Soon, Laos would return from the pyramids. Then Tashon could tell him his goals, his plan to increase his fourth-dimensional sight and abilities. And Laos could tell him what the place truly was. What was the significance of it? Why were so many higher forms constantly entering and exiting it? Was it a travel hub to farther reaches of the Fourth? Or something more traditional, like the judgment seat of heaven? No, it wasn't that. Nothing in the Fourth, in the reality of the afterlife as Tashon had seen it, suggested anything traditionally taught. Except for nothing, but that did not seem as sages of old had described it. Before he could have answers, though, Laos needed to return. *What if he doesn't return?* Tashon thought. He shook his head. *Don't think like that.*

He calmly pulled himself down to the Third, sinking through the surface of the Fourth. He paused for but a few breaths in nothing, filling himself with peaceful emptiness. He moved to leave, but the nothingness called to him, gracefully sang him back into its silence. The warning of the higher being came to mind, but he fought it. For a moment, the still and silent emptiness lulled him into motionlessness.

Need.
Want.
Desire.
Ambition.
All nothing.

Contentment, everything.
Content with nothing
Content with everything.

Tashon let everything wash away, let the contented nothing wash over him. And for minutes, perhaps longer, he was aware only that he existed.

***

Awareness of something beyond himself called to him. Need returned to his mind. The need to follow that something, to help it. To be with it.

No nothing.

Tashon forced his mind to the awareness, pulled himself to the something.

He was back in the Third, sitting on the snow-covered ground, trees towering above him.

Someone nearby gasped. "Tashon!"

Tashon turned and saw the familiar old face standing with a smokie. "Rosa," he said with a dazed half-smile on his face.

"You scared the shit out of me," she said. "You in the Fourth? For that long?"

"How long?"

"A full day, at least," she said. "What the hell you doing up there?"

Tashon nodded. "I was trying to expand my vision."

"Trying or succeeding?"

Tashon focused in on his higher vision and realized that he could see far more than he expected. In the center of the circle, his form was small, like a child. It spread out around his body, giving him a view of the entire continent. He saw all the way north, to the waterfall cliffs, just past the beach, a thin line of ocean at the end of his vision. To the south, past the forest of broken trees, the snow grew deeper and deeper until it reached towering glaciers and a vast expanse of smooth, blue ice. To the east, the yellow forest ended at the edge of a sea of red water. And to the west, past Sylvia's frozen corpse and the wreckage of the colony ship, an empty seabed littered with the bones of enormous animals. Tashon wondered if any water was left farther out, but his vision stopped short.

He looked at Rosa. "Succeeding," he said with a smile. "Seeing things I've never seen before."

"I'm sure there're plenty who'll want to hear about it," she said.

"Yeah, okay. Tomorrow?"

"Tomorrow." She nodded. "How's Laos?"

"He's... off checking out something new in the Fourth."

"New?"

"Like the Higher Spheres I traveled through, but pyramids. And thousands of souls rushing in and out. Constantly."

Rosa perked up, stood straighter. "Really? You think you could find Cosima there? Or Jonstin?"

Tashon smiled. "I don't know. Laos will tell me more when he comes back."

"I hope we can find them," Rosa said.

"Me too."

Rosa looked to the sky. "Some shit went down while you were gone."

"Yeah?"

Rosa told him if the decisions made about human, Singer and Crawler leadership. Explained the violent reaction of the Crawler prisoner and the resulting fear.

"Some shit did go down," Tashon said.

Rosa nodded. "What do you think?"

"About?"

"Our plan for mercy," she said. "Are we giving the Crawler leaders too much? Are we risking everything by letting them be out and among us?"

Tashon closed his eyes, wishing Laos were there to give his opinion. "What do you think, Rosa?"

"I... I don't know. We tried to offer mercy, and they tried to attack us."

"Only one of them did."

"Right." Rosa shrugged and nodded. "The others were angry."

Tashon inhaled, finding himself in a semi-meditative state as the discussion continued. "Anger isn't a crime. Acting on the anger, maybe. If it hurts someone. But no one was harmed. No one's wrist was broken," he said with a smile.

Rosa huffed. "Shut up," she said.

Tashon held his hands up in apology. "I know. But if you convinced everyone to execute the Crawlers, wouldn't you feel guiltier than you do about breaking Cosima's wrist?"

"But Cosima *changed*. I don't see the Crawlers changing."

"Maybe," Tashon said. "But after everything the Fourth has shown me, this all feels—I don't know—smaller. Not less important. But...." Tashon twisted a hand in the air, searching for the best explanation. "We do need to make the right decision, or try to. But there is more to existing than just our lives in the Third. So, make the best choices we can, but don't worry about them so much."

"But it's the future of the planet," Rosa said. "How can we not worry about it?"

Tashon nodded, understanding her concern. "It is, I know. I worry too. But just make the best decisions we can, and move forward."

"But what is the best decision?"

Tashon laughed softly. "I don't know. To me, mercy feels more important than justice."

"Maybe," Rosa said. "Maybe. I'm heading back to the ship. You?"

"Give me a bit," he said.

Rosa nodded and walked away.

Tashon sat down. He was struck yet again by the stark duality of words. Mercy and justice. Justice and mercy. One could not exist without the other. But was it possible to give so much mercy that justice disappeared, or became small enough to be insignificant? And, if so, what effect would a justice-free culture have on the inhabitants of Aethera? But, no, justice could never completely disappear. If it did, so would mercy. And where would that leave them?

So the question was simple, then. Which of the two should they put in higher regard? He considered the Fourth. That higher dimension that, to him, was in every way a more perfect existence than the Third. In the Fourth, which of the two was more valued?

Laos. Laos had been a terrorist. Had killed, had sought the death of all humanity. Yet he was not in any type of burning, miserable hell. He'd been given the opportunity to change, to progress. The shade of his essence was gradually becoming brighter and calmer. From what little Tashon truly knew, the universe, or whatever forces governed it, seemed inclined to offer mercy over justice.

And Tashon would follow the example set by the universe as he understood it. Though he knew he understood so little.

***

A sudden presence in the Fourth yanked Tashon from a restful sleep. He jolted to a sitting position, heart pounding momentarily, until he recognized the presence.

"Hi, Evalee." He smiled and closed his eyes, looking at her in the Fourth.

She said nothing, but Tashon sensed trepidation, noticed the slight trembling in her off-white glow. Tashon knew she had come for a reason. She wouldn't have left Smith and Abe without good cause. But what was it? She approached his fourth-dimensional essence and gently touched it. Swirling images, disconnecting and intertwining, moving and motionless, flashed into his mind.

A flat, colorless point hung, itself alone, stationary. Tashon saw the point, then saw and felt the universe from within the point. Floating in nothing but absence, aware only of itself. A realization: it could do more than float in one spot. It moved, slowly at first, experimenting with what motion was, what it could mean. Moving through absence, still aware of nothing but itself, of its new movement in relation to its previous stillness.

A new awareness: an existence of something beyond itself. With that awareness, the absence disappeared. As shapes and colors formed around it, the point looked in at itself and expanded from a flat point into a flat, oblong circle, rough around the edges. It moved on, soaking up the new colors and shapes, relishing the fact it was not alone in its existence.

Much later, it hit a bump in its path and it tumbled upward, for the first time experiencing fear. And with that fear came a sense of exhilaration that turned to joy as it found itself moving upward and forward. An invisible, cool presence rushed all around it as it continued on, feeling unquestionably *real*.

Fresh colors and forms surrounded it, pushed against it from all sides. Suffocated it, crushed it. But it fought back, twisted and twirled and *popped* into a larger shape, no longer flat. An ellipsoid, rolling ever forward, ever upward. Until thousands of shapes smaller than itself fell from above, hitting its form repeatedly, soaking into its flesh, slowly dragging it down.

It hit bottom amid a mass of other shapes, all moving in different directions or not moving at all. Motionless apathy took over as it looked up and saw the height from which it had fallen. How to achieve that height again? Seemed impossible, so it stayed there, moving only when necessary. And even then, stillness was more convenient.

But, for reasons it did not understand, it eventually grew tired of the absence of movement. Longed for the heights, the fear and exhilaration. Needed to feel real again. It returned to movement. At first, the slow, gentle rolling in nearly every way reminiscent of its first movements when nothing more than a point. Yet undoubtedly so different, for with its vastly expanded surface area it became far more aware of its surrounding. Felt the ground beneath, felt the other shapes that collided with it, moved with it, rolled over it, slid under it. It felt the push and pull of the real. It may have fallen from great heights, but it was still far more than the simple point it had been.

So on it went. Forward and upward, at times reaching heights exceeding all understating only to fall to depths deeper and darker that should have been possible. Yet on it moved until, upon overcoming a great depth to achieve a breathtaking height, its shape expanded into its Fourth form. A complex, hyper-ellipsoid far greater than the former point thought it could ever be.

Yet it did not end there. On it went, flying to massive heights, sinking to darkest depths. At times moving faster than it had strength, others wasting away in stillness. At times, the stillness providing healing, others the excessive movement inexplicably draining. Periodically, it reached new stages of transition.

Never ending.

The images disappeared. Tashon stared at Evalee. She stared at him, unspeaking. Seconds, then minutes.

Eventually, one phrase came to his mind: *endless progression.*

Chapter 13

Abe stood motionless in a field of tall, white grass that extended to the horizon in all directions. The sky above was not sky, but the large, curved face of a Singer staring down at him. He knew it was the Singer mother. She sang one note, and his right leg stepped forward without Abe willing it to do so. Another note, and his left leg stepped forward. The notes continued, and he fell into an odd rhythm of walking, the white grass brushing against his fingertips.

On he went, for how long he didn't know. The grass ended suddenly and Abe stepped onto smooth stone. The stone ended in a cliff a short ways off, but the Singer continued her notes. Faster and faster until his legs unwillingly ran him toward the edge. He tried to stop, to force his legs to be still. But it was impossible—they were following the will of the Singer. He ran off the edge into open air, and fell.

He awoke, and the dream turned into an idea that struck him hard and fast. It terrified him and, if it were true, would change the way he saw everything. He needed to breathe, to think, to convince himself it wasn't true. He walked quickly out of the Crawler throne room and into the chill morning air. Down the steps, across the ground now clear of rubble and corpses. Found a large rock. Sat on it and tried to let his reason catch up with the tumbling thoughts.

What if the Singers orchestrated everything? What if by prophesying that the humans would rescue the Singers, their Mother caused it to happen? Just as Whims's notes had caused Abe to feel no concern during their journey. It was proven that Singer melodies could encourage, almost force, an individual to feel and act in certain ways. Could Mother's prophetic melodies have brought humans to Aethera? And if such a thing were possible, what then of free will? Was it simply an illusion? Had the events of his life been predetermined by the melody of Mother? Had their entire journey to Aethera, and all the death it left in its wake, been the result of some long ago sung prophecy?

His imagining of it was as real to him as if it were historic fact. The Singer Mother, her prophetic melody dancing invisibly through space, planting seeds in the minds of humans on Earth. Filling them with the burning desire to escape their home world, to explore and settle new planets.

That, or she truly had seen the future. Which was more likely? And did likelihood, probability as human minds understood it, have any bearing on reality? It was improbable that life existed in the Fourth. Even more so that the afterlife and the Fourth were one and the same. Probability, statistics. Systems humans put on the universe to convince themselves they understood it. *But none of us understand it. Not really*, Abe thought.

But he longed for understanding. Needed it.

Footsteps approached. Abe turned his head, a soft smile spreading across his face. "Hey, Winona." Seeing her warmed him, calmed his mind if only slightly. He cared for her, but the thought that his feelings for her was caused by an outside source scared him.

"You okay?" she asked.

He looked at her, unsure if telling her was a good idea. "I... What if the Singer prophecies aren't prophecies?"

"What?"

He sighed. "The Singer Mother prophesied all of this. Prophesied *us*. That's what they say. But what if her singing about it happening *made it happen*?"

Winona laughed quietly, shaking her head. "You think it's possible?"

"That or they see the future," Abe said.

"Does it matter?"

Abe looked at her, shocked at the question. "Yes. It's about our free will, Winona."

"Maybe." She shrugged and looked to the sky. "But even if it's true, they haven't impacted every choice we've made. Haven't forced every decision."

Abe inhaled, exhaled and nodded. "I know. I do. But they have a drawing of us in their book. It doesn't make sense. I need to understand how the hell that happened."

"Okay. How? How do we figure that out? The Singers all seem to think the book is scripture. See Mother as a prophet. I don't think any will say she wasn't."

Abe scratched his head. "We need to read the book."

"So, we need to learn to read Singer."

Abe smiled. "We do."

The two looked at each other with smiles and bright, wide eyes. Excitement for the future filled Abe. As did a fear that his feelings weren't real, that they stemmed from an unknowable outside source. He looked at Winona as she stood and held her hand out to him, the sun behind her setting her body on fire. *Damn, I hope this is real,* he thought.

They walked, hands clasped together, back the way Abe had come. Up the stairs and into the dome. Lollawk stood near the far wall, talking calmly to a Singer with a black side braid. As Abe and Winona approached, the two kindly greeted them.

"What need?" Lollawk asked.

"Lollawk," Abe said. He looked at the Singer, then back at the Crawler. "You can read the Singer book, right?"

"Yes, yes."

"Do you think I, uh, we could learn to read it? Read Singer?"

The Singer chimed a happy note, excited that more wanted to read Mother's words for themselves. Abe refrained from explaining it was more for them to understand Mother's method than her message.

Lollawk laughed. "Yes. I help, yes. Excited." He pulled the book out of his pouch and motioned for them to sit on the floor against the wall.

"Now?" Winona asked.

"Why not now?" Lollawk replied.

Winona and Abe laughed and sat down. The Singer joined them as Lollawk stood in front, taking on the role of instructor.

"Hold on," Abe said. He turned to the Singer. "What can we call you?"

The Singer let out five notes. Abe let them sink in, doing his best to feel them in a way that would help him accurately give him a name. And she was a she, Abe realized. The notes clearly indicated that to be the case. They also helped Abe feel strong, supported and important.

"Teacher," Winona said.

Abe nodded in agreement, but it seemed too convenient. The Singer they came across when looking to learn the Singer language just happened to be known by her entire species as Teacher. Or he was only evoking those emotions in Abe and Winona so that they would perceive him as a teacher. Or, she was Teacher, and she happened to be there because she somehow knew beforehand what Abe and Winona would want help with.

None of those possibilities made sense to Abe.

"Yes, we teach Singer written language," Lollawk said. "First lesson: When Singers speak, all emotion. Singer emotion and logic comes with Singer writing."

"Okay, that makes sense," Abe said.

Lollawk placed the book on the floor. Three symbols crossed the cover at an angle from the top left to the bottom right.

"One symbol means one idea," Lollawk said. "Sometimes. The more... big ideas are more symbols."

Abe nodded, but the difficulty of the task at hand became strikingly apparent. When humans learned other human languages, letters and words had fairly straightforward equivalents. But would it be that way with the Singer language?

Winona pointed to the symbol on the top of left of the cover. "What does this mean?"

"'Book' or 'words.' Logically. Emotion changes with slant of symbol and thickness of lines."

Abe examined the symbol. The lines were thin, but since the symbol was new to him he had no idea of it was angled or not. Knowing how important the book was to the Singers, though, he could guess what the thin lines meant. "The thinner the line, the more it means to the Singers?"

"Yes, yes."

Teacher sang a note of praise that split Abe's mouth open in a smile. She was proud of her pupil. Abe's smile faded. He'd traveled with Whims and Braids, been among Singers. Cared for them, about them. But the idea that the Singers could drastically impact the future with only the use of their language seeped into his mind so deeply that it would not let go. It brought back all the fear he'd first felt when he realized how convincing the Singer language could be.

No, he thought. He pushed the thought aside as best he could, reminding himself of the journey he took with Whims and Lioness. The Singers were not evil. They had a language unlike any other. A language that, most likely, couldn't control the fate on any living being. But he still needed to figure out how Mother had predicted the humans' arrival.

"Is that symbol slanted at all?" Winona asked.

Lollawk clicked at Teacher and the Singer faced her palms to the ceiling. The now familiar black wires popped out of her hands. A hologram square appeared in front of her face. Within it, a grid of the symbol in question. The same symbol, repeated over fifty times, each with a slight variation. Or, Abe assumed each one was different. From what he could see, many of them appeared identical.

Lollawk pointed at the symbol in the center of the grid. "Standard," he said. Then he pointed to another iteration of the symbol, this in the bottom left corner. "Symbol on Mother's book."

Abe examined the two symbols and realized that when Lollawk said 'slant' he really meant 'rotated.' The symbol on the front of the book was rotated clockwise. "How far is the symbol turned?"

"Fifty-six degrees," Lollawk said.

"Why fifty-six?" Winona asked.

Teacher sang a note of confusion. She continued. Fifty-six, it seemed, was a significant number to the Singers, and it indicated an emotionally significant version of a symbol. Abe nodded, stood, and walked closer to the projected symbols. Many others were confusingly close to fifty-six degrees. Others looked to be one degree, or three hundred fifty-nine degrees. And all the others, each at seemingly random angles of rotation. None of which made any logical sense to Abe. None were at forty-five, or ninety, or one hundred eighty.

Winona stepped to Abe's side, and pointed at one of the symbols that looked to be about two hundred degrees. "How is the meaning here different than the one on the Mother's book?"

"Teacher?" Lollawk said.

She listlessly sang a string of calm notes. Abe instantly felt that Teacher cared for him.

"Book or words of support," Abe said.

"And kindness," Winona added.

"But that looks almost identical to at least ten other variations," Abe said.

Winona let out a breath. "Yeah. That's a lot to learn."

Lollawk let out a short laugh. "Yes, yes. Ready to memorize?"

"All of them?" Abe asked. "That'll take hours, at least. For one word."

"Yes, yes."

"Let's get started."

Chapter 14

Smith shook his head. "I don't know why I expected it to be so easy to create such an ideal society."

Johann laughed. "I hoped it would be easier too. But it's hard enough to get a group of humans to all agree on something. Now we have three species that we're trying to convince our merciful society is worth it."

Theresa scoffed. "Is it, though? Honestly think about it. Is it worth the potential risks?"

The three stood outside in the crisp morning air, freshly fallen snow under their feet. It had been a long and sleepless night, but rest still evaded them.

"*Potential* risks," Johann said. "Not guaranteed. And we're not ignoring what they did. They're still prisoners."

"But they're out among us, where they can do damage."

Smith sighed. "We've had that discussion. We don't need to again. We need to come up with some type of compromise that helps the most people possible feel safe."

"That also encourages mercy and kindness," Johann said.

"Justice is just as important." Theresa tossed her hands in the air.

"And that's where we disagree," Smith said.

"How do you define justice?" Johann asked as he leaned against a tree.

"It's giving a punishment equal to the crime. An outcome that leaves victims feeling...." She paused, turned her eyes up in thought. "Taken care of, safe. Mercy to the perpetrator shouldn't come at the expense of the victim."

"I, actually, agree with that," Smith said. "But the problem here is that all of us are the victims of the Crawler prisoners. And some of us feel taken care of and safe the way it is."

"But I don't. A lot of us don't."

"I know." Smith nodded. "Then what do we do?"

Theresa sighed, shrugged and looked at the sky.

"To set up this society of mercy was, at the start, my idea," Johann said. "But that was before we even knew the Crawlers existed. Before we knew of the threat to our species here on Aethera."

"Are you saying you don't want to keep working toward it?" Smith asked.

"No, I'm not. But with these Crawlers, the crime is so *immense*. It affected, literally, every single person on the planet. We can't ignore those who think the better option is a bit less mercy."

"We can't ignore the fear and hurt of the victims," Smith said.

Johann nodded. "Originally, the idea was to encourage mercy by allowing the victims to pass out the punishment. But with this many victims, there's no way we can all agree on one punishment."

"Then what do we do?" Theresa asked. "Put it to a vote?"

"We might have to," Smith said. "But I think if we do, that whatever the vote decides will set the precedent for how crimes are dealt with in the future."

They fell into silence. Smith considered how it might play out. If fifty-one percent decided to keep the prisoners as they were, and the rest voted for execution, what would happen? How would that forty-nine percent, left to their fear, react? Would they let that fear turn to rage against the citizens who had voted for mercy? Or, what if the majority chose execution, and the hope for a merciful future for Aethera crumbled? He thought again of the Singers. The one species that suffered the most at the hands of the Crawlers. And the one species most keen on providing mercy. As the most impacted party, would their vote count more than human or Crawler votes? So many variables and opinions. Not one choice that would make everyone at peace and free of fear. But no matter what decisions needed to be made, Smith knew there would never be such a choice.

And why did he think otherwise? There were choices him and Evalee never agreed on, but they still made it work. But how to make it work with hundreds of citizens from three different species?

Footsteps crunched along the snow behind them. Smith turned.

Rosa and Tashon approached, both seemingly lost in thought.

"Tashon." Smith patted his shoulder. "You've been gone a while."

"That's what Rosa says."

Johann smiled. "In the Fourth?"

"Lost track of time." Tashon shrugged. "They're trying to take back the mercy we gave the Crawlers?"

"Rosa told you," Johann said. "She tell you she wants to?"

Tashon looked at Rosa. "She just asked what I thought. She's scared like everyone else."

Smith tilted his head and looked at Tashon. The young man had changed drastically during their short time on Aethera. He stood calmly, arms relaxed at his sides, a contented smile on his face. A peace and joy that Smith thought impossible emanated from Tashon.

Maybe he is a prophet, Smith thought. "What do you think, Tash?" he asked.

"We show mercy," Tashon said with smile. "But not everyone agrees. Not everyone will."

"Yeah." Smith sighed and nodded once. "I know."

Johann stretched his arms above his head. "I just don't want to jeopardize our future on Aethera."

"I don't either," Theresa said.

"No one does," Rosa said. "But what gives us the best chance for humans to coexist with Singers and Crawlers?"

"Coexist safely," Theresa said.

"We are safe," Johann said.

"Johann," Smith said. "We are not going to agree on how safe everyone is right now."

There was no reason to fight over a point for which both sides had legitimate arguments. Yes, they were safe because no one was hurt. No, they weren't safe because there was no telling what might happen next time a prisoner decided to attack.

Rosa coughed quietly. "I changed my mind. I think we should keep showing mercy."

"You were against that," Smith said.

"I was." She looked at Tashon then back at Smith. "But I trust Tashon."

"Tashon," Theresa said. "Why mercy?"

"The universe offers us mercy every day," Tashon said.

"Can you maybe explain that?" Theresa asked.

Tashon closed his eyes and rubbed his head. "Of course. But I was in the Fourth too long. I need sleep. Tomorrow."

"Okay, Tash," Smith said. "Tomorrow. I'm excited to hear what you have to say."

Tashon smiled as he and Rosa walked to the ship.

Smith watched them leave, silently shaking his head. Tashon seemed content with knowing that not everyone would agree, with knowing there was no certainty in the decision that would be made.

***

Night had fallen and it was too cold to be outside. Unable to find sleep, Smith paced up and down a narrow, out-of-the-way tunnel deep in the red caves. It was going to be impossible to create the peaceful

Aetheran society he dreamed of. And why had he even expected it to happen? With all the hope, fear, guilt and rage humans carried in their souls, how could anything close to a perfect society exist? And then add in two completely two species? It wasn't going to happen.

"No," he said out loud. "No, it can at least be better than Earth."

He stopped walking for a moment, shook his head and then resumed his march. He had been confident in Aethera's future when it seemed nearly everyone was on the same page. Before their bottled up anger and fear burst out.

But is the way I see Aethera's future the only right way? He stopped his pacing and stood still, the thought reminding him of Evalee. Even with her immense talent for communication and persuasion, there were always people she couldn't reach. And, just like Tashon, she was content with that fact. He took a deep breath, leaned against the rocky wall. Blew the breath out, hoping the weight on his shoulders would leave with the carbon dioxide. Some of it did, but the pressure still felt overwhelming.

Footsteps echoed through the tunnel. Smith lifted his head and turned. Tashon approached, a gentle smile on his face.

"Smith," he said. "Evalee told me you were here."

Smith's eyebrows shot up. He lowered them and smiled. "I thought you couldn't see through the mountains?"

"I can't." Tashon shrugged. "I guess she can. Or any that live in the Fourth."

"What can I do for you?" Smith asked.

"What?"

"You were looking for me, right? What do you need?"

"Oh, no," Tashon said. "Evalee asked me to come talk to you."

Smith nodded slowly and took a deep breath. "About what?"

"I don't understand it," Tashon said. "Not all of it. She needs to go somewhere. She can't stay here watching you and Abe anymore."

"She needs to move on," Smith said.

"Maybe, but she didn't use those words. It seemed like there's an actual place she's leaving for. Somewhere... important."

"Okay," Smith said.

"Yeah?"

"Okay." Smith smiled. "I'm used to her being gone anyway. Most of the time. We're doing all right down here. Abe and I will be good."

Tashon nodded and smiled. "Good."

"But," Smith said, "if you figure out more about wherever she's going, I want to know."

"Yeah, of course."

Chapter 15

After talking with Smith, Tashon wandered through the tunnels, trying to decide what he was going to say to everyone in the morning. How to explain why, and by what means, he believed mercy was the proper order of the universe. But as he tried to organize those thoughts and experiences, his attention kept turning to the absence of Laos.

Since Tashon had been connected to the Fourth, Laos's essence had never left him for more than a few hours. And Evalee, though it was more rare to see her, would never again come to see him. The space above his third-dimensional form felt too empty, too lonely. He hadn't realized how much Laos's presence had meant to him.

He sighed and turned into a small cavern. He ducked to avoid hitting his head on the low ceiling. He sat and closed his eyes, focusing on the immediate concern that he could actually impact: instituting mercy.

Nothing called to him as he calmed his mind. He knew all too well, now, how easily he could lose himself in that grand absence. But he was also convinced that being there was the best—perhaps the only—way to quiet his thoughts. To bring him understanding. Understanding that he could pass on to all who would listen. And he had an idea that he hoped would prevent him from losing his way in nothing. He would go with a purpose, a specific idea in mind.

He pulled himself up off the ground, out of the Third. Just before his mind slipped completely into absence, he uttered his idea aloud. "Mercy and justice."

Soon after, or perhaps hours, the familiar thoughts found in nothing returned.

No justice, no mercy.

Mercy and justice coexist. Justice and mercy.
True.
True.
Which is more important?
More important?

More important.
Both.
Both?
Neither.
No, either.
Yes, either.
Justice and mercy exist.
Yes, exist.
I exist.
All exist. None exists.
Either.
Either.
Without justice?
Mercy leaves.
When mercy leaves?
Justice leaves.
Justice already left.

If justice leaves, mercy follows.
Then what is left?
Then what exists?
If mercy leaves, justice follows.
Then what is left?
Then what exists?
Existence.

I exist.

In the Third.
No, in nothing
The Fourth.
No, in nothing.
Nothing.
Yes, nothing.
Nothing cannot help me.
Nothing is everything.

Tashon fought to bring his mind to the Fourth, knowing he needed a higher perspective to come to the understanding he sought. But nothing wrapped around him, trying to compress his mind, force everything out of it.

Nothing is everything.

Tashon flexed his mind, synapses pulsing. Nothing squeezed harder. Pulling on his connection to the Fourth, he screamed, though the sound was swallowed by the emptiness, never reaching his ears. His body slowly moved, pushing through the entanglement of emptiness. Hours—or days— later, he collapsed in the Fourth, chest heaving and heart pounding.

As his heart rate and breathing slowed, he looked around. "Laos?"

No answer. No beings around save for the mass swirling in the distance around the pyramids. Tashon took one step toward the structure, then two. He felt an urge to find Laos, to have his companion back. But below him, in the Third, humans and Singer and Crawlers milled about talking about the future. Of what it should and could be, what it might look like. And some of them were waiting for understanding from the Fourth, from Tashon.

He sat down and watched the lives of those below. What answers could he give them? That justice and mercy must coexist? That one could not exist without the other? That was true, yes, but it was not enough. What existed between those two extremes? What choice would provide the best, most peaceful future for Aethera? Turning his attention to the universe as a whole, as an overseeing power, Tashon dropped onto his back and closed his eyes.

Existence. The universe. The dimensions. All of it. Tashon felt he was on the cusp of understanding, and he would lay there until he saw the answers he sought.

***

By the time Tashon came into the main cavern, a large group had gathered. He recognized many of the faces, Hutsep, Minow and Yeance among them. Rosa stood in the center, calling out to quiet everyone as Tashon walked in. They quickly went silent, each eye tracking Tashon as he made his way to Rosa. He kept his eyes forward, trying not to show his discomfort at the mix of reverence, doubt and confusion aimed at him.

As he joined Rosa's side, she motioned for everyone to sit.

"We're ready, Sage Tashon," she said.

Tashon smiled, feeling more comfortable with the title. "Thank you, Rosa." He looked at his audience. It wasn't every being who lived on Aethera, but it felt like it. He took a deep breath. "The question isn't just about mercy or justice. It's about how much mercy, and how much justice."

"We're giving far too much mercy to those Crawlers," someone said.

"We're not safe with them out here, with us," another said.

"We are," Yeance said. "And it's better for us to show mercy, even if there are risks."

A woman glared at Yeance. "You'd risk death just to give them mercy?"

"Yes," Yeance said firmly. "Now that I know life in the Third isn't all there is."

The crowd went silent at Yeance's conviction.

"That was well put. And brings up my point perfectly," Tashon said. "The universe is merciful. We are given mercy simply by being allowed to exist. To live."

"But then we're allowed to die!" a woman shouted.

"I don't believe the universe sees it as death," Tashon said. "Because the universe sees everything, knows everything. She knows that after the Third, we move on to the Fourth. Death is not final."

Some huffed while others nodded their agreement.

"But we can't only offer mercy," Tashon said. "The universe doesn't just offer mercy. There is pain and heartbreak. Restrictions, physical impossibilities. If we offer only mercy, that would mean the Crawler leaders would be free and untethered among us. We can't do that."

A woman's hand rose into the air, but spoke without invitation. "And if we did, justice would be basically gone, right? Since we can't have one without the other."

Tashon nodded and smiled. "Exactly, Rumi."

"So, what are you saying we should do with the Crawlers?" Rumi asked.

"I believe the universe offers as much mercy as she can. We should do the same."

"More mercy than we're already giving them?"

"What we're doing right now seems like the best option," Tashon said.

A man in the back called out. "But this is all just your beliefs? Some fourth-dimensional being didn't reveal this to you?"

Tashon shook his head. "No. No visions or visitations or anything like that. It's the... understanding I've come to. Based on my time in the Fourth, and in nothing. It's what I think is right, what I think we should do. But you should make your own choice."

The crowd whispered among themselves.

Rosa turned to Tashon. "You really sure about this?"

Tashon nodded. "I am. But, Rosa, if it doesn't seem right to you, you don't have to follow everything I say."

"No." Rosa shook her head. "I have faith in you."

Tashon smiled. "Thanks."

"You have anything else to say?"

Tashon shook his head. "No. I've said what I needed to. Let them make their decisions."

Rosa shook her head as she laughed quietly. "The Fourth has changed you."

"Is that good?"

"You were good before." Rosa shrugged and examined Tashon's face. "But now it just seems like you're older. Than me, even. You've grown. Yeah, it's good."

"Thanks for your help," Tashon said. "It's been important to me."

"Oh shut up." Rosa placed two fingers in her mouth and whistled loudly. The crowd went silent. "Does anyone have questions for Sage Tashon?"

"Yes, yes," a Crawler said as it gently pushed its way to the front of the crowd. "You see Crawlers up in Fourth?"

Tashon sighed and shook his head. "No, I wish I had. But in the Higher Spheres I saw so many other species. I'm sure there are Crawlers up there."

"Yes, perhaps, maybe."

"I have the same question," Triffin asked. "You haven't seen all of those who died in the Fourth. How can you *know* they're there?"

"I could be wrong. But I've seen enough to be convinced."

"But if our dead loved ones are in the Fourth, why aren't they all watching out for us?"

"I think some of them did, at least for a little while. Most of the ones who died, died before my connection to the Fourth."

"So they just watched us for a day, maybe a few? Then left?" a girl asked, her voice defensive.

"Evalee... Smith's wife. She told me there's somewhere she needed to go. I think... I *believe* the Fourth is more than just a restful afterlife. There are things to be done."

"It's not heaven?"

"Not in the normal way of thinking. But wouldn't you rather be given the opportunity to continue to grow, to progress? To me, that sounds more heavenly."

Some agreed, but Tashon could see that others didn't like the thought. Those faces seemed tired and worn out, in need of rest. Those worried Tashon the most.

"Let's meditate." He sat down and closed his eyes. Much of the crowd left, but many followed Tashon's lead.

Chapter 16

Every time Abe closed his eyes, the Singer symbols danced behind his eyelids. A full day of studying, and he could only correctly identify the correct symbol for 'significant book/words' six out of ten times. A full day, and he still hadn't gotten to the second symbol on the cover of the Singer book. He kicked a pebble in frustration as he walked around the main Crawler dome. He wanted—needed—to learn the Singer language. To understand how and why the Singer Mother had foreseen the humans' arrival, foreseen his and Winona's presence on Aethera. But in that moment it felt impossible. There were simply too many variations for a single symbol for him to memorize each one. At the rate he was going, he would never find the answers he so desperately craved.

He passed by a pair of humans talking, Londey, who had been concerned with the free will of the biotech, and another woman Abe recognized but whose name he couldn't remember. Abe tried to walk past with just a smile and a nod, but Londey stopped him.

"Abe," she said, "Cixin and I were just talking about the Singer book."

Abe reluctantly joined the pair. His mother had always taught him not to reject an invitation to conversation. "Yeah? Any ideas how it predicted us coming?"

Cixin nodded. "Their melody caused it. Somehow."

"Shit." Abe shook his head.

Cixin raised an eyebrow. "Same thought?"

"Yeah," Abe said.

"A terrifying idea," Londey said.

"And what does that mean about our free will?" Abe asked.

"You mean the free will of you and Winona," Londey said with grin.

Abe shrugged, but said nothing.

"Free will isn't my biggest concern," Cixin said. "They *might* have influenced humans, by unknown means, across the universe decades ago. They might influence some of us now."

Abe stared at her, startled that the question of agency didn't seem to bother her.

Cixin continued. "Or I should say whether they influenced our past doesn't really matter right now. The danger to me is what they might do now, or later. What if a Singer with the status of Mother decides humans shouldn't exist on Aethera anymore?"

"Oh," Abe said. Fear and guilt spread through him. He'd been so concerned with what the Singer book and language meant to him that he hadn't even considered the bigger implications. But at the same time, he did trust the Singers. Didn't he? "The Singers are pacifists. I don't think they would do that."

"It just takes one," Cixin said. "Just one of them killed a Crawler leader."

"It's possible," Abe said. "But first we need to figure out if the Singer language is even capable of all this. And, if it is, can all Singers do it? Or just one, like Mother?"

"How do we figure that out?" Londey asked.

"Winona and I, we're—"

"Having a baby?" Londey smiled widely.

Abe glared at her.

"I'm sorry." She laughed. "I'm sorry. I'll shut up."

"You're what?" Cixin asked, ignoring Londey.

"Trying to learn how to read Singer."

"How?"

"The Crawlers can read it, so we asked Lollawk to teach us."

"Just Crawlers?"

Abe shook his head. "One Singer."

"That seems problematic." Cixin rubbed her temples with her thumbs. "You see why, yes?"

"Teacher, the Singer, she could be manipulating our understanding," Abe said.

Cixin nodded. "Making you perceive it in a certain way."

"But I trust Lollawk," Abe said. "And some of the Singers. I just want to *understand* how their Mother saw the future. And if free will is a lie."

"I think I trust *these* Singers," Cixin said. "But speaking with the Crawlers about this is a good idea."

"I asked Lollawk," Abe said.

"And?"

Abe shrugged. "Lollawk didn't seem bothered by not knowing how Mother knew."

"Strange," Cixin said. "Perhaps the Crawlers are being manipulated by the Singers?"

"Maybe." Abe shook his head. "No, I do trust these Singers. I think the Crawlers have somehow accepted they might never understand."

"What if she predicted our coming in some other way?" Londey asked.

"How?" Cixin looked at Londey, then at Abe.

Abe tried to come up with a logical answer, but found none.

"None of it makes sense," Cixin said. "I don't like it."

Abe saw where she was coming from. Like everyone, she wanted the best for the future of humanity. But Abe still felt the Singers could be trusted. Should be trusted.

"What do you think, Londey?" Abe asked.

"I think it's too early to say anything for certain."

Abe sighed and nodded. "Think it's always too early for that."

"Maybe," Londey said.

"Cixin, do you really think we shouldn't trust the Singers?" Abe asked.

Cixin let out a breath. "I don't know. If their Mother's words did cause us to come here, or even caused the Ship of Nations to crash here, we need to be concerned. But I think learning to read Singer is a good start."

"Right," Londey said. "We should get as many of us trying to learn it as possible."

Cixin nodded. "Yes. That could speed up the process, maybe show us if some of the Singers are trying to control us."

They all agreed and walked back to the throne room in the Crawler dome. Winona stood with Lollawk and another Crawler. In that moment, Abe decided to simply ask Lollawk if their concerns were valid.

"Lollawk," he called as he walked to them.

Lollawk looked at him and clicked. "Abe, hello."

Winona looked at him, and his heart leapt at the sight of her. He tried to push it aside, still fearful the feelings were not his own.

"What's wrong?" she asked.

"Wanted to ask Lollawk something," Abe said. "Lollawk, when the Singers speak, do you ever feel... changed?"

"Changed? Meaning?"

"When the Singers talk, does it ever force you to think or feel or act in a certain way?" Cixin asked.

"No, no. Feel, at times. Sad. Happy. Angry. But... do? Think? No, no."

"What?" Abe shook his head. The Singer language didn't affect Crawlers the same way as humans. At least that meant the Crawlers had made the choice to help the Singers, and the humans, by themselves. Abe thought back to Whims, then Mohawk, casting a spell of peace over them as they journeyed across Aethera. Whims was full of good intentions. What if another Singer was not? Abe told Lollawk, as simply as possible, of the effect the spoken Singer language could have on humans.

Lollawk clicked. "Fear Singers?"

Before any of them could answer, two Singers walked in, loudly singing for everyone to gather outside.

Soon, all present in the Crawler city crowded outside, the dome casting a shadow on the ground. Two Singers stood in the middle, a few dozen feet apart. Their palm wires flipped open and between them a screen flickered to life. On it were Smith, Atom and Hutsep.

Hutsep clicked out a sentence or phrase in the Crawler tongue.

Smith nodded. "It's time to decide what to do with the former Crawler leaders."

Chapter 17

Smith stood in the red caves next to Hutsep and Atom. A large screen showed the mass of people on the continent across the ocean. As planned, the three took turns, each speaking in their native language. They wanted to be certain everyone clearly understood the decision that they needed to make.

Smith explained to the humans.

"We don't know what the conversations on the Crawler continent have been. But we're talking about justice and mercy. Justice—what the Crawler leaders may or may not deserve. And mercy—giving them less than they deserve in the hope this will create a culture of kindness and mercy for the future of Aethera. We've discussed many options, the most extreme of which would be public execution."

Atom interjected with a firm, whispered melody, indicating most of the Singers were firmly against that option.

"On the other side," Smith said, "the most merciful option anyone feels comfortable with is what we're doing now. They're not in a cell, but living among us on constant guard and cabled to another Crawler."

Smith stopped as the crowd on the screen whispered among themselves. Did they like the idea or not? He couldn't tell.

"There are probably a hundred other options between these two extremes. Theresa?" He moved out of the way, allowing her to join Atom and Hutsep.

"There are some of us—Crawlers, Singers and humans—who don't like the idea of the Crawlers being out with us. Too dangerous." She went on to tell them how one of the Crawler leaders attempted, and failed, to make an attack. "We should keep them locked up in a cell."

Atom reiterated that the majority of the Singers desired to offer the most mercy possible, despite what the leaders had done to their species.

Hutsep clicked in Crawler, and then spoke so the humans could understand. "We want all make own choice."

Without a word, Theresa stepped aside and Johann took her place. "Any questions?" he asked.

"Yeah," a man called from within the screen, an ocean away. "So all of us are *voting* on the punishment for the Crawler leaders? Not a judge or something?"

"Right," Johann said. "You're aware of our plan, or hope, to create a society that encourages mercy, yes?"

The man scoffed. "Yeah, if that's even possible."

Johann took a deep breath, calming himself. "Maybe. But we're trying. And to do that, we're allowing victims of a crime to decide on a punishment, with guidance from a merciful mediator."

"And we're all victims," the voice said, "so we're all voting."

"Right," Johann said.

"They don't deserve our mercy!" the man yelled.

"But they do," Abe shouted.

Smith smiled at that, as heated voices erupted from the screen. Atom bellowed one firm note that Smith felt meant 'shut the hell up.' It worked and all went silent.

"We will have time to discuss and debate in a *civil* manner," Johann said. "We'll hold a vote in ten days."

"I have a question," Abe said loudly from within the screen. "For the Crawlers."

"Ask," Hutsep said.

"I saw enemy Crawlers get imprisoned," Abe said and quickly described the brutality of what he witnessed. "Is it painful? Can we call that merciful?"

Smith considered his son's question, wondering if there was any pain with the way the Crawler leaders were tied up.

"Not pain," Hutsep said. "Short discomfort."

"Have you been locked up like that?" Abe asked.

"Yes, yes. For speaking in favor of Singers."

Again, Smith smiled. The goodness he was seeing in those around him, of all three species, continued to amaze him. Hutsep had spoken out against the Crawler leaders and the way they treated the Singers. Had been jailed for it, but still continued to risk his life for the species.

"Anything else?" Johann asked.

No one spoke. Johann turned to Atom, who sang a calming melody of parting. The screen disappeared. Smith looked at Atom, Hutsep, Johann and Theresa. Johann waved him over but Smith shook his head, telling them he needed rest. Which was entirely true. He was exhausted from the constant discussing and needed a break from all of the what-ifs and risk assessments. He made his way out of the main cavern, down a hall past the smokie charging room and to the door that led to the gray desert. A smokie joined him as he reached the door. He hadn't gone out through that door since he found Sylvia dead in the barren gray. But he needed to be away from people, away from the ship, away from all of it.

He opened the door onto a cold and cloudless night, the smokie following him as he stepped onto the familiar gray dirt. A scream burst from his throat and he fell to his knees. *Why did Tashon tell me Evalee left?* he asked himself. *Why did she ask him to?* He fell forward and lay on his stomach, wishing he could at least believe Evalee was still in the Fourth watching him, or watching Abe. *Why did she leave us?*

An icy rain fell from the sky. The smokie unfurled a thin blanket of black and fell on top of Smith, emoting a gentle warmth.

***

Churning, rolling, tumbling. Into the water, out of the water. In, instantly wet. Out, instantly dry. Up and down, in and out. Swallowed, spat up. Timelessness, tumbling and churning. Something in his mouth, down his throat, into his gut.

He fell onto a soft dirt surface. Sat up, looked around. A field of knee-high blue-yellow grass. Waves of a crystal clear ocean lapped at the edge of the landscape. Smith rose to his feet as something rolled in his stomach. Hands on his knees, he heaved and heaved until the rolling moved up his esophagus, into his throat and out of his mouth. It plopped onto the ground with a *chirp chirp*. A fish of glistening silver with long, cloud-white wings stood on six short, furry legs. He reached down to touch it, and the creature slowly flapped its wings, rising into the air above Smith's head.

It lazily turned in a circle, then stopped and meandered off down the coastline. Knowing he had no other choice, Smith followed, keeping the casual pace of his hovering guide. Grass grazed against his legs as eyeless frogs leaped into the water, leaving no ripples in their wake. Other small animals blurred in and out of his vision, yet he kept clear focus on the fishbird in front of him. The farther he walked, the less vivid everything else became.

He came to know and understand every part of the fishbird. How each leg played a part in controlling direction and speed. How each scale glimmered its own shade of silver, no scale the same color as any other. And the wings. How the wings grew longer, shrunk smaller as dictated by the strength of the wind. But always moving at the same slow pace that matched Smith's leisurely walk.

The fishbird stopped, hovered, then rotated ninety degrees and continued away from the water. Smith followed without hesitation because to follow was still the only choice.

The ground rose gradually, the grass thinning and fading until Smith walked along a smooth, black surface. He took a moment to glance back the way he had come. The grass and water had disappeared, leaving him surrounded by crystalline black ground and clear blue skies. He turned back. The fishbird had continued on and was nearly out of sight, a vague blurry silhouette in the distance.

Smith ran after the fishbird, but moved no faster than he had when walking. Yet, on he ran, heart beating in terror at the thought of losing the fishbird. But there was no catching up and, soon, Smith completely lost sight of his guide.

But he went on, never stopping, never turning. Until he, too, vanished.

***

When Smith awoke, the sun shone bright, doing little to ward off the chill in the air. The smokie was gone, but Hutsep and Johann stood silently by his side. He sat up, and then stood.

"All right, Smith?" Johann asked.

"Had to get away," Smith said with a shrug.

"It's a lot of pressure we've put on ourselves," Johann said. "No one would blame you if you decided to step down."

Smith considered it, and then thought of Abe. And Abe's children, if he had any. Of all the future generations of Aethera. He shook his head. "No. Just needed a break."

"Good, good," Hutsep said. "Like you."

Smith smiled. "Thanks. I like you, too, Hutsep."

Johann cleared his throat. "Still need a break?"

"No, I'm all right."

"All right." Johann nodded. "It looks like mercy's going to be a harder sale than we thought."

Hutsep clicked. "Not fortunate."

"Why?" Smith asked.

"Fear, I think. No one knew enemy Crawlers were still attacking on the other continent."

Smith nodded. "That surprised me too. Why didn't they tell us?"

"Why?" Hutsep said. "Not problem here. Problem there. Why worry us here?"

"Kinda makes sense," Johann said.

Smith shrugged. "What options are being discussed?"

"Many, many," Hutsep said.

"Yes." Johann shivered. "But four main ones have taken hold. Can we please go inside? Freeze my shit inside me out here."

They walked back into the caves and through the halls.

Smith spotted Yeance and Minow quietly whispering in a corner, their eyes bright as they looked at each other. He smiled and turned back to the conversation. "What four ideas?" he asked.

"Execution, full imprisonment, what we have currently. Then something between that and full imprisonment."

"Like a certain amount of time out, with us?" Smith asked.

"Exactly."

"That's not a bad idea at all," Smith said.

"I agree," Johann said. "But many still think it's too kind for genocidal tyrants."

They entered the main cavern and sat down. Small groups were clustered about, discussing the upcoming vote. The mercifully imprisoned Crawler leaders stood with their guards on the opposite wall.

"It might be," Smith said.

"What?" Hutsep said.

"Are you changing your mind?" Johann asked.

Smith shook his head. "No. But what we're doing is a risk. Can't pretend it's not."

"Yes, yes," Hutsep said quietly.

Silence. Smith considered what the future might look like if the choice of mercy was the wrong one. Criminals getting off too easy, let out in society too soon, only to commit crime again. But he also knew they would put procedures in place for repeat offenders. For those who showed a willingness to hurt or steal or maim again. And that thought gave him an idea he was shocked no one had come up with before. Or perhaps they had, and he hadn't heard yet.

He stood up and asked everyone to listen. "I know a big concern for all of us is what might happen if a Crawler leader, or any future prisoner, takes advantage of our mercy and hurts one of us."

Many echoed their agreement.

"We should take that into account. I'm not saying I want to give up on mercy. But what we're doing with the Crawler leaders is going to set up the future of Aethera." Smith took a deep breath, and then looked at Johann and Hutsep, wondering if he should have discussed the idea with them first. "One Crawler leader already showed us he or she will take advantage of that mercy. So, until the vote, I think we should keep that Crawler leader on full lockdown. If the vote comes out differently, we can change it."

Theresa emerged from the group. "I wish you'd talked to me about it first," she said. "But I think it's a good idea. Is anyone against moving the Crawler leader who tried to attack into full confinement?"

"Temporarily?" a man asked. "And we'll change it if the vote is different?"

"Yes," Theresa said.

"And all of you agree to that?" the man asked, looking from Smith to Johann.

Both men nodded.

"Yes."

"Absolutely."

"Yes, yes," Hutsep said.

The man nodded. "Okay with me."

"Everyone?" Smith asked.

All agreed, and three Crawlers surrounded the Crawler leader. It screeched, spat and stomped, but the guards were in control this time. They dragged the prisoner away as the other Crawler leaders watched silently.

Is the mercy we're offering having an impact on them? he wondered.

PART TWO

Chapter 18

In the days leading up to the vote, Tashon held countless meditation sessions. He was exhausted, but he could see the peace it gave people. For him that was worth the drain on his energy. But, thanks to Rosa, he had the night before the vote to himself. She had seen the red in his eyes, and seen him nodding off at meetings and meals. So she told everyone that Sage Tashon needed to be alone.

Tashon smiled and took a deep breath as he lay on the surface of the Fourth. The warm, swirling wind of colors blew more swiftly than Tashon had ever seen. The ground itself rolled up and down with the force of it, calming Tashon into empty mindfulness. He watched the wind swirl, twist and leap. Colorful wisps interweaved into patterns both wondrous and complex. A stream of rushing blue rolled around a windy wall of some unnameable color. Beyond that, a slowly rotating tornado of colors unlike any in the Third. He had no thoughts of the vote, of justice or mercy or of the role he now had as a sage to the people. Just the wind, the gentle wave of the ground, the slow movement of his chest as he breathed.

After a time, the moths fluttered into view on a lone strand of white wind. Tashon sat up—he hadn't seen the moths in days, maybe even weeks. Not since before the Crawler leaders surrendered. They changed course and flew to him, twirling around his head. The white strand trailed behind them and Tashon realized it was not wind, but an object carried by the moths.

As the moths circled him, faster and faster, the white string connected at the ends. The moths stopped and dropped the white circle. It landed, nearly weightless, on Tashon's shoulders. A necklace emanated a soft light. The moths landed on the rolling ground, then turned away from him, gazing at the pyramids. The pyramids. Laos.

Is something wrong with Laos?

The moths made no sound, no movement. He looked past them to the pyramids, and the structure shifted. It slowly blew apart into perfectly geometric chunks, thousands upon thousands of them slowly floating off in different directions. Tashon watched in awe at the beauty of it. Saw, understood, the beauty of a thing broken apart into a million pieces smaller than the whole. Minute by minute, the pieces spread farther from where the pyramids had stood. As the fourth-dimensional dust settled, white light erupted from the center point, streaming up and out. The wind vanished. The waving ground went still.

Tashon watched and realized the light was not just light, but souls. The essences of those since gone from the Third. He jumped to his feet, squinting to see individual souls. Some of them felt familiar to Tashon, and he was sure Laos was among them. And he knew Laos would not return. Evalee must have been among them. His parents and sister too. Maybe even the Mother Singer who had aided him, or some Crawlers who had died in the battle. Soon, the white forms simply blinked out of sight, as if popping out of existence.

No, Tashon thought. *Like they're transitioning to a higher dimension.*

Was that even possible? There was still so little he understood of the Fourth that conjuring mental images of anything higher was pointless. And there was no proof that the souls had gone to a Fifth Dimension. All he knew was that they were gone, and he believed he would never see any of those particular souls again. But it only made sense to him that the next existence would be in something even higher than the Fourth.

He took a deep breath, realizing that if he chased that train of thought he would lose sight of what he perceived as his purpose at that time: helping those on Aethera find greater peace. He looked to the moths, silently thanking them for their gift, though he had no idea what it was for. Gently, he placed one finger on the necklace. It was smooth like glass, flexible like rope. It simultaneously energized him and calmed him, filling him with a hopeful yet cautious confidence. Other than that, no clues as to its purpose.

The moths left him and he sat down. Something else caught his attention. Twelve beings were suddenly a few dozen yards away. They stood motionless, giving Tashon time to examine them. A few moments of staring, and he realized they were all fourth-dimensional Crawlers. Each stared at, and through, the translucent ground of the Fourth. Tashon cautiously walked to them, unsure where their allegiances might lie. But as he got to them, none even acknowledged his presence. Whatever was in the Third had their complete attention. Tashon looked down.

There, in the melting ice and snow, lay the Crawler leaders and their guards, heads severed from bodies. He let out a short shout and turned back to the Crawlers in the Fourth, his understanding now full. Someone, or a group, had murdered the Crawler leaders and their guards. They had taken the decision into their own hands, unwilling or perhaps unable to offer mercy of any kind.

"Who did it?" he asked the Crawlers.

One looked at Tashon but didn't speak. It just stood here, as if struggling to comprehend where it was and how it got there. Had they not heard Tashon speak of the Fourth as an afterlife? *Or maybe after death there's a time of disorientation at the sudden change of existence*, Tashon thought. He looked at them, then back at the corpses below. Time passed, but the Crawlers did nothing.

"You... you're in the Fourth Dimension," he said. "Your... souls are."

A few more looked at him and Tashon thought, perhaps only hoped, that they were beginning to understand.

"You were...." he said, and looked at the bodies below. "You died, but it's not the end."

Some of the Crawlers wandered away while the rest continued to stare at their dead bodies. Tashon tried to think of more to say, of some encouraging phrase or word but nothing he thought of made sense. All clichés based on what humans thought the afterlife would be, not what it actually was.

Tashon sighed and shook his head. There was nothing he could do for the Crawlers, but there was work to be done in the Third.

He closed his eyes and pulled himself back to the Third, back into the yellow forest. The morning sun slowly melted the top layer of snow, the setting for what could have been a peaceful day. With the sun on his face and his breath puffing clouds in the air, he started back to the ship. As he made it to the clearing, he realized if he hadn't been distracted watching the pyramids, he might have seen who killed the Crawlers.

The clearing was quiet, a few early risers milling about. Tashon would be the one to deliver the news of the murders. He took a deep breath, and went to find Smith. As he did, he realized the necklace was invisible in the Third, but he still felt the weight of it on his shoulders.

Chapter 19

Chaotic terror spread through the clearing, the ship and the caves as news of the murders spread. With Johann and Theresa close behind, Smith moved through the mass of natives and humans as quickly as possible, catching people's agreement, distaste or confusion at the act. They had to find Atom and Hutsep as soon as possible. The murders could be enough to break down the relationship between the three species, potentially leading to a war that the humans would have no way of winning. Smith thought that, maybe, the native species would blame each other and leave the humans out of it. However, even if they did, a battle between Singers and Crawlers would still have human casualties.

They ran past trees, into the red caves and down the tunnel. Human screams, raging Singer melodies and fierce Crawler screeching echoed from the main cavern.

"Shit," Johann said.

They burst into the cavern and the first thing Smith saw was that the arguing groups were not split by species. At first, this seemed like a good sign to Smith. No species hanging up on another. Then he noticed they were declining to baseless blame and profanities solely based on how another would have voted. This, Smith knew, was just as bad.

The more he examined those in the cavern, he saw that there were more silent observers than there were those shouting harsh rhetoric. *Not too different from Earth*, Smith thought. Johann whistled loudly and all went silent. Everyone looked to the three human leaders. Smith had no idea what to say and, apparently, neither did Johann.

Theresa stepped forward. "I know we're all angry or confused or afraid. Or all of those. But whoever did this was not part of a larger group."

"How know that?" A Crawler clicked loudly, slid its five tongues out of his mouth, then pulled them back in. "Many sought execution."

More shouts erupted, accusations of murder and calls to listen to reason. Johann whistled again.

Theresa sighed. "I was going to vote for execution."

More screams, harsher accusations that were, again, silenced by Johann.

"But I didn't want their *guards* dead too. They were innocent, trying to do the right thing. Maybe the leaders were deserving of death. But what's been done to the guards.... Do any of us really think it was right?"

Silence. Smith looked at Theresa, shocked by how logical she was in such a time of crisis. And Smith agreed. Who wanted the Crawler leaders dead so badly that they would kill the guards too? Or maybe whoever did it thought the guards would step aside, not do anything to protect the prisoners. Which meant that the guards died protecting the Crawler leaders. Sacrificed themselves to protect those who had sought the death of any in support of the Singers and humans.

"So you think it was someone acting alone?" a woman asked.

Theresa shrugged and looked to Smith.

Smith cleared his throat. "I would like to think that. But do we know any who could do that much damage alone?"

"Maybe," a woman said. "Maybe the prisoners tried to escape, and in the fight they all killed each other."

"No, no," a Crawler said. "How all heads gone?"

Smith nodded. If it had been gun wounds or loss of blood that had killed them, it was possible that they killed each other in an escape attempt. But it was impossible that they all decapitated each other.

"So it had to have been a group," the man said.

"Yes, I think so," Smith said.

A Singer sang a melody of heartbreaking fear and frustration. Smith shook his head, wondering if the right for mercy was over. Or, if somehow, the fight for mercy was even to blame for the murders. If the prisoners had been in a cell, they may still be alive.

Another melody rang out, overpowering the first. Atom walked into the room, flanked by Whims and Comet. The notes she sang calmed Smith, and seemed to calm the room. There was no message or meaning other than to simply *be calm*. The three Singers stopped next to Smith and Theresa.

Atom adjusted her tone, heightened her pitch. Words that Smith had come to know as 'them' and 'ocean' were a part of the chorus. They needed to tell those on the other continent about the killings. Whims and Comet made a screen, and soon it was filled with the face Lollawk, a crowd behind him. Abe and Winona were in the bottom right corner of the screen, partially obscured by Lollawk's head. Smith smiled sadly at the sight of his son, wondering how the boy would react to the news.

"Ready vote?" Lollawk asked.

Atom sang a slow, melancholy 'no.'

"No?" Lollawk asked.

Hutsep joined Atom, and clicked to Lollawk. The two spoke back and forth, and Smith could only wonder at the thoughts that must be going through Lollawk's mind. The minds of all the Crawlers across the ocean. Soon, the clicking stopped, and Lollawk screeched, the sound making Smith's ears ring.

"What's wrong?" a woman behind Lollawk asked.

Atom sang Smith's name. Slowly, partially wishing Johann's name had left her lips, Smith walked to her side.

"The leaders," he said. "The prisoners, their guards too. They were... killed. Murdered."

Silence, followed quickly by shouts and melodies and clacks. Questions and profanities, fears and allegations. Atom silenced it all with a single note. Smith looked around the room again, and realized someone was missing.

He walked to Atom and pulled her aside. "Lioness?"

Atom made a sound that Smith interpreted as a gasp, then indicated Smith should join her. She walked back to the screen.

"Now what?" Lollawk asked.

Atom sang Smith's name.

"We should.... " He stopped, had no idea what to say. There was much to be done, he knew, but how to do it after such an act?

"Still vote," Lollawk said. "What do with prisoners here?"

"That... makes sense to me," Smith said, though he wondered how the murders might affect the votes.

Atom agreed, and then called out a string of seething notes directed at whomever had committed the violent act: *you will be found.* The emotion attached to the phrase sent fear through Smith. It was the closest to violence he had ever felt the Singers to be, and for a moment, he saw how dangerous Atom would be if she threw her pacifism to the wind.

***

For Smith, it was an easy decision to make. He would cast his vote to keep the Crawlers imprisoned, with the opportunity for release should they prove deserving. And many agreed, realizing that some of those Crawlers had followed the leaders' will, not necessarily their own.

"That's still not an excuse," Minow said as they waited their turn to vote.

"It's not," Smith agreed. "If more of them had stood against the Crawler leaders, maybe there would have been fewer deaths. They shouldn't be executed because they didn't stand up to their nation's leaders."

"Maybe. But what if they aren't willing to coexist with us at all?" she asked.

"They stay imprisoned for life," Smith said.

"Right."

Smith nodded and looked around at everyone waiting to vote, listening to the conversations, trying to glean how the murders were impacting everyone's decision. Would they perceive mercy to be the problem, claiming that if the prisoners had been in locked cells they would have been safe? It wasn't an illogical view, Smith realized. But there was also no way to know what might have been. Or, were they considering justice to be the culprit, envisioning a justice-seeking vigilante to be the killer? Between the two extremes, how many were there, sitting somewhere in the middle? He sighed and shook his head.

"Smith," Minow said, pulling him from his thoughts. "This is a big moment. I get that. But why are you putting so much weight on it? We can change it if it proves to create an unintended effect."

Smith shook his head. He looked away as he spoke. "Change is always possible. But look at Earth. So much was done early on that had lasting, negative influences. And the pain suffered to change those? The lives lost? It's better to do it right the first time."

Minow sighed. "You're not wrong. It's not going to be perfect, though. All of these people were on the Ship of Nations because Humans for Humanity *chose* them because they were considered the best of humanity. I think you might've forgotten that."

Smith turned his head and looked directly at her, knowing she was right. "Yeah," he said. "I guess we're already off to a better start than Earth."

She half-smiled. "I think so."

Theresa stepped out of a side room and called Smith's name. He stood, walked into the room and closed the door. A small screen floated between four wires protruding from a table. Images representing each possible choice were on it. Below each image, what the image represented, written in all three languages.

Without hesitation, Smith made his vote and left the room.

Soon, all the votes had been cast and counted. The majority—59 percent—sided with Smith. Thirty-one percent voted for imprisonment with no opportunity for release. The remaining 10 percent voted for the execution of all Crawler prisoners.

As Smith said his goodnights and goodbyes, a thought refused to leave his mind. If they knew who fell within that ten percent, they would shorten their suspect pool immensely, and could more effectively discover who murdered the prisoners and guards. Voting, of course, was meant to be anonymous. But he wondered if there was a way to hack the system in order to find that information. *Would it be unethical to breach that anonymity to find the murderers?* he thought to himself.

Even so, he wasn't sure it mattered. Lioness, along with the last Singers, Crawlers and humans she'd been seen with, were still nowhere to be found.

Chapter 20

Abe stared at the second symbol on the cover of the Singer book. He knew it meant something akin to 'future' with its specific angle and wisps indicating a future that encompasses 'all.' He was trying to memorize every line, angle and curve of the symbol. But his mind refused to think on anything other than the murders. Yes, he'd seen death before. He'd seen the bloodied corpses of humans, Crawlers and Singers alike. But this had been after the battle was won, and whoever did it seemed to have no issue taking the innocent lives of the guards, as well. They had taken their lives, and by doing so took the vote away from everyone else on Aethera. As if the only opinion that mattered was their own. He groaned and stood up, knowing the focus he desired would not come.

Lollawk walked to him. "What wrong, Abe?"

Abe shook his head. "I can't believe what happened to your old leaders. I thought that everyone left desired some form of peace and mercy and law."

"Most do." Lollawk clicked and shuffled his feet.

Abe looked at the book, then back at Lollawk. "Does the book say anything about the murders? Or what happens now?"

"No, no. Singer promise of no violence, start and end. Middle tells that humans help Singers, that Abe and Winona make offspring."

Abe sighed and shook his head. The idea had become familiar enough not to embarrass him, but he was still far from understanding the predictive nature of the Singer book. Still had no idea to what extent the Singer language could influence outside results.

"You've really never felt forced to do something a Singer told you to do?" he asked Lollawk.

"No, no."

"Once I touched a Singer, and it told me so strongly to step away that my arm and legs moved. It wasn't me."

Lollawk clicked out a laugh. "Never touch Singer. Singer hate to be touched."

"Okay," Abe said. "That still doesn't help me understand how the hell any of this works. How I'm in their damn book, and why these murders weren't. Why any of this was seen by a Singer hundreds of years ago."

"Thousands," Lollawk said.

Abe sighed. "You have no idea how this book was written so accurately?"

"No, no. And not all accurate. Book not say Crawlers help."

Abe shrugged. "Right. Do you think it's possible by speaking those predictions, the Singer Mother caused them to happen?"

"No," Lollawk said. "Or yes."

"I just want to *understand*." Abe turned from Lollawk.

Winona walked directly to him, her eyes red and puffy as though she'd been crying. "Can we go for a walk?" She reached out and grabbed his hand.

"Yeah, of course," he said.

They walked hand in hand around the Crawler dome.

"What's wrong?" Abe asked.

A few fresh tears spilled onto her cheeks. "The brutality of the murders. Did you hear what they did to those Crawlers?"

Abe shook his head.

"Decapitated them." She took a deep breath. "Why? What's the *point* of it? Don't we all want peace? The opportunity to be granted grace and mercy? I don't get it, Abe." She pulled herself closer to his side, her tears smearing on his shoulder.

"I don't either. But at least the majority vote leaned toward mercy for the prisoners here, right?"

She shrugged. "Yeah. How can any intelligent being do that to another?"

"Gross violence happened on Earth too."

"Those were just *stories*." Winona wiped her face. "We never experienced it on the ship."

Abe nodded. He agreed that Aethera itself felt heavier than it had, but what could he do about it? He held Winona closer, pushing aside the ever-invading thought that their connection was manufactured by the Singer language. "Yeah. The stories never seemed real," he said.

She nodded, her wet cheek rubbing on his shoulder. "Tell me about something different."

"The only other thing I can think about is the Singer book."

"Me too," she said. "The second symbol means 'future,' right?"

"Right. But it's just like the symbol for 'book.' Fifty variations of it, each barely different than any other."

"Yeah," Winona said as they walked past a flock of idle biotech birds. "I was looking at it with Cixin. Analyzing every detail. And I think we're doing something *wrong*."

Abe looked at her. "Wrong?"

"I mean, applying too much *human* logic to a language that isn't human."

"Okay, maybe. But how else are we supposed to do it?"

Winona laughed softly. "No damn idea."

"Not even a shitty idea?" Abe asked with a smile.

Winona stopped walking and looked him in the eye. "I *never* have shitty ideas."

They both laughed and walked on. Those few moments with Winona lightened Abe's heart more than anything else could have. He knew it, and appreciated it. Still, he doubted its authenticity. *How the hell did the book predict me coming here?* he asked himself.

"Maybe there's a better way," Abe said. "But I don't think so. Learning how to read the language of an entirely different species, with different cultural and historical backgrounds can't be easy. We're lucky we can communicate with them as well as we can already."

"That's true," Winona said. "The Crawlers can read it. Maybe they can stab one of their cables into your brain stem and pump the knowledge into you."

"No way in hell I'm doing that," Abe said.

"Fine." Winona laughed. "Okay, don't take the easier road."

"I think that road would kill me."

"And where would Aethera be without its first parents?" she asked.

Abe shook his head, a slight smile spreading across his lips.

Winona sighed. "Abe." She stopped walking again. "I know you've wondered if how we feel about each other is real."

Abe looked at the ground, guilt and embarrassment rushing through him. "I... Winona—"

"I have too," she said.

He let out a sigh of relief. "I hate the idea of something controlling my life."

"Me too," she said. "But do you think we are? Being controlled?"

Abe shrugged. "Would we know if we were?"

"We figured out that Mohawk and Whims were altering our perspective when we walked through the forest."

"I've thought about that too. But he had good intentions." Abe took a breath. "At least I think so."

"And the Singer Mother had bad intentions?"

"I hadn't thought of that," Abe said. "I guess not. She wanted to save her people."

"So did she inadvertently control humanity's fate?" Winona wondered.

Abe looked at the sun as it began its descent into the horizon. "Maybe. Lollawk said the Singer language doesn't affect the Crawlers the same as it does us."

"Right. Could she have known how Singer words can impact human minds?" Winona pulled Abe to a boulder and they sat down.

"But" — Abe ran a hand across his head — "if it was inadvertent, how did she see us clearly enough to draw pictures of us? And how would it have reached all the way to Earth?"

"I've been wondering if we'll ever figure that out," she said.

Abe groaned. *Not understanding it terrifies me*, he thought.

"What?" Winona squeezed his hand.

"It scares me to think we'll never understand it." Abe looked at the ground and traced a circle in the dirt with his foot.

Winona looked at the circle he'd made on the ground and drew her own. She looked to the sky. "Does it scare you that you don't understand everything about the Fourth? And about what Tashon can do?"

"No, it doesn't," he said.

"Then why does *this* scare you?" she asked.

Abe shrugged and sighed. "I don't think it would if we weren't in the book. If she'd just predicted an alien race coming to save them, yeah, I'd be confused as hell. But *we're* in the book. And our decisions and thoughts and feelings might not be our own. I'm surprised I haven't shit my pants over it."

Winona laughed softly and shook her head. "I think you should hold the shit in until we have real answers."

"But you just said we might not get any real answers," Abe said.

"I did." Winona wrapped her arms around his waist.

Abe inhaled deeply, amazed by her kindness and warmth. *She seems okay if she never understands*, he thought. *Why does not knowing, never understanding, upset me so much?* He was starkly aware of the excitement he felt at Winona's touch, the warmth of her smile and the rush through his veins every time she was near. He tried to push aside the fear that it was all manufactured, false emotions placed on him to prove the truth of an ancient prophesy. But those doubts only slipped to the back of his thoughts, refusing to disappear.

That night, his dreams were jumbles of images and sounds. Tentacles from Aleron's monster piercing Crawlers and humans, accompanied by the echoing of Singer notes. His mother's limp body falling to Aethera's surface. The Ship of Nations leaving the planet where they left Colony Five. Winona, holding his hand and staring into his eyes, a smile on her face. Then a Singer melody calling her away from him forever.

Chapter 21

For the first time since gaining access to the Fourth, Tashon was frustrated with the questions of those seeking answers. No matter what he said, some of them refused to accept his answers as truth. He stood in a small group, trying to shake the sleep from his mind as he pondered his answer. Only human eyes looked to him for an answer.

"No," he said. "I am connected to the Fourth, but that doesn't give me any omniscience to know who killed them." He glanced at Rosa, sitting outside the circle, writing on a yellowed stack of papers.

"But can't you use it to figure out who did?" an elderly woman asked.

"I saw the Crawler essences after they were killed. I did, but that did nothing to help us. They were... confused, silent."

"Are they still there?"

Tashon shook his head. "They left soon after."

A man cleared his throat. "That doesn't make any sense, Tashon. Wouldn't they want justice by telling you who killed them?"

Tashon held in a soft laugh. "Perspectives change in the Fourth. Once you realize death in the Third really isn't the end, death in the Third loses much of its significance. The way I see it is that the killer rendered their Third bodies useless, expediting their move into the Fourth. I'm not saying it was right or that it wasn't murder. Not at all. I'm just saying that once it is known, for certain, that there is an afterlife, perspectives change."

No one spoke. Tashon could see the pondering on their faces as they wondered whether Tashon's words were valid. He looked to the Fourth in search of Laos, and that absence sank into Tashon's heart for the hundredth time that day. *The man I killed became one of my most trusted friends*, he thought.

"Have you heard me speak of Laos?" Tashon asked.

"The terrorist you killed," a boy said.

Tashon nodded. "Not once did he hold it against me. He became one of my closest friends."

"But you killed him in self-defense," a woman pointed out. "The Crawler guards were killed in cold blood."

"I still didn't get the impression they were out for revenge. What's important in the Fourth seems... entirely different than what we in the Third think is important."

Minow's voice rang out from the back. "And what's important in the Fourth?"

"Self-improvement," Tashon said. "That's the impression I get, at least."

"But what about the monster that attached to Aleron?" a little girl asked.

Tashon squatted to her level. "He didn't seem like he wanted to get better, I agree. But I haven't seen him, or any other monsters in the Fourth since we kicked him out of here."

The girl smiled. "Okay."

"But I've heard you say you've seen spirits of light *and* of darkness in the Fourth," a woman said.

"I have," Tashon said. "And none of those darker spirits have seemed as consuming, as powerful as whatever took Aleron."

A man sighed and shook his head. "So the one that got Aleron was... what? Special?"

Tashon shrugged. "Maybe. Different, at least. The other dark ones all seem to at least *want* to improve. But I haven't been close to any of those. They keep their distance."

"You have this connection to the Fourth," someone said, "but it seems like you don't know much more than we do."

Tashon laughed. "That's accurate. Vague impressions. What the higher being has told me. What Evalee and Laos told me."

"You talk like Laos and Evalee aren't there anymore," someone said.

Tashon rubbed the invisible necklace between his fingers. "They're not. Not where I can see them, at least. They... progressed. Went on to their next stage of existence."

"What's the next stage?" Minow asked.

Tashon shook his head. "No idea."

The elderly woman took a step toward Tashon. "So you don't know who killed the Crawlers," she said. "Or where any of the dead have gone to. What real good is your connection to the Fourth?"

Minow walked into the circle. "Hope," she said. "And peace. That's what Sage Tashon offers."

"But we still know almost nothing. Doesn't more knowledge bring more hope and peace?" the woman asked.

Tashon shook his head and looked down. "I don't know. Maybe," he said.

At that comment, many in the group left, whispering among themselves. But their doubt remained, seeping into Tashon. *Their questions are valid*, he thought. *Why do I know so little?*

As if sensing his concerns, Rosa emerged from the circle and placed a hand on his shoulder, "Sage Tashon, will you meditate with us?"

Tashon sat on the floor and motioned for them to do the same. As they got comfortable and closed their eyes, he rubbed the necklace from the moths. It sent a tingling warmth into his fingers and down his veins. He opened his mouth to begin, but didn't know what to say, his mind flooding with his questions. *I know the Fourth isn't perfect, so why haven't I seen any signs of evil or true darkness?* The doubts of those who questioned him sank into his mind, and he wondered if peace was ever fully attainable. *Why is it I've only seen the beautiful and mesmerizing in the Fourth? Have I been blind to the darkness? Or has it just not found me yet?* He knew, of course, that there must be darkness there. The light could not exist without the darkness, nor the beautiful without the ugly. *When will it find me?*

"Sage Tashon?" Rosa said. "Are you okay?"

Tashon nodded and inhaled deeply. "Clear all thoughts from your mind," he said. "Focus on one simple idea. That nothing is out there, that nothing matters. Everything matters. All equal, the same. Let all else fade." Thoughts of darkness crept back into his mind. He gripped the necklace with an entire fist. "You're in a place of nothing but white, floating. Surrounded by air, neither hot nor cold, warm or cool. Your body, your skin blends with it. Slow your breathing. In and out. In. And. Out."

He went silent, hoping they were finding calm as he fought the fear of a potential future of darkness. *I could better help them if my mind were in nothing*, he thought. But how to lift his mind to nothing and keep his body in the Third? He focused on his portion of essence in the Fourth. *Can I bring that down into nothing?* He tugged softly on it, and it resisted. But he felt he should be able to bring it down. He pulled a bit harder, and it gave, breaking partially through the surface of the Fourth. From within his higher eyesight, he saw the Third and Fourth, as always. And in between the two a wave of absence. He pulled his external essence toward the emptiness. It stretched, one end remaining in the Fourth and the other just touching the edge of nothing.

Then the end of the essence in the Fourth jerked back, yanking the other end out of nothing, the two ends slamming together in the higher dimension. The force of it whipped Tashon's head back. His skull slammed into stone. His ears rang.

"Shit." He opened his eyes and sat up.

Rosa ran to his side while the other mediators stared at him, concern and confusion spread across their faces.

"What happened?" Rosa asked.

He shrugged, unsure of how to explain it. "I tried the impossible."

"What does that mean?"

"I tried to... connect to nothing *and* stay here," he said.

Rosa sat next to him. "Here, the Third?"

Tashon nodded.

"Why?" another woman asked.

"I wanted to give you a better sense of what nothing is like. Words alone can't do that, can't give that kind of peace."

Rosa smiled, put a hand on Tashon's shoulder and looked at the mediators. "Sage Tashon took a risk to bring us more peace," she said.

"Why?" the little girl asked.

Tashon ran a hand through his hair as he thought of an answer. "I don't like being the only one to see and feel nothing and the Fourth. The only one with that type of peace and understanding."

"You want to share with us?" the girl asked.

"Yeah." Tashon smiled. "I want to share with you." Vertigo rushed into him, his head spun and he let himself slowly drop back to the floor.

"Let's give the sage some rest," Rosa said. She grabbed his hand, helped him to his feet and steadied him as they walked to a bench.

With a sigh, Tashon sat and closed his eyes. "Thanks, Rosa."

***

When Tashon opened his eyes, everyone other than Rosa was gone. She sat by his side, writing on the same stack of aging papers. Her attention was focused entirely on her task and she didn't notice he was awake. Tashon closed eyes, thinking of the aggressive woman Rosa had been when they first met. How she had changed and become his biggest advocate, and a large advocate for sharing and achieving peace.

He realized that he was a large reason for her change, and felt a surge of pride. But the pride quickly faded away as he considered what he had actually done. It felt that everything had been done to him, and he'd only shared those experiences with others. He hadn't jumped in front Aleron to save someone, like Cosima and Jonstin. Luck had simply been on his side, the ship jumping to the Fourth at just the right second to leave his mind permanently tethered to the higher plane. So why were more and more people referring to him as 'sage?' He hadn't done anything great. Nothing great had happened to him, either. Strange and beautiful, perhaps, but nothing that earned him such a title. Even when he tried to truly share what he had found in nothing with those in need, he failed.

"I'm no sage," he whispered.

"Shut up," Rosa said. "You are."

"Why?"

"A sage is one with wisdom that most don't have," she said. "Who sees the world through a different lens. A better lens."

"Different, yeah. I don't know about better."

"Open your eyes," she said.

He obeyed, then sat up.

"You see and knows things about the universe no one else does," she said. "Things that bring peace and comfort."

Tashon sighed. "I *try* to bring peace and comfort. But it doesn't seem to really be helping. I mean, like they said, I hardly know more than they do."

"Their doubt is giving you doubt." She huffed, set her stack of papers on the ground and stood up. "Outside," she said.

Tashon hesitated, but when she glared at him he quickly got to his feet and followed her out of the caves.

It was another brisk morning, and more snow had melted, leaving the ground dotted with white and brown.

Rosa gently pulled Tashon between two trees. "Close your eyes," she said. "Tell me *everything* you see."

Tashon fought the urge to roll his eyes, Rosa's staunch faith in him feeling like a burden alongside the doubts of the others. Nevertheless, he followed her directions. "I see us," he said. "The entire forest. The mountains, the desert, out to the edge of the dried up sea."

"The other directions?"

Despite his frustration with her, Tashon could feel himself relaxing. "The forest ends to the east, on the edge of a sea of red water. Then north, where we went. The rolling hills, the cliffs, the edge of the ocean we crossed. South, the desert fades to frozen tundra."

"No one else can see that," Rosa said. "Not like that."

"But what good is seeing an entire continent at once? How can that help anyone?"

Rosa shrugged. "It might not. But what you're seeing in the Fourth can, and has. You can't expect everyone to believe you."

Tashon nodded, though some of the doubts remained. The fact that he hadn't seen any true darkness troubled him. The Fourth wasn't a perfect place. It wasn't heaven, he knew that for certain. So why then did the dark forms remain at a distance? Could the Fourth continue to be a sanctuary for him, or was there something he was missing? He wrapped a finger around the necklace, and let the warmth spread through his body.

"Thanks, Rosa," he said.

"Anytime, Sage Tashon." She walked away.

When will the darkness find me? Find us? he thought, then remembered the murders. I guess it already has. Is that why I'm doubting? Because I could do nothing to find the killer? He considered the question, but couldn't find any specific reason for his doubt and fear.

But sometimes the worst pieces of the human mind creep in with no apparent reason at all.

Chapter 22

Smith sat at a table in the ship, talking about what had happened and what to do next. A conversation he felt he was always having. The type of conversation he would probably always have, as long as he was a leader on Aethera. With him were Atom, Wave, Ulot, Hutsep, Johann, Theresa and Deloi. A wide man with piercing eyes, Deloi had performed the autopsies of the murdered, with the help of Ulot.

"Still no sign of Lioness?" Theresa asked. "Or the others?"

"No, no," Hutsep said.

Atom confirmed the answer with a slow, defeated note, followed by one of fearful confusion. She did not understand how one of her own could do something so violent, so grotesque.

"But," Johann said, "is their absence the only evidence we have that it was them?"

Hutsep clicked. "Yes. Good thought."

Wave quickly disagreed. His notes indicated that, to him, the ones who disappeared were already proven guilty.

"I think so too," Theresa said. "Why else would they be missing?"

"Wait," Smith said. "First let Ulot and Deloi tell us what they found."

"Cause of death was definitely decapitation," Deloi said. "But...." He looked to Ulot.

"Crawler skin thick, hard to cut. Bone and muscle too. Thought cuts would be... word?" He turned it back to Deloi.

"Right," Deloi said. "Ulot said the cuts would be jagged, almost shredded. But each head was cut off cleanly, smooth lines all the way through. Nothing torn or broken. Ulot said that was impossible."

"Yes, not possible," Hutsep said. He clicked at Ulot and the two talked back and forth. Then, "Ulot show pictures."

Ulot placed an elliptical disc on the table and clicked at it. A dozen tiny wings popped out of its sides. It lifted up, and centered itself two feet above the table. Light flickered underneath it, and a holographic Crawler head appeared on the table. Lollawk leaned forward, his finger tracing the line where head had been separated from the body.

Hutsep and Ulot clicked back and forth, ignoring the others present. For a moment Smith wished he could at least *feel* the meaning of what they said, but soon realized two species with that ability could be dangerous. He looked to Johann, who shrugged in response. Theresa chewed her nails. Atom and Wave sat still, as if unconcerned by what the Crawlers were saying. But then he remembered they understood the Crawler language.

Hutsep and Ulot stopped clicking.

"Ulot and Deloi right," Hutsep said. "Not possible."

Wave sang, disagreeing with Hutsep. It was possible, because it had happened. Smith realized, again, the kind awareness of the Singers. Wave had no doubt understood what Ulot and Lollawk had said to each other, yet had waited until the humans also understood to respond. A simple gesture, perhaps. But one Smith thought he wouldn't have been aware enough to make if he were Wave.

"Yes, yes," Hutsep said. "Did happen. Possible. New."

"What could've done this?" Johann asked.

"Nothing," Hutsep said.

Again, Wave disagreed.

Hutsep clicked. "Nothing *known*," he said.

"What about biotech? Nanotech?" Smith asked.

Wave stood and quietly sang to Atom. The two walked out of earshot.

"The hell?" Johann said.

"Shit." Theresa shook her head. "Knew we shouldn't have trusted them."

"Silent," Ulot said. "Singers good."

Smith said nothing. He watched the two Singers, trying to catch a sound or a feeling, anything to indicate what they were saying.

Eventually, Wave walked away, down a hall and out of sight. Atom returned to the table but remained standing. She sang a slow melody, carefully enunciating each note. Smith knew the meaning of many of them. 'Old,' 'sleep,' 'idea,' 'protection.' That, combined with the usual emotional meaning that pressed into him, made it easy to discern Atom's meaning. Which was that, before all the Singers were out in stasis, some of them built a weapon of protection. From what Smith understood, it was a defensive system that would keep the Singers safe from Crawler attack while they slept.

"And this weapon could do this kind of damage?" Smith asked.

Before Atom could respond, Hutsep screeched out a series of hissing clicks. Ulot shot back his own fierce clacks, then the two stared at Atom.

"Hutsep," Smith said. "What's wrong?"

"Not true," Hutsep said. "Singers peaceful. No weapons, no. Not Singers."

Atom sang a note of shame and regret, followed by one of confession soaked in sincerity. The weapon had been designed out of fear. And Atom regretted even considering using violence against the Crawlers.

"Was the weapon ever finished?" Johan asked.

Atom indicated that it was not.

"Would Lioness know how to finish it?" Theresa asked. "Or any of the other Singers?"

Atom sang each name of the original five Singers.

"Damn it, Lioness." Smith shook his head. "I know she's been afraid, angry. But... not this."

"But where the hell is she?" Johann asked. "Or any of them?"

"Exactly," Theresa said. "And do we know for sure how many are missing? Six humans are unaccounted for."

"Eight Crawlers," Ulot said.

Atom held up three fingers and sang a lamenting melody of shame and grief. It reminded Smith of a folk song he'd heard back on Earth about a man grieving the loss of his daughter. The way Atom sang, it was as if Lioness and the other two Singers were as good as dead to her. *But what about mercy for them?* Smith asked himself.

"What kind of weapon?" Johann asked.

Atom turned away, singing for them to follow. They all walked quickly after the Singer, down halls and out of the ship into warm afternoon air. Smith continually sidestepped those asking questions, giving them only vague answers.

"Did we learn anything new?"

"No."

"Where's Lioness and the others?"

"No idea, sorry."

"What're we gonna do about the murders?"

"Working on that." Smith shook his head as they kept walking.

The entrance to the caves came into view and Atom sang three swift notes. Smokies emerged from trees on both sides, sandwiching the group between two lines of a dozen smokies each. Atom opened the door and went in first, quickening the pace.

Halfway down the first hall she stopped, kicked the wall on the left and sang six distinct notes. A seam appeared and the wall slid open, revealing a descending staircase of clean, white stone. Atom went down, the wall closing as soon as the last of them made it through. Darkness covered them until Atom flipped open her palm wires and illuminated everything with the soft blue light. Smith glanced behind them. The backside of the door was also white, and all twenty-four smokies had followed them in.

Smith turned forward. The stairs spiraled sharply to the right and soon he couldn't see Atom at the front of the line. They walked down and Smith ran his fingers along the stone. It appeared smooth, but the farther down they went the rougher it got, with no changes to its appearance. As far as Smith's eyes could tell, it was still smooth stone. But his fingers felt otherwise.

"What kind of stone is this?" he asked.

Atom sang a note that had no effect on Smith.

Hutsep clicked. "Best translate... glass-stone."

"Glass-stone?" Smith paused, leaning closer to the surface. And found that the bumps he felt were from clear bubble that grew larger the farther down they went.

"Careful," Ulot said. "Glass-stone turn sharp."

Smith nodded and removed his hand.

"Is this in the ground naturally?" Theresa asked.

Atom answered with a simple 'yes.'

"In parts all over planet," Hutsep said.

"In any pattern?" Theresa asked.

"No, no," Hutsep said.

The bumps of glass changed the deeper they got, and by the time they reached the bottom the walls were covered with translucent, pointed shards. But at that point what caught Smith's attention was the large door of shining gold. It stood over a dozen feet tall and half that in width. A third from the bottom stretched a thick, black line. Atom closed her palm lights and walked to the door, placing a finger in the middle of the line. She spiraled her finger along the surface to the left edge, then spiraled it back to the middle. From there she zigzagged it to the right edge, and traced a straight line back to the middle. She finished with three taps and five low, rumbling notes. The black line disappeared, revealing three glowing holes. Atom sang a different note into each, and the door slid up into the rocks.

Johann whistled. "That's a password."

There was no light behind the door. Atom sang a note of trepidation, and stepped across the threshold. Her foot touched down, and the center of the room lit up with a white light, leaving the ground, ceiling and walls shrouded in darkness. A glass sphere floated in front of them, within it three thin lines of bright silver, each at least five feet long. Looking at them, Smith couldn't decide if they were made of metal or light, or some online combination of the two.

Atom screeched the note for 'no,' then for 'five.' She ran forward, her foot *thunked* into something on the ground and she collapsed. With another, quieter 'no' she rose to her feet and flipped on her palm lights.

At her feet lay Lioness, motionless, covered in blood. Smith's heart broke and tears streamed down his face as Atom's shrieking melody of mourning echoed off the walls. She ran to a small panel under the sphere, pushed something and the entire room filled with light, revealing more bodies.

Two more Singers, three Crawlers and four humans. Atom went completely stiff, leaned forward and let herself fall flat on the floor. As her screeching grew louder and louder, Smith's tears fell harder and faster. He sat on the floor, vaguely aware the others did the same. Eventually Atom stopped, and the room went silent.

Smith wiped the tears from his eyes and looked around. "What the hell do we do now?"

Chapter 23

Abe sat with Lollawk in a small room, down a hall off the underground garden. The Crawler stood while Abe sat in soft dirt, staring at the almost identical symbols Lollawk had drawn with his finger.

Abe clicked his tongue in thought, then pointed to one of them. "That one."

"Yes, yes," Lollawk said. "Good. Meaning?"

"That's the easy part," Abe said. "The future of all."

Lollawk wiped the symbols out of the dirt with a foot, pulled out the Singer book, and placed it gently on the ground. He pointed at the third and final symbol on the cover, then looked at Abe. "Sure no Singer help?"

Abe nodded. "Yes. I want to make sure how I understand the book isn't influenced by their language."

"Okay. I do best I can." Lollawk traced the lines of the symbol with his finger. "This mean...no violence. What human call that?"

"Pacifism," Abe said.

"Yes, yes. Pacifism."

"What's the *feeling* behind this one?"

Lollawk clicked quietly. "Is a word don't think human have." Lollawk paused, slowly moving from foot to foot. "Means a promise that cannot break."

"Cannot break?" Abe asked. "But it has been broken, before. When that Singer killed your leader."

"It can break, yes." Lollawk clicked again, seemingly frustrated at the difficulty of communicating. "It means more they will not break. It means promise... serious. Made with entire... soul? That word work?"

"Yeah," Abe said. "That makes sense. Can I ask something?"

"Yes, yes."

"Are all Singers forced to make this promise? Or do they have a choice?"

"Choice? Yes, no. All must choose at a time. But one choose not to, sent away."

Abe nearly gasped in surprise. "Really? They banish any who don't make the promise? Where?"

"No, not made to leave," Lollawk said. "Made silent. There but not a part."

Abe shook his head. He appreciated, even admired, the Singer's staunch pacifism. But shunning someone for not making a promise didn't sit right with him. "What if a Singer commits violence?"

"Book not say. But think we soon find out."

"The murders?" Abe asked.

"Yes, yes."

"You really think a Singer was involved?" Abe had considered it, but despite his distrust of the species he still believed them to be pacifists.

"I think Singer helped, yes."

Abe shook his head. He hoped it wasn't true, but felt he hoped in vain. "Let's open the book," he said.

"Abe not memorize symbol yet," Lollawk said.

"I'll work on that later. I want to know some of what it says. Can you tell me what the first page says?"

"First, tell title of book."

Abe thought about turning it into a grammatically correct version of the title, but decided to keep it as true to the original as possible. "Crucial Book of Future For All Aethera and A Promise of Pacifism."

Lollawk softly clicked out a laugh. "Yes, good." He carefully turned over the cover, revealing a page of smooth yellow paper covered in symbols.

And immediately Abe's heart sank. Just like the cover, the symbols were organized diagonally, but the sheer number of new symbols was overwhelming, and the size of the symbols fluctuated drastically. He scanned the page quickly and counted at least fifty symbols. "Shit," he whispered.

"No," Lollawk said. "Look for symbols known."

Abe nodded and took a deep breath. He looked back at the page, this time looking it over with more care. Soon enough, he realized the smallest symbol was a variation of the one for 'future.' He pointed it out to Lollawk.

"Good, good. What meaning?"

Abe looked at Lollawk, then back at the page, squinting. The angle was slightly different than that on the cover and the lines were thinner, drawn with less pressure. "So, if I understand what I've already learned, this is referring to a near future. Or, near to whenever it was written?"

"Why think that?"

Abe scratched his head. *Why does that seem like the right answer?* He thought back to the chart of 'future' symbols he reviewed the first day of studying. Many of those also had varying line thickness, along with the vast differences in angle to which he was still getting accustomed. He flipped to the cover, studied that symbol for 'future,' and then returned to the first page. The smaller symbol was rotated to the left of the one on the cover, closer to the standard base of the symbol.

Abe sighed and turned back to Lollawk. "The lines are thinner. Which means it was of more significance to the writer. I think a closer future would seem more important. And it's turned to a different angle, closer to the standard of the symbol. Or the *start* of the symbol."

"Yes, yes." Lollawk said. "Good. Abe smart."

Abe sighed and rubbed his eyes. "Thanks, Lollawk."

"Tired?"

"I am, Lollawk." Abe stood and stretched his arms above his head.

Lollawk shuffled his feet back and forth. "Abe?"

"Yeah, Lollawk?"

"Where Winona?"

"She's with Teacher," Abe said.

"Learning language?"

Abe tried not to smile, but couldn't help it. "Yeah."

Lollawk stopped and went still for a moment, then clicked. "Understand," he said. "Smart. Want to learn if Winona understand different than Abe. Want to know if Singer change understanding."

"Exactly," Abe said.

"Abe, get rest. I read alone now." Lollawk picked up the book and began reading.

Abe said a quick goodbye and made his way to the garden, up the stairs and out of the large dome. It was midday and the sky was a soft gray, a cool breeze lazily blowing clouds through the air. All around, groups of all three species mingled about, talking about everything from the weather to the murders to the future of Aethera itself. Abe avoided all of these, choosing instead to sit on the opposite side of a large boulder, out of sight.

He closed his eyes and images of Winona instantly flashed into his mind. He huffed to himself, frustrated that he still questioned the reality of their friendship, their connection. The more time he spent with her, the more he felt he needed her. And not just to help him understand the Singers and their book. It was the kind of need that made him fear losing her, a need that filled him at once with joy and terror.

But what if it's not real?

"What if that doesn't matter?" he whispered.

If being with her brought him joy and fulfillment, did it matter where the feelings came from? He wanted to say it didn't, but he knew that was a lie. If he moved forward without knowing whether his feelings were genuine, he would always doubt their relationship. He repeated Winona's words in his mind: *But what if we never understand it?* If they never solved the puzzle, would he give her up?

"Abe?" Winona's voice came from the other side of the boulder.

Despite himself, Abe smiled. "Over here," he answered.

She quickly made it to his side and sat down. "Hiding from me?"

"From everyone." Abe shrugged.

"Brooding?"

Abe smiled. "Something like that."

She let out a small laugh. "How'd it go with Lollawk?"

"Good," he said and quickly summarized what he'd learned with the Crawler. "How was it with Teacher?"

"More or less the same," she said. "The title I got is basically the same as yours."

"Good." Abe nodded. "Did you see the first page?"

"Yeah, but the first symbol Teacher and I worked on was a new one."

Excitedly, Abe asked which symbol.

"Violence," she said.

"Violence?"

Winona nodded. "But this symbol didn't have any variations."

"Really? Just one version? Why?"

Winona smiled. "You're smart, Abe. Figure it out."

Abe squinted at her. The breeze, now with a crisper chill, blew harder. As Abe thought of the reason, he considered wrapping an arm around Winona. He'd done it before, but in that moment, the fear of his feelings was too strong, so he looked away.

"So?" Winona elbowed his side.

"So...?"

"Why do you think they only have one symbol for violence?"

"Oh, right." Abe scratched his head. "They only feel one way about violence. I don't think they would have symbol that means 'good violence' or 'acceptable violence' or anything like that."

"Right," she said. "And when Teacher sang the note for the symbol, I abhorred the symbol and everything it meant. The only symbol, and note, they have for violence is one that shows how vile the idea is to them."

Abe took a deep breath and let the thought sink in, and when it did a question arose. "What if they do have other versions of the symbol, but Teacher only showed you this one to influence how you view the Singers?"

Winona sighed. "Abe, I know their prophesy about us scares you. But you were so close with Lioness and Whims when we went to face the Crawlers. You *trusted* them."

Abe looked to the darkening sky. She was right, of course. He had grown to care for Whims and Lioness, even saw them as friends. It was with Whims that he'd learned to understand most of what he did of the Singer language. *Then why all the doubt?* he asked himself, but the answer was easy. *Fear. Of what? The impossible, the unknown.*

Frigid wind whisked through his bones. He and Winona shivered, but this time it was she who put an arm around him.

Chapter 24

Tashon lay in his living quarters on the ship, pretending to be asleep while Rosa continued to write on her stacks of pages. He thought of how, more than anything, he needed answers. Answers to the questions of those who doubted him. Questions that were making him doubt himself and what he'd seen. He knew he wasn't insane. Others had seen him disappear from the Third only to reappear somewhere else. He had carried Ballas through the Fourth and used the higher dimension to win the battle against the Crawlers. But what about all he'd seen, or hadn't seen? He was accessing the Fourth, but what if his mind was only comprehending segments of it, not acknowledging anything too complex?

But no, he was confident he could find the answers. He only needed to explore more of the Fourth, needed to expand his mind. Resolutely, he opened his eyes and sat up.

Rosa sat her stack of papers on the floor. "Good morning, Sage."

He rubbed his eyes, then looked at the papers. "What've you been working on?"

Rosa smiled. "Your story. Your words."

"What? Why?"

"Sage, you are going to end up being a significant part of Aethera's history. People are going to want to read your story, and your words."

Tashon stood up. "You really believe that?"

Rosa nodded. "You really have to ask that?"

Tashon laughed softly. "No. I just don't believe it. Not always, at least."

"Your humility is a good trait," Rosa said. "But you need to learn to trust yourself."

"If I learned more about the Fourth, that'd help."

Rosa raised an eyebrow. "You think so?"

Tashon shrugged. "Maybe."

"How're you going to find your answers?"

Tashon let a small smile creep onto his face. "I have some ideas."

Rosa picked up her papers and walked out of the door. "Let's go, then."

They quickly made their way out of the ship and into the dim light of the setting sun. They passed and greeted Singers, Crawlers and humans that, thankfully, asked no questions about the Fourth. The two walked side by side into the forest. Tashon glanced down at the papers in Rosa's arm and noticed his name written across the top of the front page. *I'm not* that *important*, he thought.

"How far you want to go?" Rosa asked.

Tashon looked around. The clearing was still partially visible behind them. "Another hundred yards, roughly."

Once the clearing was out of sight, Tashon sat between two trees and closed his eyes.

"How're you going to find your answers?" Rosa asked.

"To know more, I have to see more," Tashon said.

From the Fourth, he saw Rosa nod her head and sit down. "I'll wait for you," she said.

Tashon pulled as much of his attention as possible to the Fourth. Instinctively, he looked for Laos. But no other forms were there. No pyramids or spheres in the distance, no sign of the higher being. Just empty, rolling ground and a gentle breeze of color. *Why are they there sometimes, and not others?* he asked himself. He wondered if the structures he saw moved of their own accord, or if the Fourth itself moved. He looked at the ground, and it seemed to be the same ground that was always above Aethera.

A man approached in the Third, but Tashon ignored him, knowing Rosa would send him away or, at the very least, tell him to be quiet.

I could probably find the answers if I come back to the Fourth completely, and travel across it, he told himself. But to get the answers he needed, he knew he'd have to travel farther than he ever had, and he knew his body wouldn't survive a journey that long. No, he couldn't leave. The only way, then, was to expand his mind. The piece in the Fourth, and the piece in the Third. With a quick tug from his higher self, his body in the Third lifted off the ground. The man talking to Rosa gasped. Tashon smiled, and pulled himself completely out of the Third.

The man below swore and Rosa laughed.

For a moment, between dimensions, as always, nothing called to Tashon. But this time, with a clear purpose in mind, it was easy for him to ignore. His vision flashed white and he was in the Fourth. And even though he'd just examined the higher plane, he turned in a circle to see if anything had appeared during his brief transition.

Nothing had. *Empty*, Tashon thought. *How can it be so empty?* He knew there were far more humans dead than alive. At least twenty dead to every one alive. And if the Crawlers and Singers had existed for as long as it seemed, their number would be similar. So why was it so empty? As he thought, he looked at the necklace, visible in the Fourth. He touched it, hoping its warmth held the secrets of the universe, or call the moths to him. Only warmth came from it, spreading through his veins and bringing the slightest of calm.

He knew, of course, the reasons he'd given those who questioned him. The essences of the dead had other places to be and things to do. They went to the Higher Spheres or the pyramids or who knew where else. But his simple answers, that had seemed so mystic in days past, now filled him with frustration. Being in the Fourth, he didn't question his sanity. He knew his connection to the dimension was real, and knew all he'd seen there was real.

He just didn't know what else to *do* with it. All he had were vague quotables and half-full impressions. He looked down at Rosa, knowing she would tell him that the mere knowledge of an afterlife was enough. That he didn't need to do any more than he was. He felt the need, though. He had a connection no else did, no one else ever had, and he would use it to the fullest.

Slowly inhaling, he stretched his arms up and closed his eyes, turning his entire focus to his essence that floated in the Fourth. He thought of how he'd manipulated it to expand the view it gave him of the Third. Could he also expand his sight of the Fourth? He studied it, attempting to discern how it was connected to him, but saw nothing. If he could somehow move that part of him that was always saw the Fourth while he remained in Third, he *might* be able to find more answers with surpassing his physical limits.

"But how the hell would I do that?" he whispered to himself.

For the moment, he settled on doing something he knew he could. Less carefully than the first time, he grabbed his essence and stretched one way, then the other. It gave easier than he expected, resulting in a mass nearly double the size it had been. He dropped his hand, sat on the floor and blew out a long breath. The simple act had exhausted him, but he knew when he returned to the Third his third-person view would have a much wider lens.

What good will that do? The question came to his mind without permission, and Tashon tried to push it away. But the questioning thought was resilient, returning over and over. *What real good can I do with a wider lens?* It wouldn't help him find the murderers, wouldn't help him bring greater peace to the Aetheran populace. If they were still actively fighting their enemies, it could be used for tactical advantages. He groaned and, without opening his eyes, lowered himself back to his home dimension.

Voices erupted as soon as he touched three-dimensional ground. He opened his eyes. There sat Rosa, surrounded by at least fifty others, each species healthily represented.

Rosa stood and smiled. "Welcome back, Sage Tashon."

Through heaving breaths, Tashon gave a quiet greeting and waved his hand.

"Anyone have water for Sage Tashon?" Rosa asked.

A Singer walked to Tashon's side, handing him a conical bottle.

He took a long drink and handed it back. "Thank you," he said.

"Sage, what you see today?" a Crawler asked.

As he worked to slow his breathing, Tashon looked at the group before him, their eyes filled with hope. *Hope in me*, he realized. For them, it seemed the answer he had was enough, and they were willing to learn of the Fourth as he learned of it.

He smiled and stood. "I was trying to find a way to get answers."

"What answers?" Minow asked.

"To the questions that I've been asked," Tashon said. "Where are all those who've died? What really happens to us when we get to the Fourth?"

A note rang from a Singer, asking if he found the answers.

Tashon looked to the ground in defeat, and shook his head. "No," he said, then closed his eyes.

"What happened in the Fourth this time?" Rosa asked.

"It was empty," he said, eyes still closed. "I couldn't find anything, so I did the only thing I could think of."

A Crawler clicked softly. "What you do?"

Tashon told them how he expanded his sight of the Third the first time, stretching his view to encompass the entire continent, then went silent, examining his new view. All of Aethera spread out before him, stretching past the barren ocean, over shallow puddles of water that turned into rolling green sea, an island of growth floating through the water before the ocean split between the two continents. He saw where the green water gave way to red, where red slowly froze and merged with the glaciers. He saw the entire planet, and from the Fourth it seemed at once both spherical and flat.

"I can see all of Aethera," he said.

"How?" a man asked. "It's a sphere."

Tashon opened his eyes. "Rosa, can I use one of those papers?"

She handed one over.

"Thank you," he said, and held the paper vertically. "Aethera is this paper. The writing on it is us. And we, living on that one side of paper, can't see the other side. But from the Third we can examine the entire paper with little effort. The Fourth is more complex, but the concept is the same."

Smiles and sounds of understanding spread through the group as the idea settled in their minds. It surprised Tashon how that simple knowledge brought happiness. It wasn't an understanding of anything about the afterlife, and it didn't answer any of the big questions Tashon had been struggling with.

Yet it still brought them joy.

"Wait," a woman said excitedly. "Do you think you could expand your — what did you call it?"

"My vision, or lens," Tashon said.

"Right. Could you expand it even more?" she asked.

Tashon nodded. "I think so, yeah."

"How far?" another asked.

"No idea, really," Tashon said. "I don't think I'll know until I hit my wall."

"Do you think, maybe, that you could see the other colonies? Or even Earth?" the woman asked.

Despite the daunting nature of such a task, Tashon smiled. "I don't know, but I love that idea."

Even the Singers and Crawlers seemed enthralled by the idea. Tashon was too. But he still felt they wanted more. *No*, he thought, *they* deserve *more*.

"But knowing what's going on out there still won't answer our questions about the Fourth," Tashon said.

"Sage," Rosa said. "You'll find those answers."

"Or not," a Crawler said. "Sage already teach much. Give much hope."

All Singers present sang the same sentiment. Tears pooled in Tashon's eyes and he turned his head. After a few deep breaths, he wiped his cheeks and turned back to them, seeing the hope in their eyes. The hope they had in him, and in the knowledge he offered. Then he looked down on himself from above, saw the sagging of his shoulders, the doubt he had in himself and in the lack of knowledge he offered. *Hope and doubt,* he thought, and sat down. His hopeful crowd followed suit, each preparing to meditate, closing their eyes without instruction.

Tashon spoke whatever thoughts came to him. "Hope cannot exist without doubt," he said. "The opposite is also true." From above, he saw Rosa eagerly writing down his words. "It seems my knowledge has given you hope. I'm glad. But I've been doubting myself. My purpose. But your hope has lessened the doubt a little." Tashon paused, distracted by increased winds in the Fourth. "You know the old cliché? How two opposites are like two sides of the same coin? I don't like that. Not just because it's a cliché, but it ignores the in-between where most of us are. There are few who doubt completely. And I don't think any hope perfectly. It's more like opposites, negatives and positives, are connected by a... road. Hope on one end, doubt on the other. Everyone is constantly moving up and down these roads, a different road for each opposite. Peace and turmoil. Joy and despair.

"And, yeah, I've been far closer to the side of doubt. But you—" Tashon was cut off by an echoing, lamenting melody of loss. His eyes snapped open and he jumped to his feet.

The song of mourning grew as more voices joined in, the very trees seeming to vibrate with loneliness and despair. The Singers reacted first, sprinting back to the clearing as they screamed notes of fear and foreboding. Then the Crawlers and humans were close behind, fear gripping Tashon as he wondered what they would find.

Chapter 25

Smith emerged from the caves in a daze of confused despair, put upon him by Atom's singing. And that they'd just found more corpses in the middle of a sealed vault containing an advanced weapon created by a supposedly pacifist species. He glanced at Theresa and Johann, both to his right, and it seemed they were in a similar state of shock.

Nothing how it's supposed to be, Smith thought, recalling the words spoken by Jonstin. They moved slowly, Singers constantly joining them, contributing their own notes of mourning. Smith longed to express his confusion, fear and defeat the way the Singers did. In his current state, he couldn't even think of the words to say what he was feeling.

Soon, Crawlers and humans joined them at the edge of the clearing, the sounds of mourning reaching a near deafening volume. Then, in unison, the Singers went silent. But the void of loss remained. For Smith, the emptiness was from the dead, and from the loss of the way of life he hoped for. The murders brought their plans of mercy into question but now he felt there was something happening, hidden and secret, that threatened the future of Aethera. Or maybe not hidden, Smith realized. Maybe he'd just not wanted to see it. And what was the purpose, the goal of all the killing? If only humans and Singers had been killed, it would've been easier to determine the culprits, and their reasons. Yet, guilty and innocent Crawlers were dead, along with seemingly innocent humans and Singers. *Nothing how it's supposed to be*, he thought again, shaking his head.

A line of smokies walked into the clearing, each carrying a corpse on its back. They formed a triangle on the ground, slowly released the corpses and then disappeared back into the trees. Smith noted that the bodies weren't organized by species, and he felt that was intentional, a way for the Singers to say they still saw all species as equals. But how many of the Singers truly believed that? How many of them believed it?

A new group appeared on the opposite side of the clearing, Tashon, Rosa, Yeance and Minow among them. They stopped as soon as they noticed the corpses, and a Singer sent a questioning note to Atom. The eldest singer responded quickly, using the notes for 'weapon,' 'violence,' 'death' and 'confusion,' among others notes Smith could only guess. Regardless, though, he could still tell Atom wasn't giving any information he didn't already know. As the newly arrived Singers began their own grieving chorus, Tashon, Rosa and a man named Fylin made their away around the edge of the clearing to join the three human leaders. Minow and Yeance stayed where they were, both softly crying.

No one spoke until the Singers went quiet again.

Rosa wiped tears from her cheeks. "What the hell?"

Smith looked to Theresa, who looked to Johann, who looked back at Smith. Smith ran a hand through his hair, then explained what they'd learned, as best he could.

Fylin shouted. "A weapon?" He glared at Atom. "They said they were *pacifists*."

"They never finished it," Johann said. "Or, hadn't finished it."

"Right," the man said. "They have now, though, haven't they?"

"It wasn't all of them," Smith said.

"We don't know that," Fylin said. "Atom could—"

"I agree with Smith," Rosa said. "If Atom had been a part of this, she wouldn't have shown us the weapon. Wouldn't have reacted to what we saw down there so... intensely."

"But something isn't right here," Fylin said.

"No shit," Rosa said. "But we can't blame an entire species for that."

Fylin folded his arms right across his chest. "Why did a species of pacifists even start building a weapon?"

"Fear," Tashon said. "They didn't want their species extinct."

"And they stopped building it," Rosa said.

Fylin started to speak but stopped as Hutsep walked into the clearing and crouched down next to a Crawler body. With a soft, continuous grinding coming from his throat, he pulled a long, needle-like object from his pouch. He stabbed it into the body's forehead and traced a circle. Once the circle was complete, he stabbed the center of it and removed the disc of skin. He reached into the hole with two skinny fingers and pulled out the dead Crawler's cable, coiling it neatly on the ground. When no more would come out, Hutsep yanked it out with a *crack* and the cable popped free, revealing a spear-shaped end. Hutsep turned and clicked to another Crawler, who walked out, picked up the cable and walked off into the forest. Hutsep repeated the process with the remaining bodies, a new Crawler disappearing into the trees with each cable. Once done, Hutsep returned to the edge of the clearing.

Smith looked at his companions, who seemed in awe at the Crawler tradition Hutsep performed. He was sure their thoughts were on other things, like his own were, though he had no idea what those thoughts might be. There were so many thoughts that moment, none of them joyous.

Johann walked into the clearing and kneeled at the nearest human body. He straightened the legs, gently crossed the arms across the chest and closed the eyes. He waved Smith and Theresa out to help do the same with the others. They did so silently and efficiently, Smith feeling the eyes watching them. When they were done, the three returned to their spots along the edge of the clearing. And, despite the silence from the Singers, Smith realized tears ran down his cheek.

The Singers resumed their song of mourning, and Atom walked to the corpse of Lioness, sitting next to her, legs crossed. The mourning dropped to a whisper as the eldest Singer rolled Lioness to her side, pulled her knees to her chest and wrapped her arms around her knees. She shouted out the note for Lioness. After repeating the process for the other deceased Singers, Atom stood and silence returned to the clearing. Atom called Smith and Hutsep to join her. She said the singer name for Smith, and he knew she wanted him to speak.

He glanced at her, at the bodies on the ground, the living eyes looking back at him. And only one word came to mind. "Shit," he said, earning a few soft laughs. "Just... shit." He shrugged and shook his head. "I don't know where we go from this."

Hutsep clicked phrases or sentences to the Crawlers. Then said, "Is difficult. Must all choose path. Best path for all, for Aethera."

"But how the hell do we decide that?" Smith asked, knowing that, as a leader, he should be more positive. But he couldn't lie about how it was affecting him, couldn't tell everyone it would get figured out because he doubted it would. *Or maybe honesty and vulnerability is what they need*, he thought. *How many leaders on Earth did that?* "And really, I don't want to talk about what to do next. Not today. Let's each take care of our dead however we will. We can discuss and argue over our next moves in a few days. Talk among yourselves about it if you want. We'll hold something official later. Hutsep, Atom, is that okay with you?"

Atom answered in the affirmative.

"Yes, yes," Hutsep said. "First, before decide, should learn truth." Hutsep pointed to the triangle of bodies.

"The truth of what happened?" Smith asked.

"Yes, yes."

Smith and Atom agreed, and each leader wondered back to where they were.

For long minutes of silence, no one moved. Smith felt as if they might be stuck in that moment forever, lost in a limbo of pathless unknowing. Clouds rolled over the sun, a few leaves blowing across the clearing. He leaned against a tree, exhausted.

Eventually, three smokies walked into the clearing and removed the Singer corpses. As if that was the sign for time to resume, the clearing broke out in movement and the rest of the bodies were soon taken away.

An intense urge to speak with his son filled Smith and he looked around for a Singer he knew and trusted. He found Whims standing alone near the ship, staring into an open airlock.

"Whims, can you help me?" he asked. "I want to talk to Abe. Alone, or as alone as I can be."

Whims happily agreed to help. They walked into the ship and secluded themselves in living quarters far from any opening. The familiar screen rose from Whims's hands. A face appeared, and the two conversed briefly. Silence and movement as the Singer went in search of Abe.

While he waited, Smith wondered how Abe would take the news of more deaths. He knew his son was strong, but there was only so much anyone could take. He decided not to tell Abe. Not yet, anyway.

Abe's face popped onto the screen. "Dad!" he said with a smile, but Smith could tell something was bothering him. "How's it going over there?"

"The shits," Smith said.

"What happening?"

Smith shook his head. "I really just want to hear how you're doing, Abe. If that's okay."

Abe scratched his chin and looked around, as if ensuring he was alone. "Have you looked at the Singers' book?"

"No." Smith shook his head. "Why?"

"Some of it's about pacifism, but some of it predicted us coming here to save the Singers."

"I've heard that," Smith said.

"You heard what it says about me?"

"What?"

Abe shrugged and shook his head. "Ask Whims to show you," he said.

"Whims? Is my son in your book?"

Whims dropped his hands and the screen disappeared. He pulled the book out of a small pack, flipped to a specific page, and handed it to

Smith. As Smith stared at a perfectly accurate drawing of Abe and Winona, Whims restored the screen.

"That's you," Smith said.

"No shit, Dad." Abe rubbed his eyes with his thumb and middle finger. "Sorry, Dad. Look at the next page."

Smith turned it. "A baby?" Smith asked.

"The book says Winona and I will be the first parents of the new Aethera."

Smith looked at Abe, then back at the book. *He's only sixteen*, Smith thought. "Are you and Winona...?"

Abe's face flushed red. "No! No, Dad."

"Just had to ask." Smith lifted his hands up. "Sorry. But how did a Singer predict this?"

"They call her Mother," Abe said. "And we're hoping learning how to read the book will help figure out how."

"Any idea yet?"

"One, but it's not in the book. You know how when they talk, the Singers' language can influence us?"

Smith nodded, thinking he understood the idea. "You're saying, then, that maybe by predicting we would come save them, she sent that influence all the way to Earth, and somehow that led us all here?"

"Yeah," Abe said. "That's the theory."

Abe let out a large breath. It wasn't a terrible theory, especially since he knew how convincing a Singer's voice could be. But sending that influence light years away to another planet? Mother would have had to know about Earth, that it was populated, that the inhabitants were intelligent enough to make it to Aethera. And was that more likely than Mother actually seeing the future? *I have to ask Atom about this*, he thought. *If I ever get the chance with all the other shit going on.*

"Dad?" Abe asked quietly.

Smith heard the concern in his son's voice, and worry flooded over him. "Abe, what's wrong?"

"Winona... I care about her. A lot. But what if the two of us being here, together, and having a baby was somehow planned by Mother? What if our feelings aren't real? That they are just put on us from the influence of Mother's predictions?"

Smith laughed, but quickly stopped himself. "Sorry. I'm sorry," he said. "I think you'd be wondering if how you felt was real even if you were still on the ship."

"What?"

Smith shrugged. "I questioned it with your mom. Didn't know if I loved her, or just wanted her. Or just wanted *someone*."

Abe shook his head. "I guess that makes sense. But what if they aren't my feelings? And how did she *see me*?"

"I don't know," Smith said. "Have you asked any Singers?"

"No. I don't know if what they say will be fully honest, or emotionally manipulating."

"I think you're overthinking, Abe."

"Maybe." Abe shrugged.

"You trust Whims, right?" Smith asked.

"More than any other Singer," he said.

"Would you trust his answer?" Smith asked.

Abe looked down in thought. "Yeah, I would."

Smith looked at the Singer. "Whims, how did Mother know we would come?"

The notes Whims sang filled Smith with an impatience, as if he's been waiting forever. The notes shifted, and Smith felt as if his life had just started. Then Whims sang the note for 'time.' Smith was at the same point in his life, but could feel new and invigorated one minute, impatient and longing the next.

"Time depends on perspective?" Smith asked.

Whims indicated that was his meaning, then sang the note for 'Mother,' followed by a swirling of elongated notes. Words Smith had learned already. 'After,' before,' 'now,' and 'different,' followed again by the note for 'Mother.' Whims stopped.

"Abe, what do you think?" Smith asked.

"I think he's saying Mother saw time differently than others," Abe said.

"Right." Smith nodded. "Whims, how could she do that?"

Whims had no idea.

"Did anyone ever ask her?" Abe asked.

Whims was sure no one had.

"You all just accepted it?" Smith asked.

Whims indicated shock with his notes, surprised that they were questioning Mother's ability. Smith caught a hint of sarcasm, as if Whims were saying, "It came true, right?"

"Whims," Abe said. "Do you know how your language makes us *feel*?"

Whims sang that he did.

"But you wouldn't use that to control us, would you?" Smith asked.

Whims sang a harsh version of the note for 'no,' laced with hints of offense taken.

"I'm sorry," Smith said sincerely. "We're trying to understand all of this."

Whims quickly forgave him, and went silent.

"Sorry, Abe," Smith said. "I don't think that really helped."

"It did, though." Abe smiled. "I trust Whims. I mean, I want to figure out how Mother's prophesying worked. And hopefully the book will teach me that."

"You think your feelings for Winona are real?"

Abe laughed. "I don't know. I guess it didn't answer my question, then."

"What would you do if you found out your feelings for her were the result of Mother's predictions?"

Abe shook his and said nothing.

"Answer that, and you'll know what to do," Smith said. "Just don't get her pregnant anytime soon."

Abe chuckled softly. "Yeah, yeah. No shit."

Neither spoke, and Smith figured Abe was trying to figure out how he felt.

"Abe, I should getting going."

"To deal with the shit?"

"Yeah. Abe, we'll let everyone over there know what shit's happened soon. You'll be okay, okay? Go find Winona."

"Wait. It's that bad?" Abe asked.

Smith sensed the fear. "Abe, don't tell anyone yet. Tell whichever Singer you're with not to, either. But... more dead. Crawlers, Singers and humans. One of them is Lioness, Abe. I'm sorry."

Chapter 26

Abe held Winona tight against his chest behind a stone pillar, out of sight. Both of their faces were wet with tears. They'd just received the official news from the Singer continent. More deaths. Singer weapons. Yet the hardest part to swallow was the loss of Lioness. She traveled with them across the ocean, fought the Crawlers with them. Fought to protect her people.

And now they were saying she was one of the those who killed the prisoners and their guards.

Abe sniffed as tears slowed. "She didn't do it," he whispered.

Winona nodded against his chest, but didn't speak.

Abe took a deep breath and slowly blew it out. He looked up at the stars in the night sky, wondering if anyone in the Fourth was looking down on them. What they might be thinking. Maybe one of them was the Singer Mother, her long ago prophesy still drawing Winona to him and him to her, still making her the only place he could find comfort.

He'd spent so much time worrying the Singers were manipulating his feelings to fit the prophecy, worried that a Singer, centuries ago, had created his feelings for Winona. But with the pain of losing Lioness fresh on his mind and heart, he realized how important the Singers were to him. All this time, had it been the Singers he didn't trusting, or was it himself? Had it been easier for him to explain how he felt by crafting a story of a fateful connection forced by a dead prophetess than to simply say he loved Winona?

Thinking of it in the aftermath of Lioness's death, it seemed insane. *But what are we humans if not a bit insane?* he wondered.

Then there was still the question of that eerily accurate drawing of him and Winona. A mystery to consider another time, he decided. Because even if his connection with Winona wasn't real, he knew that if he wasn't holding onto her, he'd collapse.

They stood there until it got too cold, then made their way to one of the smaller Crawler domes. They sat against a crate, as far away from anyone else as possible.

Naturally, after yet another loss, Abe's thoughts turned to the first loss he ever suffered: the death of his mom. Thinking of that day, he said, "I think I cried more today than when my mom died."

Winona looked at him, her eyes gently gleaming. "You did cry a lot. You know why?" She rested her head on his lap.

He softly scratched her back as he thought of an answer. "Maybe I didn't want my dad to see me cry. And I felt more... empty than sad. And it's not just that Lioness died. It's that she was killed."

Winona turned her head and looked up at him. "And it means our goal of a merciful society will be more difficult to create than we thought."

Abe looked down at her and his train of thought shifted. "What would you do if we found out how we feel isn't real?"

She smiled. "I don't think I could not be with you," she said.

Abe smiled back. "I agree." He leaned down and kissed her.

Soon, she fell asleep, his lap her pillow, and he thought again of the emptiness he felt at Lioness's absence. She was a Singer he would've trusted his life with. He took a few breaths and decided, completely, that his feeling for Winona weren't contrived by Mother's prophecy or by any part of the Singer language.

***

Abe awoke to the sounds of verbal chaos outside the dome. Winona sat next him, staring at the early rays of sun coming through the entrance.

"What's going on?" Abe asked.

Winona shook her head. "Just woke up too."

Abe stood, stretched and helped Winona to her feet. Hands clasped, they walked outside into a clash of human shouts, Crawler clicks and Singer notes. Groups were scattered around, each arguing about who or what was to blame for the murders. Abe saw that it was not arguments between species, but between ideas. Singer fought with Singer about the acceptability of the defensive weapon. Human shouted at human about whether their idea of mercy had suggested too much leniency, thus leading to the killings. And Crawler screeched at Crawler with words Abe couldn't understand, though it was easy enough to guess.

Winona led him to the closest group. One Singer and Cixin shouting at Lollawk and Teacher.

"Singer not lie," Lollawk said. "Not Singer fault."

"They did lie," Cixin said. "True pacifists would not build a weapon."

The Singer next to her, with knee-length hair, agreed, singing Atom's name with seething anger.

Teacher responded quietly, referring to the Singer with the long hair as 'Blowing Leaf.' Teacher said that Atom had not let the weapon be completed. It was only in defense of the Singers in stasis.

"True pacifists give up *all* violence," Cixin said.

"Not Atom fault," Lollawk said. "Is fault of killer."

Blowing Leaf bleated the note for Lioness, claiming she must have been the one to complete the weapon.

Winona stepped forward. "Lioness wouldn't do that," she said.

"We know she killed Crawlers in the battle," Cixin said.

"Yes, yes in battle," Lollawk said. "Not Crawler with no weapon, not innocent guards."

Teacher agreed, singing that no blame should yet be placed.

"Exactly," Abe said. "We don't know what happened. Lioness could've been trying to stop whoever was using the weapon."

"She still did it violently," Cixin said. "She broke her pact."

Winona threw her hands in the air. "They're just like humans," she said. "They're not all the same. They're not perfect."

"I know tha —"

"You don't," Winona said. "Or you wouldn't be so upset that some of the Singers don't fit your view of them."

"I'm not upset,"Cixin said. "I'm pissed. This would have never happened if we'd executed the Crawler leaders. We gave too much mercy, and this is the price. It's only going to get more expensive if we don't do something different."

"Do what?" Lollawk asked.

Blowing Leaf sang notes for 'find' and 'kill.'

"What happened to your pacifism?" Winona asked.

The Singer answered with 'dead,' the note laced with hints of bitterness.

"So you're giving up on mercy?" Abe asked.

"No, no," Lollawk said.

"Yes," Cixin said.

Teacher sang an emphatic "no," aimed specifically at Blowing Leaf.

Blowing Leaf refused to reconsider.

Cixin looked at Abe. "And what happened to you? You thought the Singers were manipulating you and your girl there."

Abe's face flushed. "I forgot what I went through with Whims and Lioness. I trust them. I trusted her, and now she's dead."

"So now you suddenly know that what you feel is real?" Cixin asked. "How do you know they're not controlling you, controlling *all* of this?"

"I don't," Abe said. "I believe it's real."

"Why?"

"To believe it's not would be too much."

"Naivety at its finest," she said. "Watch. Things are going to get worse before they get better." She looked at Blowing Leaf and the two walked away.

Abe blew out a breath. "Shit. Is this what everyone's arguing about?"

"Yes, yes."

"Are a lot arguing Cixin's side?" Winona asked.

"Yes, yes. Many."

Abe looked around, taking in the anger and fear present in the arguing groups. "It really is going to get worse, isn't it?"

"I think so, Abe." Winona grabbed his hand.

"Yes, yes." Lollawk clicked quietly, gently shuffling his feet.

PART THREE

Chapter 27

"What happened to your visions?" Fylin asked Tashon. "I thought you could see the future."

They were in the clearing outside the ship, Tashon yet again being questioned by those who didn't believe in his connection to the Fourth but also demanding more of his ability. Tashon looked at the group. It was full of faces he knew didn't believe him, as well as ones he didn't have a clear reading on, like Theresa. Then there were those he trusted. Smith, Rosa, Yeance, Minow and more than a dozen others he recognized from his meditation sessions, Singers and Crawlers among them. *There are those who believe me*, he thought. *Who have found comfort in my words.* He took a deep breath, reminding himself to stay calm.

"The few visions I had," Tashon said, "were from the essence of the Singer Mother."

"Why hasn't she shown you anything else?" Simone asked.

"She's gone," Tashon said. "I don't really understand where."

"Bullshit," Fylin said. "You never saw her."

Tashon's heart rate jumped and he clenched his fists.

Rosa stepped between him and Fylin. "First, don't talk to *my* sage that way," she said. "Next, how the hell would they get safely into enemy territory if not for Tashon's vision?"

"Maybe the way they say it happened is fabricated," Fylin said.

"Sage Tashon *does not lie*," Rosa said as she stepped closer to Fylin.

"What're you gonna do, Rosa?" Fylin smiled. "Break my wrist?"

Her hand shot forward, and would have gotten hold of his wrist were it not for Tashon grabbing her shoulder.

"It's okay, Rosa," he said. Then, to Fylin, "Don't believe me, that's fine. But *do not* belittle those who do."

Fylin huffed and looked away.

Rosa and Tashon stepped back.

Theresa cleared her throat. "Okay, let's say you did see this Singer Mother," she said. "And that she showed you visions. Who's to say she wasn't manipulating your emotional state too?"

"Theresa," Smith said. "I thought we were done with those accusations."

"We were until we realized they only made us *think* they're a pacifist species," Theresa said.

Keeping his voice as calm as possible, Tashon said, "Theresa, if the Singer Mother *were* manipulating me, why was most of what she told me true?"

"Because not all of it was," she said.

"But just because she's in the Fourth doesn't mean she's perfect," Tashon said. "She made a mistake."

"No, we all made a mistake trusting the *Singers*." She said the name with such disdain that Tashon had no idea how to respond.

A Singer sang that they were pacifists, that the "five awake" were to blame for working on the weapon. The anger toward the five Singers sank into Tashon as the last note rang out, then disappeared.

Another Singer called out in defense of the "five awake," citing the fact that they didn't finish the weapon.

"But they didn't destroy it, either," Fylin said.

"Right," Theresa said. "We can't trust them."

"Theresa, you really think that?" Smith asked.

"Yes. And I'm not the only one," she said, looking around.

Many more than Tashon expected called out their agreement.

"Then what do we do?" Tashon asked. "Try to kill all of them, just because they're not exactly what we thought? That's as bad as the Crawlers were."

From the back of the group, Hutsep clicked and pushed his way forward. "No, no. Singers good. Was Singer fear build weapon."

In response, Ulot stomped his feet and clicked loudly at Hutsep. Then, so all could understand, said, "Singers not follow Singer book. Now many dead. Now no trust."

"We can't live among them," Fylin said. "Or let them live among us."

"This Singer home," Hutsep said. "Not take it."

"We need to do something," Theresa said. "Nearly half of us don't want to live around them."

"This is bullshit," Rosa said. "I thought we all were supposed to be the best of humanity. Now you're trying to segregate yourselves from an entire species."

"A species that *isn't human*," Fylin said. "We're looking out for humanity's future here."

Yeance raised his hand and spoke. "They are equal to humans, though. They don't deserve our hate or fear." He looked at Theresa and

Fylin, then scanned the entire crowd. "And how does this thinking promote mercy?"

Fylin laughed. "Are you still following through with that merciful society shit?" he said. "That's what gave room for all these murders and deaths to happen."

At that, the crowd lost control. Shouts of agreement followed by shouts of shock. It quickly devolved into a match of screaming opinions. Crawlers screeching, Singers harshly melodizing and humans yelling. Louder and louder it became, the sheer volume and anger overwhelming Tashon. His heart pounded and his head spun. Bodies moved closer together. Someone threw a punch and a Singer slapped onto the floor, unconscious. A Crawler kicked the offender, sending multiple bodies to the ground.

The sudden and intense withdrawal of peace drained something from Tashon and he felt he might collapse. Instead, he grasped his necklace, closed his eyes and pulled on his higher self. He lifted off the ground, vaguely aware that this caused a few to pause in amazement. Then he popped out of sight. That place of nothing called to him, but he ignored it. He wanted to be out of the chaos, but he still wanted to know what was happening. Plus, if he went back to nothing, he feared the temptation to escape the insanity on Aethera would be too great and he'd lose himself in nothing forever. He landed in the Fourth amidst a harsh wind that forced him to sit. Something that looked like a city stretched out in the distance and he wondered if it was the same one where he'd seen Grace and their parents during his first trip in the Fourth. And if it was, were they still there? He shook his head and looked down at the clearing.

It was quieter than when he left it, but he could see the tension in the folded arms and the narrowed eyes, in the visible gap between the two sides of the argument. His disappearance from the Third at least seemed to have calmed the physical violence.

"We knew he could do that," Fylin said. "But that doesn't mean we should trust the Singers. Or that their mom didn't mess with how he perceives reality. *If* he even saw her. A connection to the Fourth doesn't mean he's some all-knowing prophet."

He's got that right, Tashon thought. *But I've never claimed to be.*

"But that's not the problem," Rosa said. "The problem is that all of you don't give a *shit* about Aethera's future."

"You don't give a shit about humanity's," Fylin said.

Yeance casually folded his arms. "You sound like a racist tit," he said calmly. "All of you who agree with him do."

Again, the clearing erupted in screams, and Tashon decided he had to do something before they turned back to physical aggression. He focused on the small space between the two groups and pulled himself down, ignoring the nothing in between. Screams surrounded him as he appeared back in the Third, inches above the ground. He dropped onto his feet and found himself face to face with Fylin.

"I don't agree with what you're saying," he said. "And I don't agree *at all* with this fighting, no matter how important any of your own opinions seem." He turned a full circle, hoping even those who shared his views would understand his point. "After all this shit, I need to go meditate. Anyone is welcome to join." He pushed his way out of the clearing, refusing to look back and determined to get as far away as possible. But before he was out of earshot, the arguing behind him resumed.

Eventually, he was far enough away that the shouting didn't reach him, amid the thin black trees. He sat on a rock, the same one he'd been on when he first went fully into the Fourth through his own power. A group at least fifty strong had followed him, and they quickly sat on the dry ground.

Tashon smiled and took a deep breath. "Pick one thing to focus your attention on," he said. "Something of the natural world works for me. A leaf. A branch. A pebble. Anything. Focus on it until nothing else exists." He chose a knot on the side of a tree and tried to focus on it. But his attention kept going above it to a point where the tree split from one trunk into two branches that grew further and further apart. He closed his eyes and slowly exhaled, but the split in the tree wouldn't leave his mind. Then, because it's what he'd always done, he spoke whatever words came to him. "I don't like what's happening. It scares me. I thought we were all united in the plan for mercy. Maybe we were. I don't know. But not after all the murders and deaths. There's no going back, and I'm scared of what's coming."

"Is this a vision...a prophecy?" someone asked.

"No." Tashon looked again at where the tree split into two. "Just a feeling. And look at what's happening already. We're divided. I'm afraid that divide will only grow."

Nods of understanding accompanied whispers and murmurs.

"So what do we do?" someone asked.

Tashon opened his eyes and looked closely at each face before him. Most were on the side of mercy, and the side of the Singers. But he thought a few were those who were with Fylin and Theresa. Maybe he could convince them not to use violence in the promoting of ideas. Though he wasn't sure how the idea that an entire species was untrustworthy could turn into anything but violent. "What do we do?" he asked, repeating the question. "We can't force everyone to be on the side of mercy. Or anyone. Who thinks we should live separate from the Singers?"

No one answered, but Tashon saw two women look at each other nervously. "More than anything, I want to bring peace," he said. "If you don't trust the Singers, I want to hear you. *No one* will react violently."

One of the women cautiously stood and looked at Tashon.

"Kossy, why don't you think we should live with the Singers?" Tashon asked.

"It's not that I don't like the Singers," Kossy said. "But I don't think our two species are...compatible. That's the best word."

"You want to have a segregated society?" someone asked harshly.

"I know how that sounds," she said. "I don't think they're less than us, or inferior. I don't think it's *safe* for humans and Singers to live together."

"Because they built a weapon to defend themselves?" Yeance asked. "Why are we holding the Singers to a higher standard than humans and Crawlers?"

"It's that they kept the weapon from us, and convinced us they were pacifists," Kossy said. "And the real problem is how their language can change our emotional state. Even with the best of intentions, they could do damage."

Tashon took a deep breath, trying to calm himself. They had been so close to overcoming their fear and mistrust of the Singers, and what their language might do. Everything had been lined up to propel all species of Aethera into an abundant and peaceful future. *Peace cannot exist without violence*, he thought.

Minow stood up. "But how much damage could their language inadvertently do?"

"I don't know," Kossy said. "What if a depressed Singer's words make an entire group of humans suicidal?"

"Okay," Minow said. "It's possible. But wouldn't it be better to have safeguards in place so that doesn't happen?"

"What would those safeguards look like?" Kossy said.

Minow didn't have an answer, and both sat down. Everyone look expectantly at Tashon. "I don't think I can offer any peace," Tashon said. "Not right now. I need to think about what this means. What the best way to move forward is."

He stood and walked farther still. Rosa tried to follow him, but he wouldn't let her. Once he was certain he was alone, he fell to the ground and wept.

Chapter 28

Smith sat in a small cave with those he trusted most. Everything they had been working for seemed like it was slipping away. A society unlike any other that put unprecedented value on mercy and kindness. But now that dream was fading, splintering apart in the aftermath of murders and a stolen weapon. Now they faced a drifting apart of ideas and goals. That Smith knew was inevitable. But the two sides that were forming held distinctly different views and what the government should look like, and what it could accomplish.

"I don't see any reconciling this shit," Rosa said.

"There isn't," Tashon whispered. His eyes were red with recent tears. Quiet mumblings and nods.

Smith felt there was a way to move past and through the growing chasm between ideals, but he thought it wouldn't happen without more violence. *Using violence to bring about a merciful society*, he thought, shaking his head.

Minow, eyes focused on the ground, cleared her throat. "Sage Tashon," she said. "Why isn't there a way to reconcile the two?"

"Both exist," Tashon said. "One can't exist without the other. And we never wanted only mercy. We just wanted *more* mercy. Right, Johann?"

Johann nodded. "Right. There still needs to be consequences for crimes and violence. But this vigilante justice against the Crawler leaders is wrong."

"No one here disagrees with that," Yeance said. "But what do we *do*? Nearly half of Aethera's population is calling to virtually abolish mercy."

Smith shook his head. "That's not their goal, though. We have to remember that they're looking out for the safety of Aethera."

"But not *all* Aethera," Minow said. "Most of those seeking increased justice blame the Singers for this. There are humans and Crawlers that would be fine never seeing a Singer again."

"They're scared," Tashon said. "We shouldn't segregate species, I agree. But they're considering it out of fear and a loss of trust."

"So we need to restore their trust in the Singers?" Yeance asked.

"How the hell would we do that?" Johann asked. "The fact that the Singers even built a weapon is more than enough for most of them to push the Singers away forever."

Rosa scoffed. "Which is bullshit. Holding their species to a higher standard than our own."

"We're all in agreement there too," Yeance said. "But my question is, what do we do now?"

More silence. Smith rolled countless half-formed ideas through his mind but none made any sense. It seemed to him too big a problem to wrap his mind around. Which was why he brought those with him to discuss their options. Though options seemed minimal, if not absent. "We can't force any of them to live around Singers," Smith said.

"We can't let them drive Singers away, either," Minow said.

Minow finally looked up from the ground. "What if we give them a place to live, away from the Singers?"

"Maybe," Johann said. "But setting up a place where they're allowed and Singers aren't is still segregation."

"Yeah." Minow closed her eyes and dropped her head on Yeance's shoulder.

"So the best option is to try to restore their trust in the Singers," Smith said. "And their faith in mercy."

"We should try," Tashon said. "But I don't think many will come back to trust and mercy."

"Why not?" Yeance asked.

Tashon closed his eyes, meditating over the answer. Minutes passed. "Fear is meant to keep us safe," he finally said, eyes still closed. "Their fear is seeking what they perceive as safest. It'll be hard to pull them away from their natural instincts of self-preservation."

"But what of hope?" Smith asked. "Hope for something better?"

More minutes passed in silence, and Smith couldn't help but wonder at who Tashon had become. The young nanotech genius turned biotech farmer turned meditative sage. A change that Smith hadn't seen coming. Just like everything else that had happened in the last few weeks, all unseen and unknowable. *Or was it?* Smith wondered. *Was all of this seen and known by the Singer Mother?*

Tashon opened his eyes. "Fear can keep us safe, but often prevents growth," he said. "Hope can present more risks, but often takes us to places more wondrous than we can imagine."

Smith smiled, thinking of how the statement had proven true since crashing onto Aethera. The hope of raising a family with Evalee on a new planet had brought risks he'd never expected. But all he'd experienced and seen was nothing short of beautiful. "So we need to convince them to hope for a safe future with the Singers?" he asked.

"I don't think they'll listen," Johann said. "They're adamant that the Singers aren't safe. And they have Theresa and Ulot on their side. They hold a lot of sway."

"So, again, what do we *do*?" Yeance asked calmly.

"The Singers should be allowed to live wherever they want to," Smith said.

"I agree," Johann said. "But look at it a different way. Couldn't that put them in danger? If they lived among those who feared them, it's almost certain there would be attacks against them."

"You really think that?" Minow asked.

"There's already been violence," Tashon said. "The farther apart we grow, there's bound to be more."

"Give them the shittiest piece of land to live on," Rosa said. "Singers won't be allowed there."

A few quiet laughs followed the comment, though Smith knew it would never work. But what *was* going to work? "Do we think over half the population is still for the Singers?" he asked.

"Yes," Johann said. "I think well over half of humans and Crawlers still want to coexist with the Singers. Obviously, none of the Singers want to be segregated."

"But a lot of them aren't all for our merciful government anymore," Tashon said. "They're angry at Atom and the other five for even conceiving the weapon. There's a divide and it's only going to grow."

A solemn silence descended on the room. Smith looked at Tashon, sitting there as if bathed in wisdom. The sage's finger and thumb rolled around the air in front of his chest, as if fidgeting with an invisible stone.

"So then there's nothing to be done?" Yeance asked.

The group looked expectantly at Tashon, who closed his eyes and inhaled deeply, his lungs expanding.

There has to be something, Smith thought. *We can't split apart so early.*

"Remember," Tashon said, "mercy cannot exist without justice. We do need both. We gave the Crawler leaders a form of justice with their punishment, even though it was merciful."

"And we can't force them to follow our ideas of the right form of government and law," Minow said.

"But we still can't have vigilante justice," Johann said. "We need to figure out what actually happened, and who's responsible."

"I agree," Smith said.

As did the others.

Tashon stood up. "And I do think once we know what really happened, we can make a better decision of what to do next." He turned to leave.

"Where're you going?" Smith asked.

"I need to meditate."

Rosa stood. "I'll come too," she said.

Tashon waved a hand. "Thanks, Rosa. But I need to be by myself."

Rosa sunk back into her seat and watched him leave. Smith glanced at Johann, who shrugged. The possibility of a divide between those on Aethera weighed Tashon down so intensely that Smith wondered if he should be more worried about the future.

Yeance cleared his throat. "What do we do?"

Rosa threw her hands in the air. "Shit, Yeance. What's your idea?"

Smith put a hand on Rosa's shoulder. "Tashon...*Sage* Tashon just told us. Figure out what really happened, and hopefully that brings some clarity."

They stood as one and made their way toward the main cavern. When they turned into the main hallway, a line of humans and Crawlers streamed toward the exit, arms and hands full of supplies.

"What the hell?" Rosa asked.

"Not live here," a Crawler said.

"Moving out," a man said. "Can't believe some of you are staying. Get me the hell away from these music makers."

The line kept coming. Smith knew there were many against any interaction with the Singers, but seeing them segregating themselves en masse brought the divide Tashon had spoken of into clear focus. *Is it already too late to fix?* he asked himself.

Chapter 29

Abe sprinted across the ground toward a large gathering, afraid of what was happening in its center. Tensions had only risen since that morning, leading to violent outbursts from both sides of the issue. Those against the Singers acting out of fear and mistrust. Those for the Singers reacting in an effort to protect them. An entire community diminished by that single revelation: the supposedly pacifist Singers had a weapon.

Abe burst into the circle. Cixin was on top of Teacher, one hand around the Singer's throat and the other clenched in a fist, ready to strike. She threw her fist down, the cracking of Teacher's nose only quickening Abe's pace. Cixin lifted her fist again, but before she could land another blow, Abe leaped forward and knocked her to the ground. They rolled to a stop and Cixin screamed. Abe jumped to his feet, ready for a fight. Cixin remained on the ground, her chest rising and sinking shallowly. Blood trickled past her open eyes from a large gash in her forehead.

Teacher ran to Cixin and knelt by her side. Cixin protested, pushing the Singer away. But Teacher sang a note that calmed her and quickly cauterized the wound with a palm wire. Healed, Cixin pushed Teacher away and crawled to her feet. She spat on the ground, glaring at the Singer.

Abe helped Teacher to her feet, blood dripping from her face onto the ground. "Teacher helped you, Cixin," Abe said.

"She forced me to calm down," Cixin said. "She controlled me."

"If you really wanted to, you still could've attacked," Abe said. "It's not a drug. And *she did it to help you*."

"She manipulated my emotions," Cixin said, slowly walking to the edge of the circle, earning slaps on the back from her peers.

Abe shook his head as another Singer helped Teacher out of the circle. "She's a pacifist," he said. Then, guessing at Cixin's lineage, "You're no better than those cultists in Hong Kong during the Chinese civil war."

"You shit," Cixin said.

Abe held up a hand to show he wasn't done. "Yeah, those who *murdered* thousands of their countrymen. Because they refused to give up on the old language."

Cixin charged at Abe. Before she reached him, a cable snatched her foot and pulled her to the ground. Her head smacked the ground, reopening the cauterized wound.

"Shit! Damn it," she screamed.

Lollawk pushed past the crowd, harshly clicking, saliva splattering from his mouth. The cable retracted into his forehead. "Abe okay?"

"Yeah. Thanks, Lollawk."

"Good, good," Lollawk said. "Cixin?"

Cixin silently rose to her feet and wiped blood from her eyes.

"Looks like you undid the repair Teacher tried to make," Abe said.

"That was your Crawler friend, you shit."

"Wasn't talking about your head," Abe said.

Cixin flipped him off as she pushed her way past the crowd.

"Leave," Lollawk hissed at those who remained.

The spectators cleared out, leaving Abe and Lollawk alone with a few small puddles of blood.

"Getting worse," Abe said.

"Yes, yes."

"Have you seen Winona?"

"Winona learn book with Singers," Lollawk said. "In throne dome."

Abe nodded and started in that direction, but Lollawk stopped him.

"Want show Abe something," he said. "Come."

Abe followed him to a large boulder. They walked around to one side and stopped. A hole had been dug underneath the boulder, revealing a pile of bones.

"Here found Singer book," Lollawk said. "Leaders not allow any to this place. When Lollawk and Crawlers doubt leaders, sneak in. Large Singer grave, and many Singer books." Lollawk stared at the bones, whispered a click, and went on. "I first find book. Told no one. Read book when alone."

"How did you know how to read it?" Abe asked.

"Cable took knowledge from Singer prisoner. Same how learn human language."

Abe nodded. "Right."

"I read words of Mother. Saw no threat in Singers, saw lies of leaders. Lies and fear." He hissed and screeched, stomping his feet. "I not allow to happen again."

"Me either," Abe said. "We'll figure this out. We'll keep them safe. Again."

"Yes, yes," Lollawk said. "Go. See Winona."

"Are you sure?"

"Be alone now," Lollawk said.

"Okay." Abe turned and walked away. "It'll be okay, Lollawk," he said.

Lollawk made no response.

***

He found Winona sitting on the steps outside the dome with the book in her lap, a Singer, a human and two Crawlers by her side. As he approached, the sun fell lower in the sky, illuminating Winona in a soft glow. Abe stopped for a moment and watched. Her head tilted slightly to the side, a smile on her face as she listened to a Singer read from the book. He was still too far to hear or feel the melody, but everyone on the steps seemed entirely content. *This is who the Singers are*, he thought as he quickened his pace.

Winona stood to greet him as he made his way up the steps. They hugged each other tightly, the warmth and joy of her touch spreading through his body.

"I saw what Cixin did to Teacher," she said as she pulled away.

Abe sat down. "It's insane. And there was a circle around them just *watching*. Some were even proud of Cixin."

Winona shook her head. "Sounds like you saved Teacher's life."

"Maybe." Abe shrugged. "I'm glad she's okay, but it seems small with all the shit building up."

"I get that," Londey said. "It's not right. And it makes no sense."

"What doesn't?" Abe asked.

"Some of the Singers seem to be with Cixin," she replied.

"Not completely, I don't think," Winona said.

A Crawler moved down a step. "Some Singers no more pacifists. No more like idea of mercy."

"They're angry Atom lied to them," Abe said. "And they're blaming all the murders on the lack of justice. Just like Cixin."

"But the humans and Crawlers who are against mercy also seem against *all* Singers," Londey said.

The Singer holding the book confirmed the statement with a few lilting notes.

Two forms came down the stairs, an injured Singer helped by a Crawler. As they got closer, Abe realized it was Blowing Leaf, the Singer who had been with Cixin. One of the Singer's eyes was swollen shut, a line of dry blood below it.

"What happened?" Winona asked. "Cixin?"

Blowing Leaf answered affirmatively, then broke into a tirade of profane notes.

"Cixin say Singers not good for humans," the Crawler said.

Winona asked Blowing Leaf to sit, but the Singer refused with a melody that spurned the book and the Singer traditions. Blowing Leaf had no intention of returning to pacifism or promoting mercy.

"They built the weapon to protect you while you slept," Londey said.

"And they didn't even finish it," Winona added.

The Crawler beside Blowing Leaf clicked. "Singer still keep weapon. And book say Singer die before harming other. Five Singers wrong to make weapon. Five Singers need justice."

Winona sat down by Abe and opened the book "We're not discussing this right now." She turned to the Singer with the book. "We're listening to Bright Fire read to us."

Bright Fire looked at the page and began a melodious chant of a hopeful future. A future of peace and prosperity, kindness and understanding. The future Mother had foretold the future after humanity saved them from the Crawlers. *A future worth fighting for*, Abe thought. *But how do you* fight *for mercy?* He felt Winona next to him, saw and felt the contentment of those listening to Bright Fire. *This is how*, he realized.

He looked down at the book, feeling Bright Fire's notes as he tried to understand the symbols etched onto the page. The symbol for 'future' was large, in the bottom right corner. He didn't recognize any of the others. But as he stared at the page, with the melody rolling through the air, he did his best to understand the interplay of the written and spoken Singer language. Note and symbols didn't seem to be in any particular order, rather they wove in and around each other, forming an emotional image that made the meaning clear. Would he ever be able to experience the same feeling while reading on his own, without the voice of a Singer guiding him? It seemed difficult, if not impossible, though he knew learning to read their language was not the purpose of that moment. No, it was to promote peace despite differences of opinion.

Abe looked up the steps at Blowing Leaf, who had backed away but still stood within earshot, as if considering whether to really step away from the tradition of the Singers. As he thought about it, the Singer's indecision made sense to Abe. The five Singers who Burning Leaf trusted to hold up the standard of peace had faltered, creating a tool of violence. He'd lost faith in his leaders, perhaps even lost faith in the ideals that made the Singers pacifists in the first place.

But then Abe wondered if that were an inherently bad thing, to lose that faith. Was it better for an entire species to keep to one ideal, or to break into their own paths and viewpoints? He'd been taught that humanity's differences on Earth had gotten so extreme that wars were unavoidable. More importantly, though, was the fact that people were less willing to *accept* those differences. Was he making the same mistake by not accepting Blowing Leaf's view of justice over mercy?

He looked back to Bright Fire, who still sang the melody of peace, and came to a realization: he had been so lost in his own thoughts that Bright Fire's melody, and its emotions, had faded out of his mind. Then another epiphany. In the aftermath of Lioness's death, and everything it meant, the question of how he was in the Singer book lost its significance. He was there, and he was a part of Aethera's future. He would do everything he could to make it the most promising future possible.

Chapter 30

"Laos!" Tashon's voice rang into the still air of the Fourth. No echo, no response. He wiped tears from his eyes. And in his mind, the branches of the tree grew farther and farther apart.

The pyramids hovered in sight, though farther than he thought he had the ability to go. He knew Laos was gone, had most likely left as part of the mass exodus that erupted from the pyramids. He needed guidance from an outside perspective, from a source with no emotional attachment to the growing divide below. But no one and nothing came to his aid.

Nothing, he thought. He feared going there again. Feared he would lose himself in the contentment of complete absence. *I could meditate myself into a similar mindset*, he thought as he sat down. *Yes, that will work.* A lone, long strand of colorful wind appeared above him. He focused on it, and recited what he could remember from nothing.

"Nothing is everything. Everything is nothing. I am everything. I am nothing."

Inhale, exhale. The line of wind swirled and twisted.

"Hope and doubt. Doubt and hope. Both a part of everything."

A thought came to his mind, though he didn't want to voice it. He pushed it aside. And, from its non-space, nothing called to him.

"No," he said, and returned to his litany. "Chaos and peace. Joy and sadness. Mercy and justice."

The thought returned, and the call of nothing vibrated into his mind. He lay down on his back, the thought of emptiness warming his soul. To have no concerns as to right or wrong, just or unjust. To simply *be*. But no, there was so much happening on Aethera that he needed to be a part of. They wanted his help, his guidance. A word from nothing reached out to him: insignificant. With the vastness of the universe and the higher dimensions, was Aethera as significant as it seemed? And had Tashon himself not said that the continuance of life in the Fourth decreased the significance of death in the Third?

Why then was he concerned with the lives on Aethera? Would it not be better for them to die sooner, to reach their next stage of progression with more efficiency?

He sat up at the thought. "No," he said. He knew a lie when it reached into his mind and tried to lull him into apathy. He thought of the word's opposite: significant.

"Insignificant and significant." He slowed his breaths, knowing he'd had this thought before. He continued, voice calm and focused. "We might be unimportant in the vast expanse of everything. But we matter to each other. All below are important to me." He smiled at the thought and the peace it brought. And the realization that significance and insignificance existed, had to exist together, brought his mind to the answer he sought.

"Justice is as real as mercy. As needed. The divide is natural. Some lean more to one than the other. All in different parts of the road."

But what were the dangers where the road ends at justice? What dangers did we find at mercy's end?

Those on both ends of the road, and everywhere between, needed to work together.

"Yes," Tashon said.

A new wave of wind blew toward him, carrying the moths. They fluttered and landed in front of him. At their presence, the necklace grew brighter and warmer. They sat in blissful silence for a time, and the branches in Tashon's mind bent slightly back toward each other.

Eventually, he stood and the moths flew off. Amidst the black trees below, Rosa waited with Yeance, Minow, Hutsep, Comet and Atom. Tashon didn't know when the two Singers had shown up—he hadn't seen any of those first Singers since before he heard of the weapon. He closed his eyes and sank back into the Third.

"Sage." Rosa grabbed his arm as soon as his feet touched the ground.

Flushed with a gentle vertigo, he sat down. Atom and Comet fearfully sang out Wave's name, asking if Tashon had seen him.

"No, I haven't," Tashon said.

"Look, look," Hutsep said. "From above."

Tashon nodded slowly, the spinning in his head subsiding. "Any idea where he might be?"

"No." Rosa shook her head. "No one has seen him since before Atom told us of the weapon. They think... They're worried he had something to do with the missing weapons. And with the murders."

"Why?" Tashon asked.

Atom responded with notes of knowing and feeling. She *felt* it was the truth. Comet sang another note—she *hoped* it wasn't.

"Okay." Tashon nodded and closed his eyes. "I'll look."

All Aethera spread out before him, and the difficulty of the task was starkly apparent. Up to that point, Tashon had only ever zoomed in in the Third on the area he occupied. But to find Wave, he would have to pull his sight entirely off of himself, most likely not even being visible on the edges of his view. His mind seemed to tire at the thought, but he knew it must be done.

"Where did you see Wave last?" he asked.

"Leaving ship," Hutsep said.

Tashon moved his view so the ship was in the center. "What direction did he go?"

"North," Rosa said. "I saw him going north after I heard about the weapon."

"You remember that?" Tashon asked.

"He was running," Rosa said.

Tashon nodded. Without zooming in, he began a quick scan northward in search of any signs of the missing Singer. In the rolling fields, still white with snow, movement caught his eye. He took a deep breath. To get a closer view, he would take himself completely out of his higher viewpoint. After what nothing did to him, he simply wasn't sure his mind was capable. *Is anyone's mind capable of completely ridding itself of thoughts of oneself?* he wondered.

Another deep breath and he lowered the viewpoint, slowly, pausing just as he reached the edge. Then, fully committed, he focused in on the movement as fast as his mind would allow. His third-dimensional mind pulled and fought as his own form disappeared from view, forcing Tashon to slow down. But it worked, and he soon saw that the source of the movement was only a small bush creature running circles in the snow. He pulled back until Aethera was again in full view and opened his eyes, tired, yet not exhausted from the effort.

"Nothing yet," he said. "Just give me a minute."

Rosa handed him a bottle of water. He took a large gulp, passed it back and closed his eyes. He resumed his scanning, slower this time, not wanting to zoom in again unless he had to. His focus moved from the fields to the stones to the waterfall cliff then on to the ocean before he saw any more movement.

Fierce winds rushed over the green water, covering its entire surface in rolling waves. Tashon almost passed it all over, seeing no reason to assume anything moving was something other than water. But then he saw it: two long, thin lines of light speeding across the waves against the wind.

"What did you say the weapon looked like?" he asked.

"Metal sticks," Hutsep said.

"Thin metallic light," Rosa said.

"Oh, shit," Tashon whispered.

Rosa blew out a breath. "What?"

Atom and Comet mumbled nervously to themselves.

"Hold on." Bracing against his mind's disapproval, Tashon pulled his view in as quick as possible. His head pounded, but he found what they were looking for.

Wave flew over the water on a cloud of black, a spear of light on each side. And he wasn't alone. Singers, humans and Crawlers rode with him, each silently looking toward the Crawler land. Tashon recognized some of the humans, including Fylin and Theresa.

"Shit," he said again. "He has the weapons. And he's not alone."

Swears and harsh tones made up the responses.

"Even Theresa. What the hell are they doing?" He shook his head, then realized he recognized one of the Crawlers. "Hutsep, Ulot's there too."

Hutsep let out an ear piercing screech.

"Shit," Rosa said. "Sage, how close to land are they?"

Tashon zoomed back out. The pounding in his head increased, but he ignored it. "More than halfway across the ocean."

"What the hell's their plan?" Rosa asked.

Tashon shook his head. "No idea. But we need to tell Smith and Johann."

Chapter 31

Smith had spent over the last two hours wandering the halls of the ship in search of Theresa, but to no avail. Most genuinely didn't know where she was, while others seemed to be hiding something from Smith. Regardless, he was still no closer to finding her or to learning what really happened to Lioness and the Crawler leaders. Running a hand through his hair and shaking his head, he walked out of the airlock and almost directly into Minow and Yeance.

Minow smiled. "Smith!"

Yeance nodded and grabbed Smith's shoulder. "We have some good news," he said.

"Good news? Really?"

Minow nodded, her beaming smile still stretching across her face. "I'm pregnant."

Smith's eyes went wide. He looked to Yeance then back to Minow, laughed and clapped his hands once. "Abe is going to be so excited," he said.

Yeance and Minow glanced at each other. "What?" they asked simultaneously.

Smith shrugged. "Never mind." He smiled. "Congratulations. I'm happy for you. That's really good news."

"But you're still worried about all the other shit," Yeance said.

Smith nodded. "Aren't you?"

"Of course we are," Minow said. "But this'll be the first human born on Aethera. That's exhilarating."

Yeance kissed her cheek. "It is," he said.

"How long—" Smith was cut off by charging feet and shouting voices.

He turned. Tashon, Rosa, Atom, Comet and Hutsep ran into the clearing, straight to Smith.

"Smith," Tashon said while gulping breaths. "We found... Theresa. Wave too."

"They're almost to the Crawler continent," Rosa said. "With others too."

"With Ulot," Hutsep hissed.

Atom added her own notes, letting Smith know they also carried two of the Singer weapons with them.

"Shit," Smith said. "Can we catch them before they make it?"

"No, no," Hutsep said. "The sage, maybe."

They all looked to Tashon.

Tashon closed his eyes, then opened them. "I can. But we need more coming behind me. What's the fastest way to get you there?"

"Crawler vessel," Hutsep said.

"Atom? You agree?" Smith asked.

Atom agreed.

Soon they were piling as many people and provisions as possible into a vessel identical to the one Abe had left on weeks earlier. As Smith set a box of food down, someone grabbed his shoulder and forced him to turn around. A man stood there, his nose inches away from Smith's.

"Is it true?" he seethed. "One of their leaders is responsible?"

"We don't know that for sure," Smith said.

"But one of them has the weapon and is charging across the ocean."

"Yes."

"Knew we couldn't trust the bastards," the man said.

Smith stepped closer to him. "Bull*shit*. You can't say there's no trusting an entire damn species."

The man huffed. "Theresa's been saying it. Far as I know, she's one of our leaders."

Rosa and Johann walked over, and Smith realized everyone had stopped to listen to the conversation.

"Theresa's with them, and the weapon, you ass," Rosa said.

The man's anger momentarily vanished from his face. "What? Why?"

Smith shook his head.

Johann scratched his beard. "My guess is she—all of them—are turning against mercy."

The man smiled. "I don't trust the Singers, but that's a good idea. Take harsh justice to the Crawlers."

Atom approached, and the man glared at her. "And to these damn Singers," he said.

"I don't care if you trust them or not," Smith said. "Any aggression toward a Singer will be punished."

"Mercifully?" The man sneered.

"Oh, I'm giving you mercy right now just by not breaking your wrist," Rosa said.

The man huffed a harsh laugh. "We'll leave the Singers alone, for now. But they're not allowed on the ship."

Atom musically retorted that all were still welcome in their caves.

"Manipulative bitch," the man said.

Rosa's hands shot out and she had his wrist in her grip. "Just know I could've done it," she said, and let go. "Get the hell away from me."

The man puffed out his chest, and for a moment Smith thought he was going to take a swing. But then he blew out a breath and walked away.

Rosa and Johann climbed onto the vessel. Smith moved to follow, but they stopped him.

"You should stay here, Smith," Johann said.

"Why in the hell...?"

"I have military experience," Johann said. "And you're the only other human leader. You need to stay, keep the peace."

Smith shook his head, but he knew Johann was right. There was no telling what chaos might break out in coming hours and days. He needed to stay. "Yeah, okay," he said. "If you see Abe, tell him Yeance got Minow pregnant. It's a good thing."

"What?" Johann shook his head and laughed.

"Just tell him. Please."

"Okay, you got it, Smith."

"Thanks," Smith said. "And when I see you again, tell me what his reaction was."

"Uh... okay, yeah."

The vessel rose above the trees, and shot northward. Smith watched until it disappeared. When he turned to walk away, he found Minow and Yeance standing nearby. They smiled and called him over.

"You okay?" Minow asked.

Smith just shrugged and looked at the man who'd confronted him. "What's his name?"

"Hiloy," Yeance said. "He's hulled up in the ship with a chunk of humans and Crawlers. Not letting any Singers in."

Smith shook his head. "That, then this shit with Theresa, Wave and Ulot."

"Why do you think Theresa's with them?" Yeance asked.

"No idea." Smith squinted at the sun in the sky and scuffed his shoe in the ground. "Thought she'd be with the ones in the ship."

"But she was always resistant to the idea of mercy," Minow said. "I think they're seeking their own justice."

Yeance nodded. "Do you think she had something to do with the Crawler leaders and their guards?"

"I don't." Smith shook his head. "But there are a lot blaming all the death on us being too soft, offering too much mercy. And they might be right."

"What?" Minow asked, a hint of anger lacking the word.

"If they had been imprisoned, they might not have been killed," Smith said.

"But we can't know that," Yeance said. "And what about Lioness and the others found in the caves? We still have no idea what happened."

Smith shrugged, then rubbed his eyes. "I know, but I'm sure it has to do with mercy versus justice. In a way, the Crawler leaders did *deserve* death."

Minow shook her head. "But that wasn't the point," she said. "The point was showing *mercy*. More than they deserve, remember?"

"Yeah," Smith said. "But not everyone agrees. And we acted as if everyone did. I think that's what led to... whoever acting on their own."

"We wanted all of Aethera to have the same system," Yeance said. "Yeah. Maybe that wasn't the right call."

"Maybe." Smith sighed. "But how are we going to figure out what happened?"

"Wave stole the weapons," Minow said. "But how was everyone we found dead down there involved?"

Smith nodded. "Exactly. And how does what happened affect what we're doing next?"

"Let's start by talking to Whims," Yeance said. "He's the last of the original five who are still here.

Smith smiled and nodded. Rosa, Johann and Abe might not be with him, but he was glad he still had people he could count on.

They found Whims alone in a cavern, anxiously singing notes of frustrated confusion.

"Whims," Minow said calmly as they entered. "Hey, Whims. Are you okay?"

Whims smacked his own chest and wailed a guilty melody.

"You feel guilty?" Yeance asked. "For what?"

Whims sang of knowledge and wrongdoing and bad feelings.

"You knew what was happening?" Smith asked.

The Singer responded with notes for 'yes' and 'no.'

"Some of it?" Minow asked. "Did you know the leaders were going to be murdered?"

Whims hadn't known that, but he'd had a bad feeling about Wave.

"Do you think Wave killed them?" Smith asked.

He didn't have a perfect knowledge of it, but Whims believed Wave was the culprit.

"And what about Lioness? And the others in the weapon room?"

Whims went still, then slowly sang Atom's name.

"What about Atom?" Smith asked.

Atom had knowledge of what had happened, and was supposed to tell the humans.

"She didn't tell us anything," Smith said. "Why would she keep things from us?"

Whims pushed past them and stood at the entry to the cavern. He sang out a loud note, and soon a smokie joined them. Whims held his hand out to the smokie and cables popped out of his palms. The nanotech creature pointed its head at the hands, and two thin lines of blue light weaved from its nose into the palm wires. As soon as the light disappeared, Whims stood up and projected a screen from his palms.

Two sets of Singer legs appeared on screen, walking down the white stairs that led to the weapons room. After a moment of staring at the Singers, visible only from the waist down, Smith realized it was the view from a smokie's perspective. They reached the bottom of the stairs, and the smokie stopped. The Singers came fully into view as they approached the intricately locked door.

It was Lioness and Wave. Wave started opening the door while Lioness sang for him to stop. He responded harshly, but only the first note was heard. The audio fizzled and cut out, leaving Smith and the others watching it silently play out.

Wave resumed working on the door. Lioness sang for at least a minute, and Smith hoped she was telling Wave why what he was doing was a bad idea. Still, there was no way to know. When she closed her mouth, Wave turned to her and slammed his open palm on the top of her head. She backhanded him across the face, then they both went still.

Behind the screen, Whims quietly hummed to himself, the feelings emanating from him letting everyone know how uncomfortable the footage made him feel.

Wave lifted his hand again but before he struck, Lioness stepped closer, her nose nearly touching his. Wave dropped his hand and walked back up the stairs. A few minutes later, Lioness followed. They watched her legs walk up the stairs and into the red tunnel. The smokie turned the opposite way, and the video ended.

"That's it?" Smith asked.

Whims closed his palm wires, and indicated that was it.

"Must be why Atom didn't tell us," Yeance said. "Doesn't tell us anything, really."

"Except that Wave wanted in the weapon room," Minow said.

"But he didn't go in," Smith said. "Neither of them did. All we know is that he considered it and Lioness told him not to."

"So we still don't know what happened," Minow said.

"Maybe we never will." Yeance wrapped an arm around her shoulders.

Minow gasped. "Smith. We need to tell the others what's coming."

"Oh, shit," Smith said, feeling stupid that the thought hadn't occurred to him. "Whims, get me Abe."

Chapter 32

Abe stood at the bottom of the steps surrounded by all who were still for mercy and with the Singers. The sun had sunk deep behind the dome, casting everything in shadow. The top of the staircase was lined with biotech of every kind: birds, reptilian rodents, multi-winged amphibians and two large felines, one at each end.

Roughly one hundred feet away from where Abe stood, those Crawlers, Singers and humans who had given up on mercy and strict pacifism. The last group stood in the dirt, the anger on their faces clear. They were those who wished no contact with the Singers.

And in the middle of them all, with her arms held behind her back by a towering biotech feline, stood Cixin. She had attacked another Singer, and the danger she posed to all with her actions was too evident to ignore. The only problem was deciding what to do with her.

What amount of mercy, and what degree of justice?

"Why not confine her among us, as we did our former leaders?" Lollawk asked.

Blowing Leaf made a condescending note that Abe interpreted as a scoff.

"Idiotic and naïve," a man named Dinli said. "That's why your leaders and their guards were murdered. That undeserved mercy is what caused all of this."

"Mercy is mercy *because* it is undeserved," Winona said.

Abe stepped forward. "But maybe it is more merciful to put her in a prison where she'll be safer. We can't just let her be free."

"Yes you can." She grinned.

Dinli laughed softly and shook his head. "In that case, keep her out. We'll take care of her."

From the other side of Winona, Londey responded with her own forced laugh. "Killing her? You call that justice? She hasn't killed anyone."

Blowing Leaf sang of Cixin's potential for murder.

"Cannot condemn for action not done," Lollawk said.

"Let her go," shouted one of her comrades.

Justice and mercy both ignored the plea.

"You're right, we can't execute her," Dinli said. "Justice demands a punishment equal to the crime."

With a bit of joy, Blowing Leaf suggested Cixin be assaulted multiple time, then thrown in prison.

Winona gasped. "No way in hell," she said. "We can't commit the same crime against her. That would make our legal system itself criminal."

Abe agreed, though it was impossible to decide the right course of action. True, enemy. Crawlers were imprisoned under the dome, but what came next for them? Mercy seemed to ask that they have another chance at freedom, but how would they know they wouldn't hurt or kill again?

He looked at the Singer standing behind him. "Teacher, come with me," he said. The two walked to Cixin and stood two steps below her. "Teacher, do you want to say anything to Cixin?"

After a few long moments of silence, Teacher whispered a melody with one intent: forgiveness. The intense sincerity of the tune simultaneously warmed Abe and sent chills down his spine. Water pooled in his eyes. He saw the tears filling Cixin's eyes, noticed the trembling of her hands and the quivering of her lip.

Then the notes stopped.

Cixin narrowed her eyes. "Don't force your emotions on me, manipulator," she said. "Your pseudo-forgiveness means *shit* to me."

With quiet notes of defeat, Teacher walked away.

"You'll hurt another Singer if you get the chance," Abe said.

Cixin nodded firmly.

Abe looked at her, then at the bruised and beaten Singers. There was no clear answer that could provide safety for the Singers yet also mercy for Cixin. But perhaps they should only offer mercy to those willing to change. "I do love the idea of mercy," he said. "But if we offer Cixin mercy, she's not going to change. How can we offer mercy at the expense of another's safety?"

"Turning away from mercy so easily?" Dinli asked.

"No. We should offer mercy when we can. When the offender shows regret, a willingness to change."

"The Crawler leaders didn't show that," Dinli said. "Was what we gave them wrong, then?"

Abe opened his mouth but no words came out. He closed it.

"Not wrong," Lollawk said. "Not good, maybe."

Winona grabbed Abe's hand and squeezed. "Maybe what we offered the Crawler leaders was wrong, only because of what it caused. But we couldn't have seen that coming."

"Yeah we could've," Dinli said. "A lot of us voted for more severe punishments. You didn't think someone would act on their own, after what those Crawlers did?"

"I had more faith in us," Winona said.

"Naïve," he responded.

Silence. Both groups stared across Cixin, examining each other.

Are mercy and justice really that different? Abe wondered.

"Just tell me what the hell you're going to do with me," Cixin said.

"Can't trust Cixin out," Lollawk said.

"Lock her up with the Crawler prisoners," Dinli said. "Show her what it's like to be with a bunch a monsters who think she shouldn't be alive."

"Or," Abe said, "we could show mercy by putting her somewhere more...comfortable."

Blowing Leaf seethed, letting everyone know that's not what Cixin deserved.

Londey threw her hands in the air. "That's what mercy *means*," she said.

"And why are you so keen on offering mercy over justice?" Dinli asked.

"We want to build a culture focused on kindness and understanding," Winona said.

"Justice is just as important," Dinli said. "I'm not saying no mercy. But look at Cixin here. She will take advantage of any mercy we show her."

"You're not wrong," Abe said.

"What?" Londey shouted.

"Abe...?" Winona asked.

Abe squeezed her hand. "Let's be realistic. Even Cixin said she'd hurt another Singer. But that doesn't mean we treat her less than intelligent."

Lollawk clicked. "Yes. What we do to Crawler prisoners now not good," he said.

"We could treat them better," Winona said. "Should treat them better."

"This is insane," Dinli said. "They're criminals. Violent. They might not deserve death, but they don't deserve a warm bed with soft sheets."

"Sheets?" Lollawk asked.

"Comfort," Winona said. "He's saying they don't deserve any comfort."

"Yes or no," Lollawk said.

Silence returned, save for quiet mumblings from the crowd standing in the sand. All are deserving of some form of kindness and mercy, right? Abe wondered. I was taught all are equal, regardless of background or anything else. But what if those choices have harmed others? Do they deserve the same rights and privileges the rest of us do? He shook his head, reminding himself that mercy isn't about what people deserve, but about the kindness and forgiveness others are willing to offer them.

"I say we offer them some kindness and dignity," he said finally.

Blowing Leaf vehemently disagreed, as did those on her side.

"Justice is harsh," Dinli said. "As it should be. Mercy will —"

Dinli was cut off by a bright blue light bursting from Teacher's hands. The Singer opened her palms and a screen rose out.

Smith's face appeared. He spoke before anyone else had a chance, saying, "Be ready. Wave is on his way. He has a large group. And two of the Singer weapons."

Lollawk screeched. Cixin's punishment would have to wait.

Chapter 33

Tashon rose to the Fourth, excited and nervous to travel through it again. The wind blew hard, threatening to push him over as he looked for his target. In the distance, Wave and his group neared the far shore. He'd have to move fast to catch them.

The wind swirled around as he walked, constantly changing directions. After a few steps, a gust knocked him off his feet, sending him shoulder first to the surface. Uninjured, he got up quickly but the strength of the wind only grew the farther he walked. By the time he was standing above the cliff of waterfalls, the surface of the Fourth was rolling with the force of the storm.

Tashon dropped onto his hands and knees, knowing he had to keep moving but not knowing how. He could crawl, but the peaks of the ground as it moved up and down were getting higher, always changing directions. And ahead, his target moved into the mouth of the canyon that led to the Crawler city. He took a slow, deep breath, getting as close to a meditative state as possible while still retaining control of his body.

Slowly, he lifted his hand off the ground, remaining on his knees. He felt the sway of the ground, but let his body move with it, while staying upright. He lifted one leg up and forward and placed his foot firmly on the broiling surface. Still, he remained upright.

The ground rolled in all directions. Had it been the ocean below, he no doubt would have drowned. But he was above the water, above the planet itself. He told himself he could do it, and pushed himself onto both feet. He paused, trying to sense a pattern within the swirling wind and twirling wind.

There was none.

Wave was nearly into the Crawler city. Tashon needed to move. He knew he wouldn't get there without the Fourth knocking him down at least a dozen times, but he was pretty sure he could make it in time. He walked forward, his body swaying with each step. The wind shifted again and the ground under his feet dropped into a valley, then shot into a peak, sending him twirling with the wind. He spun, floated and fell in that slow yet uncontrollable way he'd only experienced in the Fourth.

He landed on his back, head pointing toward his destination. With a groan of frustration, he rolled and rose to a squat, taking another moment to watch the moving of the ground. He noticed brief moments in which the ground was smooth enough that he'd be able to run on it. Looking down at how far he'd come already, he figured he could make it to the Crawler city in about one hundred steps across the Fourth.

Another lull came and he sprinted forward, counting his steps to keep calm. After twelve, he stopped and crouched. A few seconds later the immense waves returned. *Damn*, he thought, *I could've gotten a few more steps in.* The broiling in the ground slowed and he readied for another run, but stopped as the pyramids came into view. The massive structure hovered above the ground, at most fifty steps to his right. Souls of all shades swam in and out and around it. The word 'migration' came unbidden into his mind, but he couldn't give himself time to consider why.

But I could get the answers I need if I go, he thought. He quickly shook his head and looked forward. Wave was almost out of the canyon. He'd lost precious moments watching the pyramids, and now he didn't have the luxury to wait for a smooth surface. He ran, tripping and falling and rolling nearly every other step. But he still moved forward, always nearing his destination.

Below, Wave neared the Crawler dome that stood atop the steps, the structure surrounded by two distinctly separate groups, shouting at each other across a woman detained by a biotech tiger. Tashon tripped again and landed on his side. A new wave launched him into the air, and he barrel-rolled toward the dome. As he twisted through the colorful winds, his head spun and his stomach churned. He landed on his stomach, a dozen feet from Wave and his companions, almost at the dome.

Without care for stumbling or thought of what he'd do once he returned to the Third, he sprinted nine steps. On the tenth, he let himself start dropping back to the Third. Ripples ran under his foot from two directions, and he tripped as he began his transference into the lower dimension. He popped into the Third horizontally a few feet above Theresa. Gravity took hold and he landed on top of her, both crumpling onto the black nanotech vessel.

Wave shouted in surprise, followed by a command to seize Tashon. Fylin lifted him to his feet, trapping his arms behind his back. Theresa stood as the black cloud they flew in came to a stop at the base of the stairs.

"Theresa," Tashon said through labored breaths, his head still spinning from the tumult in the Fourth. "Theresa...."

Fylin pulled harder on Tashon's arms, forcing his shoulder blades closer together. Tashon huffed and closed his eyes, quickly bringing himself back into the Fourth. The higher-dimensional storm raged harder. He took a step forward, turned around and then returned to the Third, standing in the dirt between the enemy and the Crawler dome. His head spun with vertigo, his eyes blurring. But he focused on his breathing, and it soon passed.

Wave sang out, demanding access to the Crawler prisoners.

From Abe's side, a Singer loudly declined.

"In the basement of the dome," the woman prisoner called.

"Shit, Cixin." Abe threw his one hand in the air.

The black cloud dropped to the ground, its passengers stepped off and it gently blew apart into eight smokies. The two thin weapons of light hovered above them.

"Theresa," Tashon said again. "Please."

"Tashon," she said. "It's good to see you."

Winona walked down the stairs. "You can't kill them all."

Ulot clicked. "Who say can't? One human leader, one Singer leader, one Crawler leader say can."

A Crawler stomped down the stairs and stopped as close to Ulot's face as possible, screeching and gnashing. "Vote say can't."

"I voted against killing," Theresa said. "Against my gut, against harsh yet *true* justice. Mercy made everything go to shit."

Bodies walked down the stairs, slowly forming a half circle behind Theresa and Wave, making it clear what side they were on. The divide grew wider, but Tashon felt if he handled it right, he could avoid more bloodshed.

He glanced at the two thin weapons, then back at Theresa. "We do need justice," he said. "But also mercy. We need *both*, Theresa. We can't blindly kill everyone who's done wrong."

"It isn't blindly," Theresa said. "Those Crawlers are guilty. They willingly killed. They wanted all Singers and humans *dead*."

Lollawk shuffled his feet. "Not all, not want," he said. "Some did to follow, to protect kin."

Tashon looked at the Crawler, the realization that some of the Crawlers were forced soldiers convincing him even more of the importance of mercy. "Theresa, Wave, listen to Lollawk. They were forced into it."

Wave made a sound similar to a bird cawing, then a staccato of notes that told how a Singer would have let their family die not to commit violence.

Winona and a few others laughed. "But here we have Singers threatening to murder defenseless prisoners."

Ulot clacked and stomped his feet. "No murder. Execute."

The group behind him cheered their agreement.

"Wave," Tashon said. "You must see how you're wrong here. You blame them for killing when they were forced to kill. And you come here, nothing or no one forcing you, to kill them."

Wave sent the note for 'justice.'

"Exactly, Wave," Theresa said. "Justice demands it."

Tashon closed his eyes, imagining for a moment the road connecting justice and mercy. "Justice is an idea," he said. "A concept can't *demand* anything. And justice is just one end of a line examining how we should punish negative actions."

"Committing genocide is more than a negative action," Theresa said.

Tashon inhaled again, fearing there was no way to turn them from their path. And what then? Use violence to convince them the prisoners should be offered mercy? Did Wave and Theresa and those determined to force justice not also deserve mercy? But if the only way to stop them was with aggression, wouldn't it be better to do so? He looked at those behind him, and those with Theresa. If it weren't for Wave's weapons, they'd have a chance. But he didn't want to fight them, didn't want to be the direct or indirect cause of any being raised to the Fourth. But if Wave attacked, he knew he wouldn't just stand by at let the prisoners be slaughtered.

"What if we don't let you in?" he asked. "Are you going to fight past us to get into the prison and kill them?" Tashon asked.

Wave sang one note and one of the spears of light instantly became two interlocking rings, each spinning in opposition to the other. Another note and the second weapon did the same.

"Wave," Theresa said. "Wave, wait. Maybe...."

Wave sang a staccato of anger and vengeance, and the weapons shot up the stairs and into the dome without harming anyone on the outside. A single moment of stunned silence, then echoing shrieks as the weapon went active. Tashon was blind to what the weapon was doing within the dome, and in that moment he wished more than ever that his higher vision allowed him to see inside three-dimensional structures.

Tashon followed the speeding crowd into the dome, down a set of stairs, through a garden of strange plants, then into a massacre. The spinning rings went from Crawler head to Crawler head, severing each from its body, leaving their heads dangling from the ceiling on cables. The Crawlers who remained fought to free themselves from their cables, pulling and ripping to no avail.

Abe ran in. "Lollawk, unhook them," he yelled.

Lollawk ran to the nearest living prisoner and quickly released the cable. But when he went to the next one, both weapons blocked his path. Wave walked calmly into the room and told Lollawk to stop, or he would be killed as well.

Everyone went still as Lollawk considered the right choice. Again, Tashon wished the third-dimensional structure didn't impede his ability. If it didn't, he'd be able to bounce between the two dimensions, freeing a prisoner between each dimensional shift.

Instead, all he had were words. "Wave, stop."

The weapons ceased spinning, but remained uncomfortably close to Lollawk.

Tashon blew out a breath. "They're defenseless. Terrified. This isn't justice. It's vengeance."

Theresa stumbled in, followed by Fylin and Ulot. She looked at the bodies on the ground, the heads gently swaying from the ceiling. Then turned her head and vomited. "Shit, Wave...." She wiped bile from her chin. "Is this the justice we wanted?"

Fylin shook his head, a few unintelligible noises popping from his throat.

"No, no," Ulot said. "Stop, Wave. Stop."

Lollawk stretched his arm out and grabbed hold of the nearest dangling head. "She good Crawler. Many eggs... children. Leaders held eggs... children. Made her fight."

"Are her children still alive?" Theresa asked.

"Yes, yes."

"Wait," Fylin said. "How come we haven't heard about any of this before?"

Tashon silently acknowledged the validity of question, though he still believed Lollawk was telling the truth.

Ulot clicked quietly. "Think only human have family?"

"Wave," Theresa said. "Please, you don't need to kill them."

Wave responded with another note of anger, and the weapons resumed spinning. Lollawk jumped back, putting distance between him and the rings. Another note from Wave and the weapons sped at the Crawler. Tashon jumped in front of Lollawk, arms spread wide.

"Tashon!" Abe shouted as the weapons sped toward Tashon's head.

But in the moment of potential death, Tashon felt no fear. He'd already been where he would go upon death, and it was wondrous. But as the spinning rings of light neared his head, the necklace around his neck grew warmer. With the warmth came a light that started dim, and then burst out in a wave that shattered the weapon into thousands of tiny specks of light that fell lazily to the ground. Tashon collapsed to his knees, his energy nearly gone. And, with gratitude, he saw no one had been hurt by the necklace.

Screeching in anger, Wave charged Tashon, tackled and pinned him to the ground. Reflexively, Tashon threw a punch that connected with his attacker's left eye, but it was too weak to have any effect. Wave screeched and punched, screeched and punched until, at last, Abe appeared, flying through the air and into Wave. The two tumbled into a Crawler corpse as Tashon rolled to his knees, coughing and spitting blood.

Theresa appeared at his side and knelt down. "Maybe we made a mistake," she said.

Tashon nodded and spat. "Maybe," he said. "But something isn't right. We need to figure this all out. Without violence."

Soon, Wave and all who sided with him were imprisoned, the rest left to discuss and decide what to do moving forward.

Chapter 34

Smith, Yeance and Whims stood at an open airlock of the ship, their way blocked by Hiloy.

"You can't deny the Singers access to the ship," Smith said.

"This ship is the only human structure on Aethera, and we will not let *them* in here. It *will* be kept safe from their influence."

Yeance peered behind the man's shoulder. "How many are in there, really? Far less than we have out here, even without the Singers."

"Are you threatening us?" Hiloy asked.

Whims quickly sang 'no,' melodizing that even to threaten was against true and full pacifism.

"Maybe, though," Yeance said.

Hiloy laughed joylessly. "Says the man pushing for mercy."

"The Singers deserve mercy," Smith said. "A few have turned against their pacifism. Does that mean we should turn all of them away?"

"You don't have to," Hiloy said. "Just don't bring any in here."

Whims noted that it was fine, that there was no reason to fight about it. They had the forest and the caves and the rest of Aethera. Smith looked at the Singer, amazed by the calmness and acceptance concerning another's hate toward him. Perhaps humanity could learn from that.

"I respect that," Yeance said, then looked at Hiloy. "But any violence against a Singer solely because of their species or their language will be met with... merciful consequences.

Hiloy laughed, shaking his head. "You know that does little to deter anyone from committing a crime?"

"Maybe," Smith said. "Maybe not. But the more willing you are to commit the crime and the less willing you are to change, the less mercy you'll receive."

"That's news to me." Hiloy folded his arms right across his chest.

"I just decided," Smith said. "Talking to a racist convinced me."

Hiloy stepped closer to Smith, eyes narrowed. "We are *not* racist."

"No? Then what are you?" Smith asked.

"Wait," Yeance said. "Maybe not racist. The Singers aren't a different race. They're a different species."

"Specie-ist?" Smith asked.

"I don't like the sound of that," Yeance said. "Singer-ist?"

"We're *not*...." Hiloy said.

"Anti-Singer," Smith said.

"No...." Hiloy said.

"You're not anti-Singer?" Yeance asked.

"We — fine, call us whatever you want. We don't trust *them*. They are not safe for humanity."

Whims turned and walked away, asking Smith and Yeance to follow. They did, without another word to Hiloy.

They walked silently through the trees, Smith and Yeance nodding or waving when greeted, Whims seemingly oblivious to all such human interaction. Whims led them to the caves, down the white stairs and into the weapon room. The three thin lines hung in the air as they had before, untouched as he wished the other two were.

"Why here, Whims?" Yeance asked.

Whims indicated that just a week prior, the weapon had been incomplete. So incomplete that they weren't even sure it would work when finished.

Smith nodded and scratched his cheek. "That is odd. But when you decided to stop building it, why didn't you destroy it?"

Whims's sung answer came clearly into Smith's mind: 'Would you be able to let your entire species die to protect your own beliefs?'

Yeance whistled softly. A valid question, one Smith hoped he never had to face himself.

Wave spoke again, telling them that Atom was willing to do just that. Before she left, she had asked that he destroy the remaining three weapons.

"Really?" Smith asked. "Do you think that's a good idea?"

Whims was torn. He did believe in non-violence, in the sanctity of all life.

"But at what point is it acceptable to perpetuate smaller acts of violence to prevent larger ones?" Yeance asked.

As it turned out, that was the exact question Whims had been asking himself.

"Damn." Smith shook his head. "Tashon would have good insight on this."

"He would?" Yeance asked.

"He killed someone up on the Ship of Nations."

"One of the terrorists?"

Smith nodded. "He's not sure he made the right choice. And now, knowing what he does about the Fourth and the afterlife, I'm not sure he sees death as something to fear."

"Right," Yeance said. "But you can turn that around. If this life isn't all there is, then do we actually kill anyone? Or just send them to their next form of existence?"

Smith shook his head. "No, I still think there's a moral implication to killing another intelligent being. But knowing, or maybe just believing, in an actual afterlife might make non-violence easier."

"Make it easier to let yourself be killed?" Yeance asked.

Smith shrugged. "Maybe."

Whims sang one harsh note.

Smith and Yeance whipped their heads to look at him.

The Singer then asked their opinions. Should he destroy the weapon, or keep it?

Smith sighed. "I don't know, Whims."

"If it's moral not to kill, couldn't the reverse also be true?" Yeance asked.

Whims asked Yeance what he meant.

"If not killing is the right, moral choice, then couldn't we also say it's the right choice to keep others from getting killed?"

Smith scratched his chin and clicked his tongue. "But wouldn't we do that by killing?"

"Yeah. I just don't like the idea of being completely defenseless. I agree that we should place more importance on mercy. But if Hiloy or anyone else comes against the Singers, I'm not going to let them get murdered."

Smith nodded, realizing he agreed with Yeance.

Whims shrieked a note of frustration, telling the humans that their philosophizing was doing nothing to make his decision any easier.

"Right. Sorry, Whims," Smith said. "So, keep the weapons or destroy them. Whims, which would be worse for you: to break your pact of pacifism by using the weapons, or to lose your entire species because you didn't have these weapons to protect yourselves?"

Whims let out a low moan of confusion.

"But those aren't the only two possible outcomes," Yeance said. "Whims, what if you don't destroy the weapons, and an enemy gains control of them? What then?"

More notes of confused frustration from Whims.

"That's a good point, though, Yeance. And even without *these* weapons, you could still protect yourselves. And a lot of others will protect your species, whether you choose to fight or not."

Whims sang a slow and grateful melody that slowly grew louder, morphing into an anthem of determination. He walked to an array of buttons and holes on the far wall. Just as Atom had done with the lock, Whims now went through an intricate combination of pushing buttons and blowing various notes into the holes. When done, he turned and looked up at the glass sphere that housed the weapons. The air within it trembled and twisted, the spears of light shrinking and expanding, shrinking and expanding. The forces inside the sphere grew until the glass itself shook and Smith feared it would shatter. He took a step back, but the glass held strong.

The air inside darkened, becoming a gray-purple mist that swirled faster and faster until the weapons themselves were pulled into it, their straight lines bending until they matched the curve of the vortex. The vortex shrunk as the spears were pulled into the center. Soon, the vortex and weapons were gone, the sphere empty.

Yeance shook his head and turned to Smith. "I don't understand their technology," he said. "Maybe we should've let our engineers study the weapons."

"Probably a good thing we didn't," Smith said.

Yeance shrugged. "Yeah."

Without a note, Whims left the room and walked up the stairs. Smith and Yeance followed.

***

When Smith, Yeance and Whims returned to the clearing, a mass of Crawlers and humans surrounded the only open airlock into the ship. Hiloy had ordered all the others closed or blocked off, and left the one heavily guarded. Another group, this one made up of all three species, stood farther back, silently watching what Smith was certain would turn into a fight.

Hiloy stood at the entrance, surrounded by his fellow anti-Singers, a large stick in his hand. "The ship is ours now. Anyone who sees the truth of the Singers and wants to renounce them from their lives may enter. All others, *leave.*"

A Crawler screeched, lifted a foot and slammed it into Hiloy's chest. The human's feet lifted off the ground, his head went back and he landed flat on his back. The group behind the Crawler screamed and moved as one, making quick work of the remaining guards as they charged into the ship. Screams and crashes echoed from inside the metal hull.

"Shit!" Smith ran to the open airlock and examined the prostrated bodies. "All breathing, at least."

Yeance crouched down, peering into the ship. "Should we go in?"

"Not blindly." Smith looked at those at the edge of clearing. "And maybe not at all."

"What?" Yeance asked.

Smith walked to the onlookers and found Minow among them. "What happened?"

"We were talking about the anti-Singers," Minow said. "A lot of them got more and more angry. We tried to stop them."

Yeance caught up with Smith, breathing heavily. "Why didn't any Singers attack Hiloy?"

A Singer croaked out a line of notes, explaining they hadn't wanted any to fight for them. If some wanted to exclude Singers from the ship, so be it. They wouldn't use it as an excuse to turn to violence. They were saddened enough that humans and Crawler were committing violence in the Singer name yet again.

Smith nodded, amazed at their conviction. Their acceptance of the rejection of others. Their willingness to never enter the ship again simply to avoid harming anyone. A crash rang out from inside the ship, followed by screaming and clacking.

The same Singer sang that it needed to stop, and walked quickly toward the open airlock.

"Who is that?" Yeance asked.

"Her name's Strong Earth," Minow said.

As soon as Strong Earth's feet touched the metal of the ship, she let out a screeching, ear-piercing note, and everything went silent. She went on, noting that any who truly supported the Singers would respect their pacifist decision and leave the ship. She turned and walked out. Within minutes, all who supported the Singers were out of the ship.

Chapter 35

Abe and Winona waved as Johann disembarked the Crawler vessel. Rosa stepped off right behind him, followed by Hutsep, Atom, Comet and over a dozen others. Abe grabbed Winona's hand, trying to calm himself, his nerves still refusing to settle after Wave's attack.

"Did Tashon make it?" Johann asked.

Abe nodded. "He did, but it wasn't enough. Wave murdered nearly half the prisoners."

Atom and Comet each made a note that felt like a gasp.

"Ulot," Hutsep said. "Ulot live?"

"Ulot?" Abe asked.

"Crawler with Wave," Hutsep said.

"Oh, right," Winona said. "Ulot tried to stop Wave in the end."

"Where's Theresa?" Rosa asked.

"Talking to Tashon and Lollawk," Abe said.

"She should be locked up," Rosa said.

"She tried to stop Wave too," Winona said.

"Stop Wave from what?" Johann asked.

"Massacring the prisoners," Abe said.

"Massacre?" Johann asked.

Abe and Winona quickly told them what happened, including every graphic detail of the beheadings.

Johann shook his head. "What now?"

"Tashon is with Lollawk and Theresa and some Singers discussing that," Abe said.

"I need to be part of that conversation," Johann said.

"Just you?" Rosa asked.

"No, all of us. As many as possible." Johann scratched his beard. "Probably get Smith on a screen too."

Abe turned and started toward the main Crawler dome, all occupants of the vessel close behind.

"Why aren't you with them?" Rosa asked.

"We were waiting for you," Abe said. "Tashon told us you were coming."

Johann nodded. "Right."

"Sage Tashon's sight is amazing," Rosa said with a smile.

"It is," Winona said. "But do you believe everything he says?"

"She does," Abe said, surprised Winona would ask such a question.

"Absolutely," Rosa said. "He's given me no reason not to. If it weren't for him, only Crawlers would exist on Aethera now."

"I don't think that's entirely accurate," Winona said.

Abe winced internally, knowing how much Rosa revered Tashon.

Rosa took a deep breath. "Do you question my sage?"

Abe considered speaking up, but he knew Winona could handle herself.

"No," Winona said. "That's not what I'm saying. He has seen and done wonderful things. But even without him, there still would have been a Crawler rebellion. There were those fighting for us and the Singers regardless what Tashon saw or did."

"But what he did directly caused the enemy to surrender," Rosa said.

"That's true," Abe said.

"It is," Winona said. "I'm just saying it still might have worked out without him. I'm not denying what he's done for us."

"That's logical," Rosa said.

Abe glanced at Rosa. "Why do you call him sage?"

Rosa stopped for a moment, as if shocked by the question. "You haven't been with him." She resumed walking. "I hadn't thought of that. He's been teaching us."

"Teaching what?" Abe asked.

"What the Fourth has taught him," Rosa said. "About balance and duality, the synonymous aspect of opposite. About how understanding this can bring peace. I've written down everything he's said."

It hit Abe how different life was on the two continents. The realization that he had been in his own world seeking his own understanding of the Singers' language while others sought peace and understanding by different means was jarring, yet logical. He knew, of course, that everyone sought knowledge through various methods, but until that moment he hadn't noticed the varied impact that could make on individual lives. And how two ways of understanding the universe could be drastically different, yet still coexist.

They arrived at the stairs leading up to the dome. He walked faster. A large group sat on the floor of the dome with Tashon, Theresa, Teacher and Ulot as Lollawk stood at the front by the thrones.

Theresa smiled at them as they walked in, a look of sadness in her eyes. "Welcome," she said. "Sit down. Johann, will you join us?"

"Hutsep too," Lollawk said.

Teacher sang the name of Atom and Comet.

The Crawler, the Singers and the human took their standing positions while the rest sat down. Abe found himself between Rosa and Winona.

"Abe told us what happened with Wave," Johann said. "Catch us up on what you're talking about."

Tashon nodded. "Theresa?"

"Why's he having her do it?" Abe whispered to Winona.

"Being an example, I think," she said.

Theresa cleared her throat. "We're attempting to figure out the right balance between justice and mercy."

Atom asked what options had been discussed.

"Nothing that specific yet," Theresa said. "Tashon's been explaining the importance of both justice and mercy. Both are needed, really."

"But, Theresa, you came with Wave to exact justice," Johann said.

Theresa closed her eyes, took a deep breath and then opened them. "I did, Johann. I was terrified and furious about what our mercy allowed to happen to the Crawler leaders and their guards. But the extreme justice Wave committed was too much. Tashon's right. We need a balance between the two."

"Yes, yes," Ulot said. "Wave angry. Too angry. Hurt. Too much hurt by Wave. Not good, not right."

Johann nodded.

"Yes, yes," Hutsep said. "Sage logical."

Atom sang her tentative agreement, letting all know she hoped the justice would be doled out in a non-violent manner.

"How achieve balance?" Hutsep asked.

"That's the question," Tashon said. "And I don't think it will ever be perfect. It will probably change constantly too. It will vary from case to case."

"But what laws do we put into writing?" Johann asked. "With a system that is meant to cater to each individual case, how do we account for every possible scenario?"

"And the fact that everyone will have a different opinion," Theresa said. "Because I'm assuming we'll put it to a vote before we make it law, yes?"

Abe and others in the crowd shouted their approval of a vote. But Abe felt the weight of what Theresa was saying. How could they create a system that incorporated two seemingly opposite ideals together while taking into account individual cases and opinions? It seemed impossible, even with only one species. Abe wondered how Earth had done it for as long as they did.

"Before we continue, I want to get Smith on screen with us," Johann said.

Atom opened her palms and her screen rose into the air. After a few moments, Whims's face floated in the air. Atom quickly gave Whims an explanation of what was happening and asked for Smith to join them.

Whims replied that it might be some time before Smith was able to come. Something had happened.

Abe's heart sank and he jumped to his feet. "Is he okay?"

Smith was fine, according to Whims. There was something that needed his attention.

Abe nodded and sat down. "Okay." His heart rate slowly went down, but he wouldn't feel truly okay until he saw his dad. Winona smiled at him. A soft sense of comfort poured into him, followed by the familiar doubt at the validity of his feelings for Winona. He pushed the thought aside as best he could, though he wondered if he could ever fully rid himself of the doubt he had let sink into his mind and heart. After a deep breath, he gave her a sincere smile in return. He did trust the Singers, and didn't think his emotions were being manipulated. Or, that's what he decided to think. Because, like Winona had said, he didn't want to be without her.

Whims's face shook on the screen as walked through the red caves, presumably looking for Smith. After a few minutes of waiting, Tashon left his spot at the front of the room, pulling Abe and Winona to the side.

"What's going on?" Abe asked.

Tashon shook his head. "I don't know, but your dad wanted me to tell you something."

"What? Is something wrong?"

"No," Tashon said. "He wanted me to tell you that Minow is pregnant."

Abe stared at Tashon, dumbfounded. Then he laughed. "Really?" He turned to Winona. "Really?"

Winona smiled. "You're not going to get me pregnant, then."

Abe laughed.

Tashon looked at them, confusion splashed across his face. "What?"

Before he could answer, Smith appeared on the screen.

Chapter 36

Smith listened intently while the situation was explained to him through Whims's screen. Finding a balance between justice and mercy made sense, though he knew finding a balance everyone agreed to would be more than difficult. Then there was the explosion of the light that came from Tashon and destroyed Wave's weapons. What was becoming of the sage?

But it wasn't the time for such questions. He needed to focus on the problem at hand. "I don't know what the right answer is," he said. "But I'm sure there will come times when justice needs to be leaned on more than mercy, and other times, mercy more than justice. Maybe we pushed for too much mercy for the Crawler leaders. I don't know." He paused, remembering something from his past that he'd promised not to share. But those involved were dead, and he felt it could bring clarity to the discussion. "Before we left on the Ship of Nations, Sylvia almost didn't come. She had a boyfriend who was just the kind of human we were trying to get away from. He owed an enormous debt." Smith paused, feeling he was telling a story that was not his to tell. But he went on. "To pay off the debt, he forced Sylvia into a brothel. I didn't know that was why she was there until we left Earth. But it makes me think. Forcing someone to be a sex worker... I don't think I could offer mercy to someone like that."

From what he could see on Whims's screen, the crowd understood his point. People nodded, Crawlers shuffled their feet.

Atom was the first to respond, sharing her grief for what happened to Sylvia. The Singer told of how such sinister crimes had never occurred among the Singers, so she had never needed to consider what punishment would be appropriate. But she did agree that such actions deserved more justice and less mercy.

Smith realized what surprised him wasn't the absence of sex crimes in Singer history. No, what surprised him was how quickly such a crime turned Atom away from mercy. "I know many of us hoped to create a simple system of passing out merciful judgments, but I don't think that's exactly possible."

The words pained him, but he knew they were true. No race or species was perfect. If people, regardless of species, could be trusted to be kind and decent at all times, perhaps a simple form of law and government would work. But when Wave, a leader of a mostly peace-loving species murdered dozens of defenseless prisoners, the reality of the darkness that hides in all beings stared Smith in his very soul. He wished mercy could lighten that darkness for all, but Wave had shown him that it wouldn't. *Perhaps mercy will bring light to some*, he thought.

"Smith is right," Tashon said, only part of his face visible on the screen. "I've spent time meditating on these things. I do feel, in some ways, that mercy is the natural inclination of the universe. The universe gives us life and joy and beauty. But one could also say the universe also gives us death and despair and darkness. We can't have one without the other. It won't work. But I do think it's possible to create a more merciful society."

Johann spoke from off-screen. "But not everyone wants a more merciful society. Some want more justice. How do we account for that?"

"Not know," Hutsep said.

Silence, save for mutterings from the unseen crowd across the ocean. Smith waited for one of the other leaders to offer a solution. But when none came, he realized answering his question would be far more difficult than he had hoped.

"Okay," Smith said. "This affects all of us, so everyone should spend the next few days discussing and coming up with ideas. We'll hold a more official meeting soon."

"That's good," Theresa said. "In two days?"

Everyone agreed, and the screen between Whims's hands disappeared.

Smith turned around to find Minow and Yeance standing nearby, pretending not to watch him.

He walked to them. "You hear all that?"

Yeance nodded and shrugged. "Yeah. What are your thoughts, Smith? What should we do?"

Smith shook his head and look at Minow.

"I know the three want at a society full of mercy and kindness," she said. "But what you told us about Sylvia. I think we've been ignoring the darker side of all sentient beings. We need something in place for that."

"For genocidal warlords and sex criminals?" Yeance asked.

"Any violent criminal who doesn't prove they're willing to change," Smith said. "Damn it. We should've thought of that before." Smith shook his head, guilt rushing over him. He sat down on the cave floor. "How could we think it even remotely possible to instill such kindness and mercy when darkness hides everywhere?"

Yeance sat next to him. "Sometimes it doesn't even hide," he said.

"And we didn't do anything wrong, Smith," Minow said, sitting next to Yeance. "We were hoping and working for something *better*. There's nothing wrong with that."

Smith shrugged. He hadn't felt so heavy since Evalee died. But now he faced more darkness than he ever thought he would after leaving Earth. He never expected it to be easy. But now racists were holed up inside the ship. A former leader of a pacifist species had gone rogue and brutally murdered dozens of Crawlers. And his goal for a society of more kind and merciful citizens seemed to be slipping away. And why shouldn't it? Mercy had proven ineffective. Had directly led, through one perspective, to the brutal murders.

He closed his eyes. "Mercy backfired and then shit on us." Smith shook his head again, knowing he was letting the darkness overwhelm him. Knowing, too, that there's been so many times he'd fought back against the darkness, even since crashing on Aethera.

"No," Yeance said. "Wave took the opportunity mercy provided to exact overly harsh justice. It was the choice of a sentient individual that shit on us. Not mercy."

"It was the sentient individual himself," Minow said. "But that doesn't mean mercy is pointless."

"I know," Smith said. "It's just frustrating and sad that this kind of darkness is something we have to worry about."

"It's true," Yeance said. "But tell me something. If you had gotten your hands on Sylvia's old boyfriend, would you have shown mercy?"

Smith let out one joyless laugh. "Probably not. That's why Evalee never told me *why* Sylvia was there in the first place. Actually, at first we both thought she was a dancer. But when I went to find her, to convince her to leave with us on the Ship of Nations, she was at the brothel."

"And I'm sure you showed whoever else was there plenty of mercy," Yeance said with a smile.

Smith laughed softly, shaking his head. "Actually ignored the guy in front at first. Until he tried to force me out. Then I punched him."

"And grabbed Sylvia, whisking her away to safety?" Minow asked.

"No. I got knocked unconscious."

"How'd she get out?" Yeance asked.

"She left," Smith said.

Minow raised her eyebrows. "Her boyfriend let her?"

"He tried to come get her, but Evalee stopped him. Just by talking to him." He smiled at the thought of her, and was flooded again with the emptiness her absence left. "I wish she were here to help with this mess."

"The boyfriend who forced her to work there... Did the law ever do anything to him?" Yeance asked.

Smith slowly shook his head. "I don't think so. Not that I know of."

"Smith," Minow said. "I want to create a society that encourages mercy too. But do we really want one where shit like that goes unpunished?"

"I just wish we could create one where shit like that didn't happen," Smith said.

"If we lay roots of mercy and kindness," Minow said. "Maybe Aethera will be that way, some day."

With the darkness that seemed to lurk inside everyone, Smith doubted it. "Maybe," he said. "For now, let's do what we can to set up a merciful system that also, somehow, deters citizens from hurting each other."

"It feels like a paradox," Yeance said.

Minow put a hand on his knee. "But I think we could do it and still keep the same basic structure we've discussed in place." When Smith and Yeance didn't respond, she continued. "The plan has been to allow the victim to pass judgment on the aggressor, encouraging the victim to show mercy. But maybe we could set up a system that gives the victim opportunity to choose between mercy and justice. Or maybe even some combination of the two."

"So we'd let the victim decide the level of mercy or justice," Smith said. "And the amount they're willing to show will depend on the severity of the crime."

"I like the idea," Yeance said. "But how we do we prevent victims passing too harsh judgments out of anger?"

"With some type of mediator," Smith said. "Like we've discussed before. But with laws for certain crimes, stipulating minimum and maximum punishments."

"I thought you didn't want that much written controlling a merciful society," Yeance said.

"I wish we didn't have to, but" —Smith shrugged— "it's better than what's happened here. The darkness seems to require some type of law to keep the rest safe."

Minow and Yeance answered him with silence, and Smith felt it was because they knew the truth of what he said. Minutes went by in silent pondering.

Then Minow slapped a hand on the floor, the sound echoing off the stone walls. Tears filled her eyes as she rested her head on Yeance's shoulder and put a hand on her stomach. Smith realized that, more than anything, they all wanted the same thing: the best Aethera possible for future generations. That nearly all, no matter where they stood on the road between justice and mercy, had that as their main goal.

We should focus on that shared goal, Smith thought. *Not on the methods that separate us.*

Chapter 37

Tashon walked through the chill evening air with Abe and Winona. The sage found comfort in the discussion, in the break from fourth-dimensional study and the seemingly complex matters of mercy and justice.

"The Singers foretold you coming," Tashon stated it as fact, for that's how he saw it. "And a baby with you."

"That's not a question," Abe said.

"Was it supposed to be?"

Winona laughed softly. "We just expected you to be more surprised."

Tashon smiled and shrugged. "After the Fourth, nothing *surprises* me. It is amazing, though."

"Do you think the Singer Mother actually saw us in a vision?" Abe asked.

Above, clouds slowly rolled in front of the moon, making it difficult to see. But from above, Tashon had a clear enough view to ensure nothing snuck up on them.

"She might have," Tashon said.

"Do you think her prophesying it in the Singers' language somehow made *all* of this happen?" Abe asked, then smiled nervously at Winona.

Tashon stopped walking, looked at Abe and Winona, then up to the night sky. He thought of those times his emotions had been influenced by Singer notes. Could the Singer Mother's voice have been such to influence everything that led to the creation of the Ship of Nations, and after?

"It's possible, maybe," Tashon said. "What've you learned from the book?"

"Just how to read some of it," Winona said. "Then everything got bad, and we haven't read much lately."

Abe nodded. "I still want to know how we're in the book. It's just not as important as it was."

Tashon could tell not knowing bothered Abe, ate at him. But what peace could be given when one sought an understanding that might never be found?

After another minute of thinking, Tashon asked, "You want to know that your feelings for Winona are real?"

Abe flushed red. "Yeah. Or... I did, at least. I still do, but I'm not sure the answer matters at this point."

Tashon raised his eyebrows. "Really? Why?"

Winona shrugged. "I don't have any better options," she said.

"Hey," Abe said.

Both laughed, and Tashon saw in their eyes the care they had for one another. To Tashon, that was real.

"Remember when we were in Whims's influence in the yellow forest?" Tashon asked.

"How could I not?" Abe asked.

"Right. We were able to pull ourselves away from the calm he put us in," Tashon said. "Do you think you could pull yourselves out of how you feel?"

Abe and Winona looked at each other, and then looked away in thought. The moon reappeared, casting the three in a soft glow.

"No," Abe said. "I just tried. I can't change it."

"I can." Winona looked at Abe, her expression blank. "I can barely even remember who you are now."

Abe's mouth fell open. "Wh-what?"

Winona burst into a fit of laugher.

"You're terrible," Abe said.

Tashon shook his head, smiling. "She really is, Abe."

Winona let out an end of laughter sigh. "I know," she said.

Soft laughter rippled through the small group. When it died out, Tashon realized that, for a few minutes, he'd been free of all the thoughts that had been weighing on him. And as he acknowledged it, all the weight rushed back into his mind. Mercy and justice, the extremes and all the gray in between. He knew mercy couldn't exist without justice, but the balance needed to be right. They—all of Aethera—needed to do everything possible to prevent the hate-fueled murders committed by Wave.

He said goodnight to Abe and Winona, then walked as far from any sentient creature as possible. With a stone pillar towering over him and blocking the moon, he lifted himself to the Fourth.

In opposition to his mind, the Fourth was calm and still. No wind or colors blew, no shapes or structures floated by in the distance. He'd searched the above Aethera for answers and found close to nothing. Tashon felt that if he could just expand his mind, reach that much further, everything would become clear. With a wider view of the universe, he hoped the universe itself would grant him great understanding.

With a deep breath, he stretched and pulled at that piece of him that was outside of him. He focused on what he could see in the Fourth, attempting to expand his range of vision in the higher dimension as well as the lower. As he did, keeping part of his sight on the entire planet before him, the other on the Fourth, the edges of his vision widened bit by bit. And his view soon included the empty black that encompasses all planets.

And there, above the lifeless vacuum of third-dimensional space, the Fourth was completely and beautifully alive. Hundreds of beings, black and white and every shade between floated, sped or lazed about dozens of structures that defied the three-dimensional mind. A city of sorts, scattered about with the spheres and pyramids with which Tashon had become familiar. But then there were the Fourth's version of every other shape possible. A seemingly organized jumble of Fourth cubes folding into cylinders, rolling into spheres, tumbling into octahedrons.

A city similar, though immensely larger, to the one Tashon had found himself when the Ship of Nation's tesseract engine was damaged. That city had also been above the vast emptiness of third-dimensional space. For whatever reason, it seemed those in the Fourth did not congregate above or near those alive in the Third.

If there were answers to be had, that's where Tashon would get them. A long walk, especially in the Fourth. But the wind and ground remained calm, and Tashon wouldn't return to the surface of Aethera until he had some knowledge or insight to share.

He gazed in the direction of the city, but saw nothing with his naked eyes. *Doesn't matter*, he thought. *I know it's there.* And it didn't matter how long it took him to get there. Because if he didn't, he'd only return with the same ideas he'd already shared, and to him those answers were not enough.

Or are they? he wondered. He considered the question as he walked slowly and steadily to his destination. The answers he had told of the coexistence of mercy and justice, of the need for a balance between the two. And a balance between all opposites. But how to balance it? What could he do, more than give mystical half-wise explanations, to improve Aethera's future?

No, the half-formed answers he had would not work. He increased his pace, his steps confident on the unmoving ground. Within minutes, he stood over nothing but black. With no planet beneath, there was no gravity. And with no gravity, the surface on which he walked resembled a rocky terrain. Semi-translucent hills and "boulders" with angles and corners impossible in the Third.

"That's why I can't see it from here," Tashon said aloud.

He scanned left and right to find the easiest path forward, but all routes were encumbered with obstacles. The smallest shape was just taller than himself and rose at a steep angle, though it had small crack he could use for footholds and handholds. At first, it was easy, like clambering over a rock in the Third. But when he reached the extra side, the edge that could not exist in the Third, he became disoriented. After climbing up the angled vertical surface, he should have been on top of the shape. Or, in the Third he would have been. Instead, he found himself on his stomach, somewhere between vertical and horizontal, his mind unable to comprehend how to move across it.

Gravity pulled from two directions. The way he had come, and from within the shape. It was if he was stuck. But if that was the odd gravity or his confusion, he wasn't sure. *Deep breaths*, he told himself. He slowly got himself into a calm and meditative state. Nothing called to him, but he pushed the thought away easily. Then his mind reached back to Aethera, and he momentarily considered giving up on his quest.

"No," he whispered.

He focused more intently on his breathing, on the pull of gravity, the weight of his body. Of how the pull of gravity had its opposite in push, how it pulled from above and below. Through trial and error, he eventually shimmied his way up and along the surface until he rolled along, down and off the opposite edge. He hit the ground soft enough to avoid injury, but the vertigo from the fall left his head spinning. Slowing his breathing, he focused on motion and stillness. Motion and stillness.

Motion.

Stillness.

The vertigo vanished and he rose to his feet. In front him, the ground gradually sank into a shallow valley full of glowing, multifaceted crystals. He moved forward, eyes wide with the beauty in front of him. Across the valley, atop a much steeper hill than the one he now descended, stood a lone, towering structure. The same crystals that covered the valley protruded from the sides of the tower in every angle possible, creating something akin to glowing cactus. But it was a made structure, wasn't it? Tashon wondered if there was natural vegetation in the Fourth. And what had made all the structures in the city to which he walked? It made sense that the beings occupying the Fourth were the builders of all of it. But the thought of the ethereal beings building such complex buildings was difficult for Tashon to comprehend.

Or were the crystals and tower some type of organic material? When plants and animals died in the Third, did their essences also rise to the Fourth? Tashon reached the floor of the valley, weaving his way around the crystals. They seemed natural to him, but what would they have been in the Third? Or were there things natural only to the Fourth?

He mentally played between the opposites of natural and made. Was there a difference?

With a sigh, he shook his head and walked faster. It wasn't the time to get lost in thought. He cleared the valley floor and paused, staring at the climb ahead of him. Not a cliff, but more than a hill, he'd have to go up on all fours. He dropped down and climbed, moving as fast as possible against gravity's pull. The higher he got, the softer the ground became.

Gone was the firm floor he'd come to understand as the Fourth's surface. Instead, replaced by a warm and cold substance that his hand and knees sank into as he progressed ever upward. He never feared it would swallow him. No, his appendages would sink in an inch or two, never trapping him, only making it difficult to continue at a steady pace. He pulled his hand up, the ground pulling back with its dual temperature thickness. The way it pulled at Tashon's skin convinced him it would be wet, but each time he pulled a hand out, his skin was dry. By the time he was halfway up the slope, his arms and legs ached from constantly fighting against the soft ground.

He stopped to take a break, his determination fading. Did he really need a deeper understanding? What good would it do, really? And why couldn't he trust those on Aethera to figure it out themselves? In that moment, he had enough energy to pull himself back to the Third. Could he pull himself back to Aethera without moving from his spot on the hill? Maybe he could.

Or he could keep going, with no assurance that he would find what he sought.

Yes, he would keep going, despite the uncertainty.

On and up he went. At some point, he realized it was getting harder and harder to pull back out of the ground. His muscles shook from the strain, and he wanted nothing more than to let his entire body drop to the ground. But if he did that, he was certain he would be stuck to the ground forever. So he moved on, his pace ever slowing, his desire to continue ever waning.

Yet, on he pushed until, exhausted and trembling, he pushed himself onto the top of the hill and crawled until the ground once again became hard. He collapsed at the foot of the tower.

An immense apathy filled him, the desire he had so recently felt, washing away. The tower with all its protrusions loomed over him, its various colors glinting and blinking in unknowable patterns.

Apathy. To simply stop caring, let the concerns of Aethera's future plague his mind no more. A certain bliss in that idea, and an even greater bliss at the thought of laying where he was and never moving again.

For what could he do to blend mercy and justice in a way that pleased everyone? What could anyone do to make that a reality?

It's an impossible reality, Tashon thought. *Too many opinions. Too many variables.*

The tower seemed to grow up and out as he lay there, though he barely noticed it.

All he could offer those on Aethera was partial understanding of a higher meditation and brief stints of calm peace through meditation. Nothing extraordinary, nothing they couldn't live without.

A black form appeared above him, emanating a deep and consuming darkness that he hadn't felt since his first time in the Fourth. The dark shape descended and enveloped Tashon, filling him with the darkness he'd thought had gone from the Fourth. Nothing but heavy sorrow and deep uselessness filled his soul and he went limp. How could he find the answers to solve Aethera's problems? It was impossible. He might gain some wisdom or insight, but nothing that would sink into the hearts of all on Aethera. Nothing that would produce real and lasting change. *Pointless*, he thought. *They'll all decide to think and live how they want to. My input doesn't matter. Getting half-cracked answers isn't worth this effort.* The darkness gripped tighter, making it hard to breathe. Yet the tightness around him felt somehow comfortable. Giving into something that would make it impossible for him to move forward or fight for anything ever again seemed like the most logical decision Tashon could make.

Or was it?

No, Tashon thought. Then, *Yes. I'm so tired.* He closed his eyes, succumbing to the comforting cool of the darkness. He hugged himself tightly, and his hand brushed against the warm necklace around his neck. *The moths*, he thought. Warmth and light spread into his fingertips, his palm, his forearm and then all the way through his body, slowly peeling the darkness off him. The darkness lifted into the air and flew off.

Tashon opened his eyes and stared up at the tower. Each crystal on its surface split into two, as if cells reproducing. The tower then duplicated itself, and Tashon found himself in shadow. Something about the new tower, which stood farther from him than the original, seemed more appealing. Tashon didn't know what it was, and part of him wanted to stand up, walk to it and discover how it differed. The other part of him wanted to remain where he was.

Motion and stillness.

Desire and apathy.

"Is there ever one end of two extremes that's always right?" he asked himself aloud.

A shadow of light flashed on top of the far tower.

Tashon sat and looked up. A form lifted off the new tower and gracefully descended. A spiraling being of sharp edges and smooth curves, of blacks and whites and grays. Spherical, cubical and conical all at once. By the time it stopped, a dozen feet off the ground, it was both larger than the towers and smaller than Tashon.

And for the first time since being attacked by Aleron's monster, Tashon truly questioned if what he saw was real or only in his mind.

But one can still gain great understanding from beings that exist only in the mind.

The being hovered, every particle of its form in constant motion, the most beautiful sight Tashon had ever beheld.

"What of the balance between justice and mercy?" Tashon asked.

Two cubes of opposing colors formed on one side of the living mass. They spiraled around each other, one chasing the other. They stopped and reversed roles, the chaser becoming the chased. Back and forth they went, at times nearly colliding and other times so far apart Tashon could only see one at a time. After a few minutes of analyzing the movement, Tashon noticed the colors changing on the cubes. When one cube neared the other, each would slowly become more the color of the other. When they grew apart, they would return to their original colors. If they were to ever touch, Tashon assumed they would each become the same color.

But after hours or days or, perhaps, even weeks, the two never touched.

And, eventually, Tashon realized he'd been given the answer he sought.

Whether by an exalted being or his own mind, he had no idea.

PART FOUR

Chapter 38

Abe and Winona sat in the shadow of a half-collapsed dome, the Singer book open on the ground. They stared at the page of emotionally-charged symbols in an attempt to determine its meaning. But Abe couldn't focus. The need he had felt to understand Mother's prophecy as the Singer language had faded to a want. A curiosity focused more on improving relations with the Singers than on deciphering the source of his feelings for Winona.

And after Wave's massacre, it seemed less important. And the three species could communicate whether Abe could read the Singer language or not.

Abe rubbed his eyes and looked at the cloudless sky. "Any ideas on mercy and justice?"

Winona closed the book and looked at him. "Maybe. I want mercy and, in turn, kindness, to be central to Aethera's future. But is there such a thing as too kind?"

"I don't know," Abe said. "But what is kindness? When I tackled Cixin off Teacher, I was protecting Teacher. What I did was a kindness *for Teacher*. But it wasn't kind to Cixin."

"But it needed to be done," Winona said.

Abe nodded. "It did. And it's the perfect example of why mercy can't always be the first option."

Winona clicked her tongue. "Unfortunately, justice and punishment are going to have to be a part of Aethera's future."

"Yeah," Abe said. "Especially for Wave. And Cixin. It's just... Why do sentients do shit like this to each other?"

Winona blew out a long breath, shaking her head. "Fear. Hate. Ignorance. Maybe something we don't even have a word for. Some just seem more prone to violence than understanding. Anger than forgiveness. But I think the point is to create a society where at least more of us naturally go to mercy and kindness."

"It is," Abe said. "But the problem is figuring out what the hell to do with those like Wave and Cixin."

"Let's talk about solutions then," Winona said. "Instead of talking about all the shitty problems."

Abe stood up and held his hand out. "Okay. Let's walk though."

She grabbed his hand and stood up. They walked slowly, Abe trying to enjoy the warm afternoon sun.

"Can't we just make it law to show mercy?" Abe asked.

Winona laughed softly. "If only. I don't think it would work."

Abe shrugged. "I know."

They kept walking. No ideas came to Abe. He understood the importance of both mercy and justice. But how to incorporate both into a governmental system, in a way that promotes mercy? For a moment, Abe missed when he was obsessing over understanding the Singer prophecy. For that he at least had a plan to reach understanding: learn to read Singer. But he saw no way to understand the complexities between mercy and justice, nor how to put them into practice.

Winona squeezed his hand and stopped walking. "Abe, you know we don't have to figure this out ourselves, right?"

"I know," he said. "You're right." He smiled at Winona, filled with a warmth he couldn't describe. "I love you," he said. And he knew, somehow, that the feeling was his own.

Winona kissed him long and soft, then pulled away. "I love *you*."

Abe leaned in and kissed her firmly. Their lips parted, their tongues gently playing on the other's. Abe slid his hand under and up her shirt.

She put a hand on his chest and pushed him away. "Abe, you're not getting me pregnant, remember?"

Abe whipped his hand out of her shirt, then laughed. "You're right. I'm sorry."

"No, don't be sorry. Let's be smart."

Abe took deep, slow breaths, trying to slow his heart rate and calm his body. "Of course," he said. "I do love you."

"Yes you do," she said. "I love you too."

***

Rain poured from the night sky. Abe sat with Winona, Rosa, Londey and Lollawk within a dome. Around them, some talked and others slept.

"Rosa, where's Tashon?" Abe asked.

Rosa shrugged. "I looked everywhere. He must be in the Fourth."

"How's long since you've seen him, though?" Abe asked.

"This morning," Rosa said. "He's never been gone this long."

"Are you worried?" Winona asked.

Rosa shook her head, but Abe could tell she was only trying to hide her concern. He decided to pretend he believed her.

"Lollawk," Londey said. "Wave and Fylin are imprisoned, right?"

"Yes, yes," Lollawk said. "All restrained."

Londey nodded. "What are we going to do with them?"

"That's the question," Rosa said. "What do we do with all further maniacs who would massacre the defenseless?"

"And commit lesser crimes," Winona said.

"Yes, yes," Lollawk said. "Mercy... justice."

"What system can we put in place to encourage and increase mercy and kindness?" Rosa asked.

"Question," Lollawk said. "Why one system only?"

Rosa's eyebrows shot up. "Because... we want all Aethera to be a kind and merciful planet."

"Not all want it," Lollawk said.

"Of course we do," Rosa said. "Are you saying some want Aethera to be unkind?"

"No, no," Lollawk said. "Many say safety over kindness."

"And they're not completely wrong," Londey said. "What if some of the Crawlers we showed mercy to had gotten free? How much damage would they have caused because we couldn't stomach a harsher punishment?"

Abe looked at the floor. Was it naïve and soft to want to offer mercy? Was it weak not to pass harsh judgments?

"But mercy is meant to provide opportunity for change," Winona said.

"I know that's the goal," Londey said. "But it's not going to change everyone. I want everyone to be kind and understanding, but I also want my grandchildren to be safe from the likes of Wave."

"And Wave did what he did because he was seeking justice, not mercy," Rosa said.

Abe began understanding both sides, and he wasn't sure he wanted to. It only made decoding which side to be on more difficult. But did he have to be strictly on one side or the other? "Rosa," he said, "Wave was seeking extreme justice. We would never set up a system that allowed something like that."

"That's a good point," Winona said, smiling at him.

Rosa sighed. "It is. But where does it leave us?"

"Two systems," Lollawk said. "One more mercy, one more justice. Work together."

The group looked at one another, and none objected to the idea.

Chapter 39

As soon as Smith finished talking to those across the ocean, he made his way back to the ship with Whims and Crawler Klen. He hoped he could talk to Hiloy, that he could somehow mend the divide that had grown between them. And convince all in the ship that they need not fear the Singers.

Smith found Hiloy just outside the ship, pacing up and down the clearing, muttering angrily to himself. Humans and Crawlers stood at the open airlock, talking among themselves and passing items back and forth that Smith didn't recognize.

"No, no," Klen said quietly.

"What?" Smith asked.

"Those Crawlers weapons," Klen said.

"Hiloy!" Smith stepped in front of the pacing man, forcing him to stop.

"Oh, Smith." Hiloy's eyes darted back and forth, his fingers twitched. "You've come to reason. You've come to join our fight."

"What the hell are you doing?"

"Oh, we're going to the caves. We're taking the power from the Singers." Hiloy walked to the airlock and grabbed a white rectangle with a thin handle. "By force. Before their notes can force us to stop."

"Hiloy. Strong Earth stopped the fighting in the ship," Smith said. "There was no violent intent."

"You give them names as if they deserve to be among us," Hiloy said. "And how do you know there was no ill intent? The humans stopped fighting at the sound of the notes, but the Crawlers did not. Many of my people were severely injured by Crawlers as they stood still, forced to pacifism."

"You have Crawlers with you too," Smith said. "They did the same to my people."

"Yes, that is true." Hiloy shrugged and examined his weapon. "But the other truth is still truth."

"What truth?" Smith asked.

"The Singers must not be allowed to...."

Hiloy kept talking, but Smith stopped listening. They would try to take the caves, that had become obvious. Smith looked at Whims and Klen, and the three ran for the caves. As they entered the tree line, Smith took one quick glance behind him. Hiloy and his soldiers charged after them.

"Shit! Faster," he called.

They ran on, kicking dirt and leaves up behind them. Just as Smith thought he would collapse, they burst through the door, closed, locked it and braced it with their bodies.

Silence, save for the sounds of heaving breaths.

An explosion from outside shook the door, but the three held firm.

"The hell was that?" Smith asked.

Whims had no idea.

"Is Crawler weapon," Klen said.

Smith braced against another explosion. "Shit," he said.

Dozens of smokies rushed down the hall toward them. Whims sang notes of instruction, and the smokies formed a wall of black that stretched from floor to ceiling, leaving a hole in the bottom just large enough for them to get through. Another burst shook the door. Then another, and a crack split across its red surface.

The three ran from the door and through the black wall. At Whims's command, the hole filled in.

"Whims," Smith said. "Go get anyone who will fight."

Whims hesitated.

"Go!"

The Singer turned and ran down the hall.

"We have more than they do," Smith said to Klen. "If they get in, we can beat them."

"Too many not want fight," Klen said.

"What?"

"All that fought in ship now promise pacifism," Klen responded. "Will use smokies to keep enemy out, but not harm enemy."

Smith shook his head and swore under his breath. He respected their commitment, to a degree. But with death possibly storming down the hall any minute, his fear convinced him the pacifists had something wrong with them. How could they turn against their natural survival instinct? A self-mastery superior to any Smith thought he could achieve. But did Smith desire that type of self-mastery? Would it have allowed him to show up at the brothel in an attempt to save Sylvia?

Another explosion shook the walls, and the sound of rocks tumbling to the floor sounded on the other side of the smokie's barrier. Shouts and footsteps followed.

"Shit in hell," Hiloy's voice rang out. "Can any of your weapons get through this?"

Smith took a deep breath. "Hiloy!"

The other side went quiet, then hushed unintelligible voices move through the makeshift wall. Smith looked at Klen. The Crawler was silent and motionless.

"Hiloy," Smith said again. "There are a lot in here who aren't going to fight back. Are you planning on massacring them?"

"They're not all pacifists," another voice answered. "Look at Wave. And the weapon the five created. And... that bitch forcing us to stop fighting."

"Strong Earth did that to *promote* pacifism," Smith said.

A Crawler hissed and clicked. Klen clacked back.

"Smith," Hiloy said. "We don't trust them. What if Strong Earth and Wave worked together? They could render us motionless and murder each of us without any resistance."

"One Singer out of a thousand broke the promise," Smith said.

"And others have controlled us," a woman said. "Manipulated us."

"And we will show them that manipulation will not be tolerated," Hiloy said.

A Crawler clicked again, and a glowing green square appeared on the wall of smokies.

Klen hissed. "No, no."

"What?" Smith said.

White smoke swirled out of the square as more formed across the wall.

"Run, run," Klen said, turning and stomping down the hall.

Smith bolted after the Crawler. Something popped from the wall and a small white disk flew past Smith's head, imbedding itself in one of Klen's legs. The Crawler faltered but did not fall, adjusting its four-legged gait to account for the injury. More *pops*, more discs flew after them. One clipped the top of Smith's ear and he instinctively slammed his hand against the wound. *At least it's my bad ear*, he thought. A few more sliced him and Klen, but none stuck into flesh.

The popping ended seconds after it started. Smith stopped to catch his breath and turned around. Thin lines of white smoke swiveled up to the ceiling as the green squares faded and disappeared.

"Can they get through?" Smith asked.

"Maybe," Klen said.

Whims ran toward them, followed by a long line of humans, Crawlers and Singers. *Singers?* Smith wondered. *I thought they weren't going to fight.* The hall was packed in tight, making it hard for Smith to pick out individuals. He saw Yeance, and his heart sank. *What if something were to happen, and Minow was left to raise a child without him?* Smith shook the thought away. They had enough bodies, he told himself. And the smokie barrier was still holding.

Jine, a staunch, white-haired woman, pushed her way to the front of the crowd. "Can they make it in?" she asked.

"Think so," Klen said.

"Do we have any weapons?" Smith asked.

Jine shook her head. "No weapons."

"What?"

Whims sang that the caves were a place of peace.

"No fight here," a Crawler said.

"Then what's your plan?" Smith asked.

A boom shook the walls. A bubble formed in the barrier, trying to force its way forward. It stretched until Smith thought it would burst, and then disappeared, the barrier intact.

"We stand our ground," Jine said.

And the mass pushed past Smith, forming a tight, tangled web of bodies that reached from wall to wall and over fifty bodies deep. Klen clicked quietly and walked deeper into caves.

Whims sang a single note, and in unison all lowered to their knees, giving Smith and Klen a clear view of the barrier they hoped would hold strong. Then, as if Smith's subconscious became aware of the significance of what was about to happen, his mind captured everything in horrifying detail.

A sound like the cracking of thunder ripped through the hall. The black wall blew out, sending metal rods careening through the air. One hit a woman in the head and she collapsed. Two Singers picked her up and carried her to the back of the crowd, the space they had occupied filling in almost immediately.

Projectiles flew through the air. White disks, giant thorns and metal spheres shot out with no regard to the defenseless pacifists. A white disk sunk deep into June's temple. A thorn impeded itself in a Crawler's eye, then exploded, covering those nearby in blood and brain matter. Yet still, they stood their ground. Flesh burst and bodies dropped. Smith tried to push through the crowd, wanting to do something to end the massacre. But they wouldn't let him through.

Hiloy ran forward, disk after disk flying from the weapon in his hand. The rage on his face was that of an animal: bloodshot eyes, saliva dripping from his mouth as a primal scream rose from deep within him. On either side of him, screeching Crawlers with their own weapons and their own faces of twisted madness.

A Singer voice rose above the screaming and the pounding of weapons. A melody of peace and acceptance.

Hiloy and his soldiers charged into the kneeling crowd, killing as if unaware they refused to fight back.

More Singer voices joined the first, the melody overpowering all else.

Hiloy faltered and stopped in front of Whims. The Singer looked up and met his eyes.

"No," Hiloy whispered, lifting the weapon to Whims's forehead.

Whims held steady, his melody rising and shifting to incorporate a new meaning: forgiveness. No matter what Hiloy chose to do, Whims forgave him.

Then all went silent. Smith softly shook his head. A tear rolled down his cheek. His heart skipped and his breath caught as he waited for Hiloy's decision.

Hiloy's hand trembled as he looked into Whims's eyes, and for a moment, Smith imagined Hiloy would make the right choice.

"No." Hiloy pressed the end of the weapon into Whims's skin and fired.

The back of his skull blew out, the disk sinking into the chest of the woman that knelt behind him. Both bodies went limp. A scream of pure rage poured from Smith, and he knew if he were closer to Hiloy he would have beaten the man to death.

Instead, he stood there screaming as the Singers resumed their chorus of peace, acceptance and forgiveness. How could they willingly accept such depravity? *Why* did they so willingly accept it?

Hiloy slowly lifted his gaze and stared at Smith. The look of insane rage was replaced with one of confusion, as if Hiloy had just awoke from a dream. And, in a sense, perhaps he had. A dream in which Singers couldn't be trusted, in which the only way to feel safe from them was to murder them. But if one lived within such a dream reality, what would he do when the truth of what he he'd done dawned on him? He slowly turned around, eyes wide as they took in the bodies and the blood, all from the side that refused to fight. His mouth moved, but no sounds came out. With slow, mechanical movements, he lifted the weapon and pointed it at his head.

And fired.

***

Smith stood in a housing corridor on the ship, eyes wet with tears. He wanted to scream at everyone locked inside the housing units. Tell them of the stupidity of their fear and hate. Ask them if they felt better now, after what they'd done. Ask if their actions had assuaged their fear, lessened whatever pain they were feeling. But he knew the answer was that it hadn't.

As he walked past the prisoners, one in each unit, he heard the sobs and the mumbling of apology. And in others angry shouts of those who were unable to accomplish their goal. As soon as Hiloy killed himself, a horde of smokies surrounded the attackers and trapped them in a black cube. They had run out of ammunition for the weapon that broke through the smokies the first time, and it seemed the smokies knew it.

"All of you idiots," he whispered and shook his head.

A song of regret rang out to his left and a shout of anger to his right.

"And that's the difference between those who earn mercy and those who don't."

He left the ship to find a Singer. It was time to tell the other continent that even more murders had been committed.

Chapter 40

Tashon awoke at the base of the tower. The being he had seen, or perhaps only imagined, was gone, as was the second tower. He stood up, his head and his body invigorated. In the distance to his right lay the city of impossible shapes. He could find all the answers he could want in that city, but it was no longer his destination. He had the answers he sought.

With a smile, he turned to his left and looked down the hill. Trying to walk down would be treacherous, so he sat and scooted forward until his legs hung down. He pushed forward and gravity took over, pulling him down through the soft ground fast enough to avoid sinking. As he slid faster, he became suddenly and immensely aware of the smallest details. The wind blew his hair from all sides, and Tashon felt how two strands pulled away from his scalp in the same direction. He felt how the ground gradually became harder as he slid farther down, felt the smallest of bumps rush underneath him.

He stopped as soon as he hit the bottom and somersaulted onto his back. Laughter swam from his lungs as he lay there, watching the wind gently blow all around him. He inhaled, and learned that each color of wind had a different smell, none of which had its likeness in the Third. Smells entirely new.

If only he could lay there forever.

"No."

He rolled over and pushed himself up, taking in how amazing it was to look *down* at the blackness of third-dimensional space from a higher plane. With a smile, he walked through the field of crystal-like growths, this time noticing how light reflected off each face the shapes.

"Light?" he said, looking up. "Where's the light coming from?"

He realized that in all his time in the Fourth, not once had it been dark. But it was a question for another time. He contentedly walked out from among the crystals, carefully clambered down the oddly-angled boulders, and caught his first glimpse of Aethera for the first time in what he knew was just under thirty hours.

The longest he'd ever spent in the Fourth, yet it didn't bother him. *Nothing* seemed to bother him except, if only slightly, the fact that nothing bothered him. Shapes appeared ahead of him, just above Aethera. He knew them to be living beings of some sort, and excitement swelled in his chest.

Had Laos returned? Or Evalee? He'd even be glad to see the Singer Mother. He drew closer, and his heart dropped. It was the essence of Whims, surrounded by twenty-seven others, each glowing light-gray or brighter. Singers, humans and Crawlers all recently gone from the Third.

He walked to Whims, the smile gone from his face. "What happened?"

Whims told of segregation and of a fight that was stopped by melody. Then of a massacre that they attempted to stop with pacifism, acceptance and mercy.

"But it didn't work," Tashon said.

The essence of a woman joined Whims. *"But it did,"* she said to Tashon's mind. *"They stopped. Had we fought back, they would've killed many more."*

Tashon nodded. To a point, she was right. But twenty-eight sentients still had to sacrifice themselves for the attack to stop. And what good did it really do? He examined each individual essence, and sensed that none held a grudge against those who killed them. They were content with the fact that their lives in the Third were over.

Whims's entire essence smiled at Tashon, sending him compassion and gratitude.

"Thankful for what?" Tashon asked.

"You taught us how death is not the end," the woman said.

Tashon smiled and nodded, grateful for their gratitude, glad to know his words had eased their transition from one dimension to the next.

Whims swished back and forth, and then asked Tashon where they were meant to go.

Tashon shrugged and shook his head. "I've never figured out for sure where everyone goes. But there's some sort of city that way." Tashon pointed. "There are hundreds of others there, at least."

One by one, the newcomers drifted toward the city, each bidding farewell and thanking Tashon in their own way. He watched them go until they were out of sight. When he turned around, he jumped at the appearance of another being, this one small and emanating immense darkness. Tashon stepped back, memories of Aleron's shadows rushing through his mind.

But the being didn't move, didn't even seem to notice him. It floated there, head down and slowing spinning around. Tashon took a cautious a step forward. Still, the being didn't react. Another step closer, and Tashon became certain it was the essence of a human.

But which human? All who died in the caves had done so in peace and forgiveness. None had exuded the immense despair that radiated from the being before him. Though about the despair felt... familiar. A mix of the despair the once embodied Laos, and that had once filled Tashon in those moments he considered suicide.

Then it clicked.

Tashon closer. "You tried to get rid of all the Singers," he said.

The being turned to Tashon. "*I led the attack.*"

The words themselves created a flurry of billowing black that momentarily obscured the being. But where Aleron's monster had been filled with rage, this being was filled with guilt and sorrow. Tashon felt no fear of the darkness, nor anger at the being. Instead, he was filled with the inexplicable desire to provide comfort.

"What's your name?" Tashon asked.

A short pause, then, "*Hiloy. But why should the sage care who I am?*"

A slight frown crossed Tashon's face. "I almost killed myself once."

"*And I went through with it.*" The words were bitter.

"I'm sorry. I didn't mean to condescend. I mean to say, I've felt something of the despair you felt."

A laugh burst from the darkness. "*Because you killed one man in self-defense?*"

Tashon opened his mouth to speak. No words came to mind.

"I heard your story of how you killed one man who would've killed you. Of how you befriended him once he was here. But I killed dozens of defenseless innocents as they knelt on the ground."

Tashon took a deep breath. "So did Laos—the man I killed—on the Ship of Nations. He killed men and women who only wanted to live out a happy life on the ship. He fought to destroy his *entire species.*"

Hiloy twisted and wretched. Tashon thought he might be crying, but wasn't sure what that looked like in the Fourth.

"And he wasn't stuck in one place when he got here," Tashon said. "He improved. Became better."

"How?"

"First, he forgave me for killing him."

Hiloy screamed, sending particles and strings of darkness flying out in all directions.

And Tashon realized the difficulty Hiloy would have in following that advice. Laos was able to begin improving by first forgiving someone else. But Hiloy would have to first forgive himself, and Tashon knew forgiving oneself could be immensely more difficult than forgiving another. So how could he provide comfort to Hiloy?

He remembered what Whims had told him. "Did you feel Whims's forgiveness?"

Hiloy's form sagged, black despair dripping to the ground. He didn't respond.

Maybe it didn't matter if Hiloy had felt the forgiveness. And, Tashon realized, Hiloy probably didn't believe he'd been forgiven anyway. He most likely thought it was an attempt at manipulation. Tashon walked to Hiloy and sat down, deciding Hiloy just needed company.

A breeze gently blew past them, bringing with it a comforting warmth. Below, on Aethera, a row of sentients emerged from the caves, carrying the bodies of the murdered. Tashon's heart dropped again, and he looked at Hiloy, feeling no hatred or anger for him. It was obvious the man regretted what he'd done, and was that not a reason to offer mercy? And where was justice? Nowhere to be found, not hovering in the Fourth waiting to punish the wicked. The only possible justice he saw was the pain Hiloy was putting himself through as he tried to come to terms with what he'd done.

"Hiloy, if you could go back in time, would you do it again?"

"I hope not. I almost stopped it. A few times, I thought that I should stop it. I should have stopped it, Sage."

Tashon inhaled and nodded. "Yes. It wasn't right, what you did. But... you did it out of fear. Out of a desire to protect humanity."

"Mostly fear, Sage. I should've accepted the Singers. But their language terrified me."

"I know, Hiloy," Tashon said. "What you did was terrible, but —"

"No, that's it. What I did was terrible."

"But your life isn't over. You're not gone from existence. You can move forward. Progress. Improve."

"Again, how?"

Tashon sighed. "I don't know. But there's a city, or something, that way."

"Others are there?"

"Yes."

"The ones I killed?"

"Yes. Others too."

Hiloy silently hung in the air.

Tashon looked down to the Third. Grieving had begun, the dead placed in the clearing the way they had been before. He considered going down, leaving Hiloy by himself. But they didn't need him to grieve. He felt he needed to stay with Hiloy, to show Hiloy not all was lost. That despite all he'd done, Hiloy was still a living being deserving of compassion. But Tashon knew he could say nothing to help the man.

So he sat, watching the gentle breeze, noticing how each color felt different on his skin. Some more soft than hard, others more rough than smooth. Some felt wet, others barely noticeable, as if they could disappear at any moment. And he wondered if life in the Fourth would ever feel as fleeting as life in the Third. Tashon believed souls could move to higher dimensions. But what caused that progression? Was it another type of death, or a transition of choice?

"Sage, why are you still here?"

Tashon thought for a moment. "So that you're not alone."

"Thank you, Sage."

Tashon nodded, but didn't know what to say. He'd only done what he felt he should. "You're welcome."

"The city's that way?"

"Yes."

"I think I'm ready to go."

"Are you sure?"

"No. But I want to see it. And maybe I can find help there."

"I think you will."

"I hope so."

Hiloy slowly floated away, still dark with despair. But Tashon thought it was the slightest shade brighter.

Chapter 41

Yet again, Abe was ripped apart by the news from the Singer continent. First Lioness and now Whims, dead. Murdered out of hate and fear. And everyone there had simply knelt and let it happen. Abe couldn't decide if he was amazed or angry with them. Whims had journeyed with them to the Crawler land, had kept them fed and warm when their future wasn't certain.

He rolled onto his side and looked at Winona. Somehow, she'd fallen asleep. Abe gently kissed her forehead and stood up. Everyone else in the dome was asleep, or pretending to be. After one last glance at Winona, he walked out of the dome and into the brisk night air, quickly finding a step to sit on. Others were scattered about the stairs, alone or in small groups. Abe didn't know if he wanted to be alone or not. He didn't think either one would make him feel better.

"Damn it," he whispered, rubbing his eyes.

Why did it keep ending in death? On the Ship of Nations, death was always reserved for the elderly who gracefully and peacefully passed on. But from the moment they landed on Aethera, death had come swift, harsh and soaked in blood. He'd seen what felt like ten times the amount of death he'd only heard of during all his years on the ship. Pointless, soul crushing death. And what could he do about it?

"Abe," a voice said.

Abe looked up. "Hey, Johann."

The bearded man sat down. "You all right?"

Abe shook his head.

"You were close with Whims."

"Yeah," Abe said.

"So what're we going to do?" Johann asked.

"What?"

Johann scratched his beard. "About justice and mercy."

"That doesn't seem that important right now," Abe said. "There were more killings, Johann. Whims, Lioness — they're dead. Justice and mercy can't bring them back."

"It's more important than ever," Johann said.

"I'm so tired, Johann. I thought mercy was the right way. But my friends keep getting *murdered*." As he said it, Abe's grief morphed into rage. "Why the hell is this happening? It's *bullshit*. My mom. My aunt. Two of my closest friends. I just...." He huffed and stopped talking.

"Abe," Johann said. "Whims used his last breaths to forgive his killer. Wouldn't you say forgiveness when none is deserved is the same as mercy?"

Abe sighed and closed his eyes. Johann was right. It was mercy. But that mercy had gotten Whims killed. And, as far as he understood it, Lioness died trying to convince Wave to offer mercy to the Crawler leaders.

Johann looked up at the sky. "And what are we going to do with the ones who attacked the caves? Mercy? Justice? Something in between? Or maybe something different."

"Different?"

"Vengeance, perhaps," Johann said.

"Like Wave," Abe said.

Johann nodded. "It's tempting, isn't it?"

Abe shrugged. He was heartbroken and angry, but not homicidal. "I don't think so. I get why none of them fought back, I do. And maybe it even saved some lives."

"Maybe it did," Johann said. "But, damn. What do you think should happen to them?"

"Hiloy thought he deserved death," Abe said.

"What do *you* think?"

Abe looked at Johann. "What do you think?"

Johann held his gaze, and then laughed softly. "Not sure, really. The first question is, do any of them regret it? Is there a willingness for change, for restitution?"

"If they know a willingness could give them a softer punishment, couldn't they just lie?" Abe asked.

"They could," Johann said. "We'd still keep an eye on them, of course."

"Right. But what does this mean for the system overall?"

"I don't know. I want it to be a simple system, but I don't see how it can be," Johann said.

"Me neither, especially since a lot of others are going to push for harsher justice."

Johann stood up and stretched. "Lollawk talked about one system of mercy and another of justice, working together."

Abe nodded. "It could work."

"I saw him go down into the garden, I think. Want to come?"

"No," Abe said. "I just want to be alone."

Johann smiled and patted his shoulder. "Okay. Come find us later."

"Okay."

Johann disappeared inside the dome.

Abe clasped his hands around the back of his head and hid his face with his elbows. The man who had killed Whims was dead, but knowing that didn't make Abe feel any better. There was still a group out there who thought the Singers shouldn't exist. And Abe didn't think he could trust any of them to change. Not enough to give them the opportunity for change. But that wasn't mercy, was it? He didn't want them out like the Crawler leaders were. He didn't want them executed, either.

A scream erupted from his throat, then he dropped his head in his lap. After a few minutes of silence, a hand pressed against his shoulder. He looked up and Winona was sitting there, a smile on her lips and a sadness in her eyes.

He smiled back.

"I was going to ask if you're okay," she said.

"None of us are okay." He wrapped his arm around her and pulled her close.

A shout rang out from inside the dome. Abe and Winona ran inside as the shouts turned into laughter. And there, in front of the thrones, stood Tashon. Rosa hugged him, then Abe and Winona followed suit, embracing the sage.

Once the greetings were done, Tashon asked everyone to quiet down. "Let's get the others on-screen," he said. "I've had some ideas in the Fourth."

***

Abe sat with Winona and the rest of the continent's populace on the steps of the dome, straining up at Tashon and Teacher. The sage stood in front of the door. The Singer's screen was out, showing the faces of Smith and Klen. But Abe was sure all eyes were focused solely on the Sage. Something had happened to Tashon. He seemed taller and stronger, yet calmer and more humble than the previous day. As if an invisible but recognizable light surrounded him.

Tashon smiled and his eyes sparkled. "I went to the Fourth to find clarity. Everyone was fighting about justice and mercy. And we needed to figure something out. But I'm going to tell it backward. On my way back, walking through the Fourth to Aethera, I saw the essences of Whims and all who were killed. I talked with them."

Hushed whispers spread through the crowd. A soft wave of relief spread through Abe knowing that Whims wasn't completely gone. But just as with the others he'd lost, knowing they were in the Fourth didn't fill the void their absences created.

"I talked with them. They're all okay. Content, and they've forgiven Hiloy and the others for what they did. I told them where I thought they should go. A city. But then...." Tashon paused and took a deep breath. "After they left, I found Hiloy."

Louder murmurings poured from the listeners. Exclamations of anger and confusion.

"That bastard," someone said.

Tashon turned to the source of the voice. "No." He shook his head. "He was distraught. Burdened with guilt that I think few of us could even understand. What he did *was* wrong, and I'll never say it wasn't. But, seeing him there, visibly drenched in despair for what he'd done, I couldn't pass judgment on him."

Someone huffed. "I could have."

Abe thought that he could have too. Hiloy had led the attack that killed twenty-eight unarmed and peaceful sentients. But what good would he do by passing judgment? *None*, he thought.

"He showed regret," Tashon said. "Were he still here, I think he would've worked to change and to repair the damage he caused. And based on what many of us have said, we would have offered Hiloy some sort of mercy because of that. We should consider this when deciding punishment for the rest."

Abe shook his head. Tashon stood up there, appearing to have gained years of wisdom in less than a day. And so confident in the words he spoke that he was unfazed by the concerns and doubts of others. Abe found himself wishing he had that kind of conviction. He did firmly believe in kindness and mercy, but knowing that others like Cixin questioned it frustrated and angered him.

Tashon continued. "But before I spoke with Hiloy and Whims, I went looking for answers. To figure out how to balance justice and mercy. I walked through the Fourth until only space was below me. I can't really explain what I saw. But I learned that the way we've been looking at mercy and justice isn't quite right. It's not two sides of the same coin, not even to extreme ends of a road. It's more complex, more *fluid* than that. Naturally, these two extremes play off each other. Yes, I do think justice and mercy are natural forces. Concepts that exist in the universe whether or not we acknowledge them. And we try to balance them, decide the right way to put these concepts to use. But...there is no one right way.

"Like I said, they are fluid. Ever changing. At times, we could consider them two ends of a road, at others merely two pieces leaping and dancing around each other. Or maybe in a moment they're motionless, one staring at the other."

"What makes them move and change?" Rosa asked from the front of the crowd.

Tashon smiled. "That was a bit... unclear. But they move, I think, every time someone acts."

"So they control what happens to us after each action?" another asked. "Kinda like fate?"

Tashon shook his head. "No. Fate doesn't exist here or in the Fourth. It's more like the universe is somehow aware of each action we make, and justice and mercy move to indicate how the universe perceives that action and the sentient."

Abe raised his hand. "So what does it mean for us? What do we do with this?"

"Right," Tashon said. "I think that with each case we face, we should try to understand where mercy and justice are, as forces, for whatever action is in question."

"How the hell would we do that?" a woman asked.

"Discussion. With each other, with the criminal, with the victim. Do our best to pick the best punishment."

Scoffs and laughter, agreements and soft cheers.

A man stood up. "But what about law? Does that mean there wouldn't be any laws specific to crimes?"

"Yes," Tashon said. "The law would be the acknowledgment that all humans—all sentients—can change and are deserving of some degree of mercy and compassion."

"So you're still saying mercy is more important than justice?" the man said.

"I'm saying that the universe itself places more importance on mercy. If it didn't, how would any of us still be here?"

The man sat down, obviously not convinced.

Abe looked around the crowd, listened to the whispers, watched the nodding and shaking of heads. Perhaps Tashon had convinced some, but the populace was still divided.

Lollawk clicked loudly. "Not all agree. Need two systems. One mercy, one justice."

Tashon looked Lollawk in the eye and smiled. "I like that idea."

Chapter 42

Smith ran a hand through his hair as he stared at the Singer screen in the center of the cavern. Lollawk's suggestion *did* make sense, but how would they make it work?

"Atom? Hutsep? Theresa? What do you think?"

The view on the screen shifted to show the Singer and the Crawler.

Atom sang her agreement.

"I am," Theresa said.

"Yes, yes," Lollawk said. "Wait. Talk with Ulot." Lollawk disappeared from the screen, and two distinct Crawler voices chattered back and forth.

Smith looked around the cavern, nodding and smiling at those who caught his gaze. Yeance left Minow's side and joined Smith.

"What're you thinking, Smith?"

"It's not a bad idea," Smith said. "But how would it work? Two systems within one larger system, or two independent systems? Two branches of a single system?"

"I don't know what Lollawk is thinking, but—"

Lollawk came back on the screen. "Ulot want lead system justice, with human and Singer."

"Okay," Smith said. "I think this is a good idea. But is anyone against it?"

No one answered.

Smith smiled. It seemed that when both sides of an issue were given credence, the people were far less likely to fight. *Two systems*, Smith thought. *Why didn't I think of it?* But if he were honest with himself, he knew why. He had been so convinced that the system he viewed as right was factually the best way, despite knowing that many of those for justice had sound reasoning to support their views. Reasons like safety and crime deterrent. Those were not bad or evil motives. True, some may take advantage of such a system. But the same could be said for a system based on mercy.

"Then let's get two groups together," Theresa said. "One to get each system planned out and in writing."

"How will these two systems work together?" Johann asked from off the screen.

"Justice here, old Crawler land," Lollawk said. "Mercy there, old Singer land."

"Two independent nations," Smith said. "How would they work together?"

"Maybe they wouldn't be wholly independent," Theresa said. "But each system's head is based in each nation."

"And work together on bigger crimes," Smith said. "But smaller ones, like theft, can be handled within each nation as they see fit."

"Okay. And any who want to be a part of laying the systems down should be allowed to," Theresa said.

"Yes, yes," Lollawk said.

Atom sang a peaceful approval, followed by a wave of gratitude that the three species were moving forward.

All said their goodbyes and the screen went black.

Smith stood up. "Okay," he said. "If anyone wants to be a part of planning out the details of our system, let me know. If anyone wants to go to the Crawler land, be a part of their system, you won't get any judgment from us."

Klen walked to the center of the room. "Vessel leave soon." The Crawler turned and walked to the exit.

"I'm sure discussion will start right away," Smith said. "But we'll officially begin once the vessel from across the ocean arrives. Probably in the morning."

***

Another cold night, though warmer than it had been in a long time. Smith walked alone through the trees, his thoughts focused on Evalee and on the future of Aethera of which she wouldn't be a part. He imagined her planning a system of mercy with her keen insight on human behavior. And Smith was certain she would have the same understanding of Singer and Crawlers, were she there. So as he walked, he played through his mind the direction a conversation with his beloved Evalee might take.

"Perhaps Crawlers are more prone to violence and Singers to peace," she would say. "But we don't know that for sure. Their current dispositions could be social and cultural. So there's no way to know how future generations of each species will think and react. We need to be sure these stereotypes are not subconsciously incorporated into either system."

Smith smiled. He knew the thoughts were his own, but they felt truer when he imagined Evalee saying them. And they were worthwhile thoughts to have, he realized. He liked both species, but he knew he had biases toward each.

In his mind, all Singers were eloquent, calm and peaceful. A species he would never have to worry about. Yet he knew that those ideas were false. Wave had proven that. And, in a way, so had Lioness. Then there were the Crawlers, a species that had fought to save human and Singer life. Smith had even seen Crawlers allow themselves to be killed by Hiloy's fanatics in order to protect their own pacifism. Yet, at first thought, Crawlers still felt to Smith to be a violent and dangerous species.

But those are just feelings, he thought. *Not truth.* He would have to ensure that all present when organizing their system of mercy kept that in mind.

Evalee's voice returned to his mind. "Yes, always be aware of your own biases and do you best not to let them impact your decisions," she would say. "Now, mercy and kindness. Never thought this idea would come from Johann." Her imagined smile lit up Smith's soul. "But it's a good idea. Do you remember on the Ship of Nations, the young woman who had a miscarriage? She blamed herself for it, locked herself in an airlock and had her hand on the open button. She blamed herself, and felt that she didn't deserve any grace or mercy. Remember that there will be those who don't want to accept mercy. Perhaps put something in place to help those people."

Smith nodded and smiled, then made his way back to the caves for a few hours of sleep.

Chapter 43

Tashon awoke early, ready to get back to the land of the Singers. Ready to truly get the system of mercy up and running. When he walked out into the early morning mist, a Crawler vessel was already being prepared for departure. It would be rejuvenating to take the boat across the ocean instead of traveling through the Fourth. The higher dimension was beautiful and exhilarating, but he needed to take the time to remind himself of the beauty that existed in his own world, his own dimension. Abe and Winona, leaning against the side of the vessel, called to Tashon.

He joined them with a smile. "You both ready to go home?"

"Home?" Abe said.

Tashon raised an eyebrow. "If you want a place that has mercy and kindness as the foundation of its law, wouldn't that be the Singer land?"

"Yeah," Abe said. "But we're not sure we want to live there."

The idea surprised Tashon. From everything he understood, Abe and Winona wanted a system of mercy as much as he did. "Why?"

Abe sighed. "Shouldn't there be kind people here too?"

Tashon almost laughed, but held it in. He looked around at those who would remain in the Crawler land, and knew their system of justice would work too. He also understood where Abe was coming from, even though Abe's reasoning was incorrect. "Abe," he said. "Those who want a system of justice, of harsher punishments aren't evil or vindictive. They're not like Wave or Hiloy. They just have a different idea of what system of law and government will be best."

Winona bumped her shoulder into Abe's. "Told you," she said.

Abe smiled. "Yeah, yeah. I don't know, something about it just worries me."

"About what?" Tashon asked.

"It just feels like, if there are two separate nations, it's inevitable they'll go to war at some point in the future," Abe said.

Tashon nodded. "Maybe. But if we had one system for all Aethera, it wouldn't be long before those against that system rose up and started a civil war."

Winona smiled. "I told you the sage would have the answers."

Abe laughed softly and shook his head. "He does. Thanks, Sage."

"Of course." Tashon turned and saw Rosa carrying a box to the vessel. He ran over and got it from her.

"Thanks, Sage," she said.

"What's in it?" He asked.

"All the papers I've been writing on," she said.

"I've seen you writing," he said. "What about?" He thought he knew the answer, but wanted to be sure.

"About you," she said. "The great sage. How he came to be and what he's taught us."

Tashon nodded as they approached the vessel. "Looks like I have something to keep me busy on the journey," he said.

"You want to read it?" she asked.

Tashon wasn't sure whether he wanted to or not, but he would read it nonetheless. "Yeah," he said as he set the box on the vessel.

Soon, the vessel was over the water. Tashon, sitting on the floor nestled between two crates, opened the box. A stack of crinkled papers over two inches thick was bound in the top left corner by a metal ring. With the sound of rushing wind heavy in his ears, he took a deep breath and started reading.

The first page read:

From Apprentice Farmer to Wise Teacher
The Early Days and Teachings of Tashon the Sage

Tashon turned the page and read on. Most of what he read he already knew, for he had experienced it himself. But what struck him was the way in which Rosa wrote about him. She treated him with a sense of awe and reverence, comparing him to Buddha and Muhammad, suggesting that perhaps all the great teachers throughout history had somehow obtained the same connection Tashon had received.

He flipped to the last page, and there found scatterings of new handwriting. Paragraphs written by those Rosa referred to as 'witnesses.' Others telling of the comfort and peace Tashon had given them. He closed the book, placed it back in the box, then closed his eyes. Of course he'd seen everyone meditating with him and listening to his words. He'd hoped they kept coming because they found peace in what he did and said. But having those hopes confirmed in writing was overwhelming. He leaned his head back against cool metal, and shed a few tears of gratitude.

Soon, he drifted into that middle ground between sleep and wakefulness, leaving his third-dimensional mind half-aware of his surroundings. His mind in the Fourth remained fully aware and, as if remembering Tashon's desire to widen his vision, it stretched itself and its lens bit by bit. The images came to Tashon as if via a dreaming reality. His view expanded outward in all directions, the blackness spreading out until, at last, another planet appeared and the expansion ceased.

It was a planet covered in lava and volcanic explosions. Tashon's mind focused in on the chaotic beauty of the uninhabitable sphere. His mind pulled in, and Tashon as through his physical form flew over glowing red rivers, past towering, glowing mountains. The heat of it all twisted into his skin, though it did not burn him. He wondered if anything lived, or could ever live, in such a place. Once the volcanic processes ceased, what would become of the planet? In millennia or more, would it be inhabitable? Or it would be a place always devoid of sentient life? Slowly, his mind pulled back and the view focused again on Aethera. Tashon opened his eyes.

Rosa stood over him. "We're here, Sage."

As he stood and rubbed the sleep from his eyes, he couldn't help but remember a question he had been asked just days earlier: What if he could see all the way to Earth?

"Sage," Rosa said. "You all right?"

Tashon blinked rapidly. "Yeah, just waking up."

Rosa smiled. "Okay. Let's get going. Can't wait to start a society of mercy and kindness."

"Let's do it," Tashon said.

Tashon watched Rosa as they stepped into the clearing, remembering the woman she was when they met. The woman who'd snapped Cosima's wrist with barely a thought, now advocating for immense mercy on a national level, for even the most violent of criminals. And somehow, she credited him with that transformation. *I don't deserve that*, he thought.

Then Smith was there, waving and smiling. It was time to get to work. Everyone followed him into the caves.

***

Once the group of sentients was gathered, Smith started by welcoming them all and asking if there were any questions before they started. For once, no questions came to Tashon. No doubts, worries or concerns. He smiled and waited silently until he had something to say.

"What are we going to name this country?" Abe asked.

"Yes, yes," Lollawk said. "What us all called? Not Singer, Crawler, human. Us all together."

"Mercy Nation?" Rosa tried, earning a few soft laughs.

"And call ourselves the Mericfuls?" Johann asked, then chuckled. "Sounds pretentious."

More laughs. Tashon soaked in the lightness of the air in the room. The calm of everyone there, the confidence that there was indeed a hopeful future for all Aethera. It was a palpable peace, and he relished every second of it.

He looked to Johann. "This idea of a merciful society came from a comic book, didn't it?"

"Yeah," Johann said. "A tribe in a comic book used a similar system."

"Comic book?" Lollawk asked.

"A book, a story told with words and pictures," Johann said.

Lollawk clicked softly with another Crawler. "Yes, yes," he eventually said. "Art."

"Yes, art," Johann said.

"And what was the name of that tribe?" Tashon asked.

"Ah," Johann said. "It was Rolthans. The Rolthan tribe."

"Wait," Minow said. "Wait. Are we naming our new nation after a fictional tribe in an old comic book?"

"We're considering it," Smith said.

Yeance wrapped an arm around Minow. "I like it," he said. "The great nation of Rolthan."

"And it gives credit to the inspiration of the idea," Tashon said. "That seems important."

"Anyone against Rolthan for a name?" Smith asked.

"Name sound good," Hutsep said. "I am Rolthan."

"Good. Rolthan it is, then," Smith said. "We're all Rolthans."

Next, the discussion went into what-if scenario after what-if scenario as the group discussed how their merciful law would address specific crimes.

Eventually, Smith raised a hand to call for silence. "This won't get us anywhere," he said. "I like discussing how future situations might play out. But we need to get some concrete aspects of this system in writing. Words that future generations can look to when problems arise."

"We need a foundation," Minow said.

"Right," Yeance said. "Like, set tenets that will be the base of everything."

Smith nodded. "Okay. I think the first one should be this: All sentients are deserving of some level of mercy and grace."

"Yes, yes," Lollawk said. "Good."

Others acknowledged their agreement.

"Good," Smith said. "Other ideas?"

As the silence of thought spread across the crowd, Rosa pulled out a new sheet of paper and began writing.

Tashon closed his eyes, thinking of his time with the twisting being in the Fourth. An idea struck him. Perhaps it was a new idea, but Tashon felt as if he were only just remembering something he had seen beneath that tower. "We don't aim to get rid of justice, only to lessen its negative impact on ourselves and our nation," he said.

"That's good," a woman said. "Though not technically a tenet."

Tashon laughed. "Good point. But I think it's important to remember."

"It absolutely is," Rosa said, writing on her papers. "What about this: No two sentients are alike. Mercy is given on an individual basis."

Everyone agreed, and Rosa wrote it down. Again, Tashon was amazed by her transformation.

Minow raised her hand and started talking. "Let's look at the base of *why* we want a merciful society. What's our goal?"

A Singer sent out notes of respect and kindness, along with a desire for all to be filled with those emotions.

"That kindness also encourages understanding," Rosa said. "Empathy."

Atom weaved together notes of peace. First, of individual peace, but then peace between neighbors, and eventually between all sentients.

"Mercy leads to empathy, empathy to peace," Tashon said.

Rosa wrote the sage's words down before anyone could tell her not to. "That's our next tenet," she said with a smile.

"That's three tenets," Smith said. "A good start. But Tashon said we're not trying to completely get rid of justice. Are we saying there will be cases in which justice supersedes mercy?"

Silence as everyone sought their own answers. Tashon thought back again to the tower, to the being that bestowed so much understanding. He hoped some other idea would come back, but nothing came.

"Individual," Lollawk said. "Can individual change?"

"I think he means *will* the individual change," Abe said.

"Yes, yes."

"We've talked about it before," Abe said. "Repeat criminals are given harsher punishment, more justice. And those who aren't willing to change or admit they did something wrong."

The conversations went on long into the night, and by morning they had a written document they felt confident would be a good foundation on which to build Rolthan, their new nation.

Before turning in for a few hours of sleep, Tashon read through it.

***

Rolthan
Nation of Mercy.
We don't aim to get rid of justice, only to lessen its negative impact on ourselves and our nation. To encourage the mercy that will lessen said negative impacts, the following tenets shall govern all further laws:

> *Everyone deserves a degree of mercy and grace.*
> *Mercy is individual.*
> *Mercy leads to empathy, empathy to peace.*
> *Individuals can change.*

The main focus of law on Rolthan is to protect civilians, encourage change in the criminal and inspire empathy in all. Illegal acts include theft and assault or violent acts of any kind against sentient or property. When a sentient commits such an illegal act, the law requires the following steps to be taken:

1. The criminal be taken into custody.

2. The criminal be given the opportunity to explain actions.

3. The victim be given the opportunity to meet with and understand the criminal. This will not be required if victim does not wish it.

4. With the guidance of a mediator, victim will be given opportunity to pass merciful judgment on the criminal. The victim is not required to do so.

5. Mediators will be volunteers who have shown to be honest citizens of Rolthan.

6. The amount of mercy a criminal is given will be dependent on the following:

> *A. Whether or not the criminal regrets actions.*
> *B. Whether or not the criminal is willing to make restitution for actions.*

C. *Whether the action is the criminal's first, second, and so on. First time actions will be offered more mercy.*

D. *The more violent or harmful an action, the less opportunity for mercy.*

E. *To some degree, the input of the victim will be considered.*

We understand these laws are vague. That is because we cannot foresee every possible scenario, and we trust all who follow to use these tenets and laws to guide them in offering mercy and kindness to all Rolthans.

Rolthan
The selection of leaders.

Rolthan will be led by a tribunal, one representative each from humans, Singers and Crawlers. These will be chosen by popular vote. Their role is twofold. First, to guide the merciful decisions of cases of the more extreme crimes. The tribunal will decide which cases to get involved with themselves. Second, they will deal in affairs with our neighboring nation of justice, (insert nation name here). All dealings with our neighbor nation will be openly shared with all Rolthan citizens.

As Rolthan grows, more leadership positions can be added.

Chapter 44

After most had retired for the night, Abe remained awake with Winona, Rosa and Johann. They slowly walked through the lesser traveled halls of the caves.

"Do we really think this will create a safe home?" Abe asked.

"I do, Abe," Rosa said.

"I *want* to think so too," Abe said. "But nothing like this has been done before, except in Johann's fictional world."

Johann smiled. "That's true. But the people who live here are choosing to live here because they want something new. They want this to work."

"And the people who don't want this system will live across the ocean," Winona said.

"Yeah," Abe said. "This is all just so... calm. And simple. So few laws. Is that really enough?"

"More laws only make more criminals," Johann said.

They reached the end of the all, turned around and kept walking.

"Huh," Abe said. "I guess that makes sense."

"The only laws we want are ones that keep everyone safe," Rosa said. "And we've done that. We'll wait for everyone to look at it, but I think we have what we need."

Abe nodded. "With how vague it is, we're putting a lot of faith in future generations."

"As we should," Johann said. "I saw terrible shit back on Earth in the military. Shit, I've seen it here. But I still think the majority of sentients are good."

"I think so too," Winona said. "We thought all of the Crawlers were murderous, but it turns out a lot of them are good and kind."

Abe shrugged and nodded. "Yeah."

They walked on in silence, Abe wanting to be fully convinced in their society of mercy but still doubted its long-term success. But he didn't have a choice, not really. Unless he wanted to live across the ocean, in a land ruled by strict justice. That sounded far worse to him than living in a land of mercy, even with the problems that could form in that land. They made their way back to the main cavern. Abe lay down on a white bench, and fell into a dreamless sleep.

***

The clearing was filled with those who planned to become citizens of Rolthan. Abe shared a stump with Winona. Smith, Johann and Atom stood in the center. A screen sprang from Atom's hands, displaying the faces of Ulot and Theresa. According to Theresa, all were present there as well.

"Why make call?" Ulot asked.

"To share our nation's plan with everyone, then to give you the chance to share yours," Johann said.

"Then, everyone can decide for certain which nation they want to be a part of," Smith said.

"We'll share our founding documents," Theresa said. "But before citizenships are finalized, there's something that needs to be decided."

"What?" Smith asked

Before Theresa could respond, Atom sang the note for Wave with a feeling of uncertainty.

"Yes, yes," Ulot said. "Wave kill here, kill there."

Abe looked at Winona and shook his head. He hadn't thought of how Wave's murders would be handled. He'd assumed mercifully, but Ulot was right—he had committed the murders on both continents. But how would the two ideals mesh together in a single case? It seemed to Abe that only the sage would be able to make that decision.

"You're right," Smith said. "And it'll show us how well we can work together."

"Let's hear what you've written down," Johann said. "Then we'll share ours."

Theresa nodded and looked at a paper she held in her hands. "We, the nation of Caxsion, lay out the foundation for our great and safe nation as follows. Above all else, we are a nation that protects its citizens. A nation of law and justice. Crimes will be met with imprisonment and, in extreme cases, execution." She paused and lifted her gaze.

Abe stared into her eyes, larger on the screen than in reality. There was a fierceness in them, the determination to do what she thought needed to be done. But no sign of the anger Abe expected to see.

She continued. "Crimes include theft, emotional abuse, physical abuse, assault of any kind, including rape. Violent acts of any kind, from a single hit to murder. Punishments will be decided by a chosen group of citizens and a hired judge. The minimum punishment for each crime is as follows: theft, one week imprisonment...."

She continued into a long list of crimes, and Abe lost focus. Yes, Theresa and those of Caxsion wanted a nation of safety above all else. And he understood that, knew the importance of feeling safe in one's own home. But as Theresa continued on with her list, Abe felt Caxsion would only limit crime out of fear for punishment. But Rolthan would be a nation in which crime was avoided out of a kindness for one another. Or that's what Abe hoped. *Is that naïve?* he asked himself. *Can an entire nation of sentients really live like that?* He liked to think so, but he'd also seen the natural feelings of confusion and fear turn into unfettered aggression. There was no perfect government system, he decided. The best one could do was follow what felt right, what seemed would have the best possible outcome for future generations. And for Abe, that was Rolthan's system.

Theresa finished reading, then asked Johann to read his document. Abe listened, partially, while also wondering how the two nations would agree on what to do with Wave. It was obvious Caxsion would want him executed. Would they be willing to lessen their punishment to appease Rolthan? Would Rolthan be willing to let Wave die for his crimes? Wave murdered Lioness, and Abe didn't think he would ever be able to forgive that. *Does one need to forgive to provide mercy?* he wondered. Another question with no clear answer.

"Thank you," Johann said. "Does Ulot want to read it in the Crawler's language?"

Ulot clicked, and recited the document seemingly from memory. Next, Johann read Rolthan's foundational document, followed by Lollawk and Atom in their native tongues.

Smith cleared his throat. "Okay. Wave. He did commit murders in both nations. So what do we do?"

"Meet middle space," Ulot said.

"Neutral ground," Johann said. "But where?"

"The floating island?" Smith asked.

Countless Crawlers loudly clicked and clicked.

"No, no," Lollawk hissed. "Have said no go there before."

Abe looked at Winona, who shrugged and shook her head.

"Okay," Smith said. "The only other option I see is the over the ocean."

"Yes, yes," Ulot said.

"Right in the middle," Theresa said. "Each nation can bring an elected spokesperson."

"Then how will we decide what happens to him?" Smith asked.

"After each nation's representative has had a turn to speak, we can discuss options together, as neighbor nations," Theresa said.

They set a time for the trial over the ocean and ended the conversation.

Smith turned in circle, looking at everyone in the cavern. "Any suggestions for Rolthan's spokesperson?"

Before Abe realized what he was doing, a name jumped from his throat. "Tashon."

Chapter 45

Tashon looked at Abe, then at Smith.

"Anyone disagree with Tashon speaking for Rolthan?" Smith asked.

"No, no," Hutsep said. "Good choice."

"The best choice," Rosa said.

"Tashon, is that okay with you?" Smith asked.

He wasn't okay with it, exactly. But he knew it was what he needed to do. "Yeah," he said. "I'll do it. But I want input from everyone. It's not just my option about Wave that matters."

"But you have insight we don't," Rosa said.

"And I've given that insight to all of you," Tashon said. "Others will have ideas on how to put that insight to use. And ideas of their own."

Rosa smiled. "You're right, Sage," she said.

Tashon nodded. "What ideas do we have?"

Londey stood up. "A confession," she said. "We saw Wave kill the prisoners on Caxsion. No one actually saw him murder the prisoners and guards here. No one saw him kill Lioness."

Something that hadn't occurred to Tashon. Yes, based on all the evidence it was likely that Wave was responsible for the deaths of Lioness, as well as the former Crawler leaders and their guards. "You want us to know for sure," Tashon said, "before we pass punishment."

"Yes," Londey said and sat down.

"That's why I want ideas from everyone," Tashon said. "A confession wasn't something I would've thought of."

"Question," Hutsep said. "What punishment should give Wave?"

"Are we going to let him be out, like the Crawler leaders?" someone asked.

"Would that even be safe for him?" Johann asked.

"We can't decide a punishment right now," Rosa said. "We need to hear what Wave has to say. We need to see if he confesses. If he regrets what he did. If he sees it as wrong."

Atom sang that she hoped Wave would regret what he did.

"Do you think he will?" Smith asked.

Atom had no idea.

Tashon nodded. "We all are here because we believe in mercy," he said. "So I think we would agree that execution is not an option. And we also have to consider Wave's safety."

"And his mental and emotional state leading up to the attacks," Johann said. "I think understanding someone's thought process and emotions is important to determine the right level of mercy."

Tashon smiled. Another good thought that he didn't think he would have had on his own. "Anything else?"

Everyone looked around, as if expecting someone else to answer.

"Nothing?" Tashon asked.

Rosa stood and walked to Tashon, placing a hand in his shoulder. "We trust you, Sage. You understand what we want Rolthan to be."

"Okay." Tashon blew out a breath and nodded. "Thank you."

***

Tashon stood in the Fourth, staring down at the green Aetheran ocean. In a few hours, he would be standing down there, explaining to all Aethera why Wave deserved any degree of mercy. And then tell what degree of mercy the murdering Singer deserved. And that couldn't be determined until he had a chance to talk to Wave. And what if Wave didn't confess to the murders in Rolthan? Would he turn the Singer's fate entirely over to the justice of Caxsion?

He turned and started pacing, back and forth over the green water. They wanted him to be the sole spokesperson for their nation. A young man with little life experience, doling out reasoning for merciful punishment? *They trust me*, he reminded himself. *Just stay at peace.* With a half-smile, he turned his gaze from the ocean to the Fourth.

It was empty. Quiet. For once, he realized the good in that. Didn't feel concerned at the absence of souls. He knew they were gathered farther out in the Fourth. Perhaps one day he could see his mom or sister again. But in the back of his mind, the darkness that attacked him at the tower swam, reminding him that darkness can always be found. Whether he was looking for it or not. He rubbed the necklace between his fingers, thankful for the physical protection the moths gave him. Wishing they could also give him more wisdom. Then a thought came to him. *You don't need more wisdom. You have what you need.*

Tashon knew it was true. He could do it. He would put forth the best case for offering Wave mercy, and whatever happened after was out of his control. He smiled and sat down, bringing his mind into peaceful meditation, waiting for his time to speak on Wave's behalf.

***

Two vessels hovered side by side over gently rolling waves. Tashon stood on one and Theresa on the other. Johann, Smith, Rosa, Lollawk and Atom accompanied Tashon. Theresa had brought Ulot, Fylin and a few others Tashon didn't know by name. Wave stood between the two vessels on top of a small disk of black. On a separate disk was another Singer with a screen extended to show the proceedings to all of Athera.

"Theresa," Tashon said. "Before anything else, I have a few questions for Wave."

"Okay," she said. "Go ahead."

Tashon took a few steps to his left to get a better view of the Singer. "Wave. We found over a dozen murdered sentients near and in the Singer caves. The Crawler leaders. Their guards. Lioness and others in the weapon room. We all believe that you did it. But no one alive saw it." Tashon paused to slow his breathing. "Wave, did you?"

Wave sent out a quiet, trembling "yes." The note felt wet with tears, dripping with regret.

Tashon turned to Theresa and the other Caxions. "Wave regrets what he did."

"That doesn't change that he did it," Theresa said. "Doesn't change what justice calls for."

He looked back to Wave. "Was anyone with you on your continent? Did anyone help you, like they did here?"

Wave sang an emphatic "no."

Tashon nodded, deciding he wouldn't push the issue. Whether Wave was telling the truth or not, those who helped him attack the prisoners on Caxsion would be at the sole mercy of the new nation of justice.

"Okay, Theresa," Tashon said. "You speak first. What does justice call for? And why?"

Theresa nodded. "Wave killed, murdered in cold blood, dozens of Crawlers, along with humans and Singers. Justice demands a judgment equal to the crime."

Tashon wanted to interrupt, to tell her that justice was ideal that existed the universe, an ideal that did not demand anything. But he stayed peacefully quiet, waiting for her to finish.

"What I have to say isn't overly complex," she said. "Wave murdered out of uncontrolled rage. We can't trust that Wave wouldn't do it again. We call for execution."

"Why not imprisoned for life?" Tashon asked.

"We discussed all the options we felt would serve justice," Theresa said. "And execution is our conclusion."

Tashon nodded. "What about compromise? Rolthan and Caxsion are meant to work together. Do you think the two new nations could come to a compromise on what to do with Wave?"

Theresa turned around and talked quietly with others on her vessel. She turned back. "Let's hear what you have to say first."

"Okay," Tashon said. "You justice demands execution. We see it differently. Justice and mercy are concepts that exist in the universe. They don't demand anything. Joy and despair don't demand anything. The universe doesn't even demand anything. So, we're not seeing we owe it to mercy to pass a softer judgment on Wave. We're saying the universe is merciful, and that as part of the universe, we are meant to be merciful beings. But the universe doesn't demand it of us. Humans—sentients—-make demands, the universe doesn't. The merciful universe doesn't make demands. It allows us to live, to search out what we think is true and right, and follow it. And I—we—are saying mercy is what's right and true."

Theresa looked quizzically at Wave. "What mercies are you offering him?"

"According to you, Wave deserves execution," Tashon said. "The point of mercy is to give less than what is deserved. So we could offer a life imprisoned. But part of what Rolthan stands for is the fact that people—sentients—*can change.* So we suggest a punishment that will give Wave that opportunity."

"Okay. And what would that punishment look like?" Theresa asked.

"Imprisoned," Tashon said. "Possibly for life. But we would provide him with opportunity we think all sentients are entitled to. Social interactions, education, and therapy. All of these with the aim to help Wave overcome his obvious guilt, and to encourage change. He could earn his freedom back."

Theresa shook her head and sighed. "Let us talk. Maybe we can compromise." She turned and formed a circle with the others on her vessel.

Tashon did the same. "What do you think?"

"I don't want any kind of compromise," Rosa said. "You said what you think the best is, and we stick to that."

"Politically, that's a terrible idea," Johann said.

Smith nodded. "That's true. If we're unwilling to work with them now, it won't set our nations up for a civil relationship in the future."

"No, no," Lollawk said. "Listen to the sage."

Atom sang a wavering note between agreement and disagreement. She saw the validity of sticking to the most merciful option possible, but also the wisdom in compromising with Caxsion.

"Sage Tashon," Rosa said. "What do you think?"

Tashon shrugged and shook his ahead. He looked down on them from above, the two ships staring at a lone violent criminal, all hovering over the ocean, waves now gently splashing the metal sides of their vessels. A storm formed off in the distance, but it would be hours before it hit where they stood. He felt the need to do everything he could the way the universe did it. To live in harmony with the universe to the best of his ability.

"We can compromise to a degree," he said. "But we'll only compromise to something we're all okay with."

"Sage," Rosa said. "Can I ask why? I thought you were about following what the universe would do?"

"The universe, Rosa, doesn't follow any pattern or rules. Yes, it is more merciful than just. But there's no equation for this, only our intuition and judgment on what is best. And Johann's right. We need to consider how this interaction will harm or benefit future generations."

Rosa nodded and looked out to the sea.

Tashon turned around and looked at the Caxsions, still deep in conversation. "Is everyone else okay with a compromise, if we need to?" he asked, without turning back.

No one objected, though he could sense Atom and Lollawk's hesitation.

Soon, Theresa left her group and returned to the edge of her vessel. "We're open to meeting somewhere in the middle... but this is in no way condoning what Wave has done."

"We don't condone it, either," Tashon said.

"Right." Theresa nodded. "First, if you want to keep Wave alive, he needs to be kept on Rolthan."

Tashon looked behind him, receiving affirmative gesture. "Okay." He turned to Theresa. "We'll keep him on Rolthan."

"That was... easier than I thought," Theresa said.

"It's a fair request," Tashon said. "And it'll be easier for us to make sure he's living comfortably if he's imprisoned with us."

"Good. And hopefully that makes our next request easier." Theresa paused and blinked slowly. "We don't want Wave to have the chance for release."

The idea hit Tashon's stomach with a physical force. He looked down, tried to think and found himself wishing everything existed in nothing. To exist and build and grow in a place with no good nor evil, no lack nor excess. A place where opposites meant nothing. *Then life would mean nothing,* he reminded himself. He signaled to Theresa that he needed a minute, and turned so that he faced no one. He could make a bold stand, then and there. A stand that said Rolthan will always give criminals a chance to change, to gain their freedom. And, in some ways, making that stand felt good. It seemed right to defend the ideal that all can change, that all deserve mercy. But was there a way to make that stand that wouldn't create tension between the two new nations?

Tashon shook his head and looked to his friends. "Atom, how many more years — rotations around the sun — will Wave live?"

After a moment, Atom sang that Wave could live for at least another four hundred years.

Confined for four hundred years. Tashon couldn't accept that. "If I — we — were to accept that offer, it would go against the tenets we put at the foundation of Rolthan. It would go against what we believe to be true: sentients can change."

Theresa whispered something to the other Caxsions, and then turned back to Tashon. "If you don't accept, we'll hear a counteroffer."

Tashon smiled. "If he's on Rolthan, then we should have more say in his fate," he said. "We will give him every opportunity for joy and change that we can. If we decide he's ready to be free, that he has changed, we will give proof of his change to Caxsion. He also will never be allowed to leave Rolthan, even if released."

Theresa nodded. "It's not unreasonable. Give us some time." She returned to her fellow Caxsions.

Wave sat down on his black disk, looking toward the distant clouds.

Feeling a pang of empathy, Tashon walked as close to Wave as he could get. "Wave, are you doing all right?"

The answer felt like a shrug.

Tashon nodded. "I've killed before. The pain of that, the guilt... You can get over it. You can gain forgiveness. Mercy."

Wave sang defeated notes of self-hatred. He broke his promise of peace and murdered dozens of sentients. Mercy was not for him. Neither was forgiveness.

Tashon crouched down and looked at the green water. "Wave, I almost killed myself after I killed. It was just one person, so I don't know exactly how you're feeling. But, Wave, I forgive you. Whims and Lioness were my friends. I cared for them. But I forgive you, Wave." Warm peace washed over Tashon as he said the words and realized he meant them, with all that he was.

And it seemed that Wave also felt the sincerity of the forgiveness, for he stood and sang weeping notes of humility and gratitude.

Tears pooled in Tashon's eyes.

Then Wave sang a question: *Will I forgive myself?*

Tashon sighed and shook his head, knowing the feeling well. "Wave, out of all those who will be willing to forgive you, it'll probably take the longest to forgive yourself. But it'll come."

Wave sang another "thank you" and went silent.

Tashon wiped his eyes. *He'll be okay*, he thought as he walked back to where he was. He examined the scene from above, looked at himself standing there, doing everything he could to provide mercy to a pained and broken sentient. *Exactly where I'm meant to be,* he thought with a smile.

Theresa left her group and looked at Tashon. "If he's stays in Rolthan, we'll agree to him having an opportunity at release," Theresa said. "But Rolthan must also agree to send updates on his status once a year."

"Yes." Tashon smiled. "We can do that."

Atom sang. The disk holding Wave flew gently to Rolthan's vessel and deposited him right next to Atom. Halting notes of piercing regret tumbled from Wave as he simultaneously gave thanks and asked for forgiveness. Atom silenced him a single, loud note. She placed a hand on top of his head and closed her eyes. She forgave Wave, wholly and completely. Then asked if he wanted to re-enter the pact of pacifism.

A slow, wailing 'yes' floated from his lips. Atom dropped her arm.

Tashon blinked and wiped a tear from his eye. The immense and unwavering love Atom had for Wave was inspiring, and Tashon had no doubt that someday Wave would see freedom again. He turned to say something to Theresa, but the Caxsion vessel was already halfway to the horizon.

Chapter 46

The cavern had become a place of joyous celebration. Humans hugged and smiled. Singers sang and Crawlers stomped their feet. All talked excitedly about Rolthan's future and about the good their system of mercy would do for countless sentients. And for the first time since leaving the Ship of Nations, Abe felt completely at home.

He leaned against a wall, looking at the crowd. In the middle of it all was Wave, sitting on a bench, hands secured behind his back. Sitting around were those of the anti-Singers who had shown that they sincerely regretted what they had done with Hiloy. Not one sentient present seemed angry with them, or even fearful. The criminals never had more than a minute or two alone before another sentient would sit down and give a few forgiving, encouraging words.

Abe knew that every Rolthan professed to believe in mercy and kindness, but seeing it in action was still shocking. No one present had given in to hate or anger, even though the criminals in the center of the room had killed the friends and family of many of them. It felt surreal and impossible, an idealistic dream that could burst any moment. Yet it was real.

A hand grabbed his shoulder and he turned around to see a smiling face. "Winona."

She kissed his cheek, and then examined the room. "Did anything like this ever happen on Earth?"

"Not that I ever learned about," Abe said.

She nuzzled her head into his shoulder and gave a contented sigh. Abe wrapped his arm around her. And a new scene of darkness flashed into his mind. A violent criminal, mercifully set free, murdering Winona. Then the pain of burying her the way his dad buried his mom.

"Abe?" Winona said. "Abe what's wrong?"

Abe blinked and Winona stood in front of him, staring into his eyes.

"I'm okay. I just had a flash of doubt, I think."

"Doubt about what?"

Abe looked around the cavern. "All of it. Are we being naïve?" As soon as he asked it, he felt guilty for questioning the system they'd fought so hard to create.

"Maybe," Winona said. "This could all come crashing down in fifty years, or four hundred. Or it could be the start of the greatest nation the third dimension has ever known. There's no way to know."

Abe nodded. "You're right. It's just so new. And it's scary to think what could happen if it goes wrong."

"It is," Winona said. "But do you doubt so much that you want to go to Caxsion?"

Abe shook his head. "No. I'm just nervous about the future. Yeah, more nervous than doubtful."

"I think everyone's nervous," she said. "But it's worth the risk, isn't it?"

Abe nodded as a spot opened up next to Wave. Steeling himself, he grabbed Winona's hand, walked to the Singer criminal and sat down. Wave immediately sang forth guilt-riddled apologies for what he'd done, note rolling into note.

"Wave," Abe said. "I... I don't know if I'm ready to forgive you. Lioness was my friend. I cared about her."

Wave acknowledged the pain he'd caused, and confessed that he felt most guilty for killing Lioness. She was the best Singer he knew.

Abe nodded. "Thanks, Wave. I want to forgive you, I just...."

Winona squeezed his hand. "We will be able to, eventually."

Wave indicated that he'd already been offered more forgiveness than he felt he deserved.

Abe smiled slightly at the comment, knowing that was the point of Rolthan. "That's mercy, Wave. And I think that, somehow, there's a true contradiction in the idea of mercy. Everyone deserves mercy."

"But mercy is getting less punishment than we deserve," Winona finished. "A true contradiction. You sound like the sage."

Abe's face flushed red and he smiled.

A note echoed off the cavern walls and all went silent. Atom, Lollawk and Smith walked to the center of the cavern.

Smith held up a small stack of papers. "Our tenets and laws." He smiled. "Signing, writing your name on something, is a human tradition. When you sign your name to something, you're committing yourself to it. Saying you believe in it and will follow it, as best you can. Atom, Lollawk and I think that's how we should make citizenship official. Sign your name to Rolthan's tenants and laws. We'll put it all together in a book."

"Yes, yes," Lollawk said. "And first citizen is Wave."

Atom grabbed the papers from Smith, and then walked to Wave. She reached behind his back, undid his restraints and handed him the papers. Abe looked down at them. Three columns were on the paper, one for each of the three languages. Without moving his gaze from the paper, Wave wept notes of gratitude. He made no move to sign the paper.

"Wave," Abe started to speak, but was cut off by notes of refusal from Wave.

Rolthan was a place for the kind and merciful, and Wave sang how he was neither of those things. He had murdered out of vengeance, and felt he had no place being a citizen of a nation built on mercy.

"Wave, Wave," Lollawk said. "Not those things yesterday. But can be those things today, tomorrow."

Atom agreed with Lollawk, reminding Wave that he renewed his pact of pacifism.

"All of us here," Smith said, "have done things out of hate or fear or vengeance. No one is perfect. Putting your name down simply means you believe in the society we're trying to create, and that you'll do your best to support it."

Abe smiled and nodded at his dad. As the two locked eyes, warmth washed over Abe and he felt that, despite everything, he was grateful for where he found himself. He squeezed Winona's hand and turned back to Wave. Silently, he lifted his hand over the paper, palm down. One black wire shot out and emitted a thin, blue line of light. One symbol appeared on the paper in black, and Wave's wire retracted.

"The first citizen of Rolthan," Abe whispered.

Chapter 47

After all had signed Rolthan's founding document, Smith found himself on top of the ship with Johann, Rosa and Abe. He stared at the darkening sky above the mountains, remembering his first day on Aethera. Arriving on its surface amid flames and death, he never thought everything would turn out as strange and beautiful as they had.

"A new nation," Rosa said.

"With a system based on a comic book written decades ago," Smith said. "An insane idea, Johann."

Johann smiled. "Maybe. But I'm excited to see it grow."

"My mom would've loved it," Abe said.

Smith wrapped an arm around his son. "Yeah, she would've."

"And she'd probably do a better job leading it than you, Dad."

Smith laughed. "Yeah, I think you're right." He imagined his wife standing next to them, wondered what she might say and do. He wished she were there, yet realized he was okay that she wasn't.

"All right, I'm going to look for Sage Tashon," Rosa said, then disappeared into the ship.

"I never expected to leave the Ship of Nations," Johann said. "But I was forced to, and I've been a part of creating a society I've always wished existed."

"You thought that much about a comic book?" Smith asked.

Johann nodded. "The idea of mercy and kindness above all else seemed important. It never left me, even when I was forced to kill in war. *Especially* then."

Abe turned to Johann. "Do you think it was destiny you ended up here, Johann? That we all did?"

Johann stroked his beard in thought. "Maybe, Abe. I don't know. I think certain things could be considered fate. But nothing outside our control. You say fate made your ship crash. But fate didn't make you do everything you've done since then. I think that if there is a fate, it can put us in situations, but it can't force us to act in any certain way."

Smith smiled. "I think so too. Any of us could've given up a hundred times, but we chose to keep going. Those were our choices, not some force from beyond controlling us."

"Yeah," Abe said. "That makes sense. I like that way of looking at it. And my mom always said that everything depends upon how you choose to perceive it. I'd forgotten that until now."

Smith looked at his son, seeing Evalee's eyes and smile. "Your mom was wise, Abe. Wiser than me, I think."

"I don't think so," Abe said with a smile. "I know she was."

Smith gently smacked the back of Abe's head and they both laughed.

"Time to get some rest." Johann patted Abe's shoulder, nodded at Smith, then walked back inside the ship.

Smith sat down at the edge and let his feet dangle over the side. He patted the cool surface next to him, and Abe sat by his side.

"Abe," he said. "I think we've found something great here."

"Something beautiful," Abe said.

"Like Winona?" Smith bumped his shoulder against Abe and smiled.

Abe smiled as his face flushed. "Yeah, she's great, Dad. I don't think I'd be doing as well as I am without her."

"You're not worried about your feelings being real anymore?" Smith asked.

"I was, I know," Abe said. "But then Lioness was murdered, and then Whims. I felt that loss. And I don't think a prophetic Singer could make me feel that. Then I thought if I lost Winona, the pain would be there, be real. And if that's real, why wouldn't the joy she brings me be real? And if my time with her could be cut short, why waste time wondering whether how I feel is real?"

Smith smiled. He couldn't have asked for a better answer. "Life isn't the shits anymore?"

Abe smiled, then shrugged. "No, but...."

"What?"

"I'm still nervous, about the shits coming next, you know?"

"Yeah, I know. Me too, sometimes. But we made it through worst shits I've ever seen."

"There've been a few good shits mixed in, though."

Smith smiled. "There have been. And we made it through. And I think we'll make it through whatever other shit the universe has for us."

"Hell yeah we will," Abe said.

"Hell yeah," Smith repeated.

They fell into comfortable silence. The last few weeks played through Smith's mind. The death, the sorrow and the darkness. Then the discoveries, knowledge and beauty. He still missed the hell out of Evalee. But he was excited as hell to see what the future held.

Chapter 48

Tashon stared down at Aethera, a planet now made of two nations, each embodying its own ideal. He watched as citizens of Rolthan and Caxsion moved about excitedly, with joy and hope for a bright future. As they should, for Tashon knew that neither nation, neither system was inherently wrong. And for the time being, with the leaders who were in place, both would be quality nations in which to live.

It's not systems themselves that make governments bad and corrupt – it's people, Tashon thought.

He smiled as a warm fourth-dimensional breeze drifted through and around him. He loved Aethera, but nothing could beat the higher plane in terms of true peace. He thought of the darkness he'd seen in the Fourth, and realized it also contained evils the Third would never understand. *No*, he thought. *Everyone down there has seen more than their own share of darkness.*

Below, Rosa walked out of the ship, asking where she could find the sage. Tashon smiled and shook his head. The title still felt too big for him, too important. But felt the love with which Rosa used it, and he couldn't deny the warmth that gave him. He closed his eyes and was about to pull himself back to the Third, when a sound pierced his ears and surrounded his entire essence. The sound itself was quiet and would have been unnoticeable in the Third. But carried by the Fourth wind, it vibrated into his bones, his veins and his cells. And as soon as it hit him, he felt the meaning of it: a call for help.

Somewhere off in the universe, something was dying, sending a plea across the cosmos for any that would listen. Once certain he wasn't needed below, he closed his eyes and focused on the near-silent sound.

It became more clear and, in every way possible, entirely more than sound was in the third dimension. The sound was warm and heavy, sad and familiar. For a moment, he wondered if it were meant specifically for him, but discarded the idea quickly. Nothing about the meaning and feeling behind the sound indicated a name or an intended recipient. No, it was a dense and wild call for help, regardless where it came from. For without help, whatever it was would die.

Tashon did not doubt the validity of the sound. It was an SOS that needed to be answered. Would there be anyone else who *could* hear it? Just to be sure, he examined those below him. None made any indication that they heard what Tashon heard.

Again, the tingle of something familiar about the sound. He focused on that familiarity and soon understood that he had some prior connection to the dying source of the plea. When that knowledge came to him, so did the conviction that he had to follow the sound to its source and try to save it. He reached his view out as far as he could, just past the lava planet, but could not find it. Something told him that it was past his current galaxy, light years beyond the planet around which they orbited.

A long journey, entirely in the Fourth. But one he was now certain he needed to make. He looked down at Aethera. At all those who had made his time there mean something. The sentients who had kept the darkness from swallowing him whole. It pained him to do it, but he pulled himself back to the Third to say goodbye to all of them.

The End

ACKNOWLEDGEMENTS

Thank you to my Heavenly Father and Jesus Christ. Thank you to my beautiful wife and best friend, Meaghan. Thanks to my parents, and all my wonderful family. Thanks to Luke Dylan Ramsey, this book would not be what it is without his aid and insight. Thank you to Carol Powell and Josh Allen, the two best writing teachers I could have ever asked for. Many thanks to Dave Lane (aka Lane Diamond) of Evolved Publishing for believing in this series as much as I do. Thank you to my editor, Becky Stephens, and to Sam Keiser for providing the phenomenal cover art. And lastly thank you, reader, for taking the time to read this book. I hope you join me again as the journey on Aethera continues.

ABOUT THE AUTHOR

Author J.S. Sherwood has a passion for stories that show the existence of peace and beauty even in the darkest of times. He spent many years teaching English at the junior high, high school, and college levels, and now brings that love of great writing to bear in his own books.

When he isn't reading or writing, he's spending time with his wife, five kids, and two dogs in Arizona. Most likely they're outside, soaking up the fresh air and sunshine.

For more, please visit J.S. Sherwood online at:
Website: www.WorldsByJSSherwood.com
Goodreads: J.S. Sherwood
Facebook: @js.sherwood.7
Twitter: @SciFiSherwood

WHAT'S NEXT?

J.S. Sherwood is hard at work on the rest of the "This Foreign Universe" series, through Book 9. Please stay tuned to developments and plans by subscribing to our newsletter at the link below.

www.EvolvedPub.com/Newsletter

MORE FROM EVOLVED PUBLISHING

We offer great books across multiple genres, featuring high-quality editing (which we believe is second-to-none) and fantastic covers.

As a hybrid small press, your support as loyal readers is so important to us, and we have strived, with tireless dedication and sheer determination, to deliver on the promise of our motto:
QUALITY IS PRIORITY #1!

Please check out all of our great books,
which you can find at this link:
www.EvolvedPub.com/Catalog/

Thank you!

www.ingramcontent.com/pod-product-compliance
Lightning Source LLC
Chambersburg PA
CBHW031216260626
47169CB00007B/2084